D   QUEST
(PHOENIX THRONE
BOOK TWO)

HEATHER WALKER

Heather Walker

Dragon Quest

Heather Walker

DRAGON QUEST (PHOENIX THRONE BOOK TWO)

HEATHER WALKER

Heather Walker

CHAPTER 1

Elle Watson ran for her life.

The natural adrenaline urged her forward, despite the burning in her legs. She hurdled over fallen tree trunks, slashed through brambles, and snapped off branches in her wake.

Something was after her.

She didn't know what it was, but she *felt* it.

She would give anything for her sidearm. She usually wore it in a holster under her business suit jacket, but she'd taken it off and put it in her handbag at Hazel's house. The last thing she expected was to need a damn gun for a "conjuring spell". Although Elle wasn't judgmental like her friend, Carmen, when it came to Hazel's unusual extracurricular activities, she couldn't help but loathe Hazel a little right now. Her "witch" amigo's choice of spell had gone *horribly* wrong.

It had all happened so fast. There was a blinding flash, and then Elle was somewhere else, here — wherever in God's name that was. She was surrounded by dense woods, and as she'd got to her feet, that's when she had felt another presence. So, she'd hit the ground running, not daring to turn around emptyhanded.

She bolted this way and that, but wherever she turned, whatever the thing was behind her followed. Cruel, mocking voices sounded from the branches of the canopy overhead, chittering and chuckling. Elle tried to tell herself that she was just stuck in some weird dream; really, she was still sitting in the circle with the other girls and had merely dozed off as they'd closed their eyes and chanted.

However, then the realist in her snapped her out of such thoughts:

No, Elle. This is real. You know it is.

Finally, up ahead in the distance, she saw an open expanse of clear sky —

not blue but dusky gray. Her heart leaped at the chance to get out of the dank, dark forest. She headed for the opening and managed to break through the last screen of foliage before cresting a rise. From the top, she looked out over rolling fields. A river curled between the hills below her, and a black fringe of more woods bordered the fields beyond.

The landscape seemed to call to her. It breathed safety. *Why?* She had no idea. She only understood, deep in her gut, that she would be safe over there.

She barreled down the slope, her eyes gazing past the river to a shallow gravel ford a few dozen paces down the bank. She headed for it, and soon the heels of her boots hit the edge of the water. The foam splashed around her ankles, but she charged across, eventually taking one giant leap onto the other bank and leaving the forest and its apparent danger behind.

Elle didn't stop running until she gained the upper flats of the fields beyond the hills. Then, she staggered and dropped from exhaustion. She had never run so damn fast in her life. Her breath strained through her parched throat, and her chest ached. She made a mental note to add more cardio to her workout regime, then laughed at herself for thinking such a "normal" thought in a context like this. Who knew if she was even still in the States. She prided herself on being prepared for anything, but running for her life in a place that didn't even seem, well, modern-like... No, she hadn't trained for that scenario.

She knelt on her hands and knees, still fighting to catch her breath. Her straight brown hair hung around her face, and the ends of her bob brushed her cheeks when she wheezed.

When she finally got her breathing under control, she pushed herself upright and brushed off her pantsuit. Before her, the clear daylight shone over the field. She hadn't realized before that point how cold it was — sprinting like a racehorse while consumed by an adrenaline rush will do that.

She glanced back from the hilltop. Dense woods crowded to the river's edge where she'd just crossed to safety, and she wondered what it was that had chased her. In its place now was inviting fields with nodding wildflowers and rustling grasses all around her legs. She set off heading nowhere. She couldn't see a house or any sign of human activity. No roads or fences crossed the fields. No livestock browsed or grazed on the lush, rich grass.

It's all so strange. Where the hell am I?

Elle knew that she couldn't stay where she was, and she couldn't go back, so she just kept going. She headed for the woods on the far side, as they didn't give her the same sense of foreboding as the other forest. Maybe she'd just panicked and hallucinated the "invisible creature" stalking her?

She arrived at the first trees and stopped, surveying the field behind her again, but she still didn't see anything.

Where is everyone?

Now that she had some time, she thought over her circumstances more in-depth. She saw herself sitting on Hazel's carpet. She watched as Hazel arranged the objects for her spell. Hazel wanted to send Elle and the other girls to King Arthur's court at Camelot. Elle didn't ask why; after all, she didn't think it would really work. Hazel always came up with these crazy ideas, and although Elle thought Hazel was a little kooky, she supported her. That's what friendship was – taking an interest in each other's passions. If Hazel wanted to dabble in magic, who was Elle to stop her? It wasn't harming anyone – well, until now.

So, naturally, Elle wasn't fazed by the incantation Hazel had told them all to say. But now, she replayed the whole scene in her mind. Carmen, ever the hard-nosed detective, had shown her distaste from the start, although more subtly than usual. Sadie, the top doctor, on the other hand, took an active interest in every detail of every situation, no matter how bizarre. And Grace worshiped Hazel and wanted to be just like her – if only Grace could muster the courage to do it.

Then there was Hazel herself. Hazel was always a bit of a misfit, even back in their college days. Hazel adopted every trend and fad she came across in her endless search for something to make sense of the world. Carmen had often told Elle on the sly about how Hazel would never succeed in her "mystical quest", but boy had Carmen been proven wrong.

Hazel's spell worked.

Which means... crap. No, no, no. I can't be in Camelot!

For a few moments, panic plumed within Elle. There was no sign of the girls here nor anyone for that matter, so how was she going to get back home? She was utterly alone. Gradually, she calmed herself — convinced herself that if she was here, then the other girls must be too. And that they couldn't be too far away as they had all been sitting so close together in the circle.

That makes sense, right?

Elle bit her bottom lip as her thoughts then changed to Camelot. If this was the land of King Arthur and the Knights of the Round Table, then where were all the knights, castles and landsmen? There ought to be someone around, at least.

She surveyed the sky, but she couldn't even figure out what time of day it was. A thick mat of shining white hung above her now, but Elle couldn't exactly call it cloud. The light streamed through the mat to illuminate the world in a hazy, dreamlike mist.

Turning her attention back to the ground, a few trails cut into the forest ahead.

Someone must have made them. They must lead somewhere, she figured and so logically chose one and sought to find shelter before nightfall, whenever that came. Then, she would sit down and try and figure out a game plan from there.

She entered the wood at an easy walk. She took her time and inspected everything around her. She studied the path for tracks, but she couldn't see a thing. Not one sign of animal or bird life disturbed the stillness.

At one point, she squatted down next to the path and took hold of a large stone embedded in the dirt. She pried it out of the ground. Not a single woodlouse, worm, or creepy-crawly squirmed underneath it against the black soil. She stared down at the flat, damp dirt. Something strange was definitely going on. She knew that for certain now.

She put the rock back and walked on, but slower than before. She chose each step with care and studied the silent forest all around her. She still didn't get any sense of danger from this place, although it did make her skin prickle, now that she knew it wasn't your "stock-standard" forest.

Maybe all those stories about King Arthur's time told the truth about magic and witches and fairies and whatever else? Maybe someone like Merlin really did exist, and Elle had stumbled into his domain. Maybe the animals and birds and bugs wouldn't live in the same forest with him for fear he would enchant them. Maybe he *did* enchant them so their noises wouldn't wake him up in the morning.

Really, Elle? she scolded herself. *Do you actually believe that?*

Well, in all honesty, anything seemed possible given what had happened, and she couldn't turn back. She would get hungry and cold pretty soon. She couldn't let the fear take over again. She had to stay lucid and rational.

She continued to stroll through the trees, her mind drifting to the four important client meetings she had tomorrow morning. As the CEO of an investment house, chaos would rain down if she was a no-show for the day. Elle chuckled.

Ha. Oh, to be a fly on the wall for that scenario...

Soon, the path undulated, dropping into hollows and curving over hummocks. It crossed streams devoid of fish, and no tracks of deer or rabbit or raccoon marked the soil. An unnerving notion crossed Elle's mind.

Maybe this isn't King Arthur's Camelot...

Camelot, understandably, would have animals and people and life. This place... well, didn't.

She stopped in her tracks. If she wasn't in Camelot, where exactly was she? If the spell worked and sent her somewhere, then magic must really work. And that in itself was a *massive* bombshell.

"Magic... Magic is real, huh?" she whispered aloud, everything she'd ever known suddenly thrown into question.

Elle looked over her surroundings with different eyes. If she was in some magical realm, what other magical things would she discover here?

Shaking her head, fighting back the panic once again, she resumed walking. The path never ended or changed much. More forest, trees, streams, leaves, and bushes surrounded her everywhere.

Elle sighed. Just when she seriously considered going back the way she came, the path broke out in a little glade fringed with trees, and a grassy lawn sponged under her boots.

"Finally, a change of scenery," she muttered under her breath, then halted mid-step.

Clear white columns of something resembling a fungus stood all over the grass. Their translucent fabric let the daylight stream through. Elle cautiously wound her way between them and stared, awestruck, at the sight.

No... that can't be possible...

Each pillar held a person suspended in clear, solid fibers.

A woman stared out at the world with her mouth frozen in the middle of a startled cry. Her hand pressed against the fibers, but she couldn't escape.

Another column held a gray-haired man wearing rustic, country clothes. He held a pitchfork in one hand, and the same surprised expression on his face.

The fibrous cylinders all contained people in various aspects of shock. One of them even held a calf. The animal gawked out at the world as if it had just picked up its head from munching the grass.

Elle walked from one column to the next in a daze. She studied each person in turn.

What could do this to these people?

She inspected the white fibers more closely. Were they some kind of fungus that shot up out of the ground to catch their prey in a net? The captives didn't show any signs of decomposition. They looked fresh and very much alive.

Elle looked at the ground on instinct. Maybe more of these "fungi" were beneath her feet, biding their time, waiting to rise up and ensnare her too?

Time to go! she decided, but as she began to pace away, a final figure made her falter.

It was a tall young man with shoulder-length, chestnut-brown hair. Elle couldn't see his eyes because his head was thrown back in a display of agony. His hands were raised like he was trying to defend himself from something. He wore a dark green kilt that came to his knees, a leather pouch on a belt around his hips to cover his crotch, a long, curved saber in a scabbard from the wide leather belt around his waist, and a simple linen shirt with another length of plaid crossed over his chest A rough scraggle of beard darkened his jaw like he hadn't shaved in a while.

Elle noted his chiseled muscles. She saw enough "masculine muscle" from the guys who weight-lifted at the gym back home to understand that this man was strong and maintained his fitness.

Out of all the people trapped in the fibers, it was he who Elle was drawn to the most.

How on earth did he wind up like this? she inwardly lamented.

Without thinking, Elle put out her hand to touch the white fibers holding him. The fabric scratched her fingers. It felt like rough wool, but the moment she touched it, it started to disintegrate.

She yanked her hand back, but a chain reaction spread from the spot where she'd laid her hand. The fibers peeled back and evaporated into steam.

Almost quicker than a blink, the whole column vaporized, and the young man collapsed in a heap at her feet, coughing and gasping for air.

He peered up at her, and at that moment, with such vulnerability in his soft-hazel eyes, Elle swore that she had never seen such a handsome man in her life.

CHAPTER 2

Robbie Cameron thought he was hallucinating when he stared up at the striking woman.

It's merely a trick, he told himself, a cruel falsity from the evil that had trapped him.

He looked away from her and retched onto the grass, excruciating pain wracking his whole body. He squinted his eyes shut against the bright light of day. As long as he kept still, it didn't hurt so much.

He waited a moment until things settled down enough to catch his breath.

His long hair concealed part of his face, shading his eyes from the majority of the light.

Then, a soft, female voice spoke to him: "Are you all right?"

He pried one eyelid open and spotted a pair of black leather boots on the ground in front of him. He rallied his courage to glance up again, but pain stabbed his insides worse than ever. He huddled down until the wave passed.

Yet that one glance told him all he needed to know: the woman was no illusion.

When he finally dared to fully regard her, he saw she had plain brown hair, and wore black trousers, black boots, and a black jacket over a pristine white shirt. He couldn't make out much of her body under those clothes, but he could tell that she had some sculpted muscle where women didn't usually.

Robbie closed his eyes again. He didn't need to see her to understand who and what she was. He'd already met Carmen, the strange woman who appeared out of nowhere wearing strange clothes like this woman's – the only difference being that this woman's attire was slightly more feminine-looking.

Robbie thought fast, his memories swarming back to him. He'd been trekking across the Highlands with his brothers on a path to an enchanted castle. They had to break the curse plaguing their family, and they'd lost forty men fighting wraiths, and God knew what else. The Fire Trilogy, that mysterious book his brother, Angus, got from some ghost queen, said Angus would become King. He would sit on the Phoenix Throne and free the ghost people from their invisible prison.

Once inside the castle, the party had found a door that opened onto a field. They crossed it to a ring of standing stones, but before they could do anything, an earthquake shook the ring into a sinkhole. Robbie saved Angus from falling to his death in the fiery inferno underground, but the instant he saved his brother, Robbie fell into the same hole.

Robbie had hung by Angus' wrists and begged his brother not to let go. Angus and Carmen fought hard to save him, but they couldn't pull him up. He fell... and wound up here.

He studied the individual blades of grass around the woman's boots.

And where is here?

The fire in the sinkhole had burned his legs and blasted up his kilt. Something terrible had then extended a scorching tendril and seized him by the ankle. It pulled him out of Angus' grasp and dragged him to his death. He remembered everything now.

Except he didn't die. He woke up here, at this woman's feet.

How is that possible?

He dared to survey his great surroundings. That's when he saw the others. Two dozen white forms dotted the glade all around him. People in different aspects of surprise and fear stood behind the clear, solid mats of fibers.

He must have been one of them. He must have gotten trapped in one of those pillars of... whatever it was. Somehow, he got transported here from the fire demon's lair under the standing stones.

He tried to sit up, and a lightning fork of pain shot through him. He pitched forward on his hands and knees. He howled through gritted teeth, and a dribble of saliva ran down his lip to disappear in the grass.

The woman spoke again: "How did you get here?"

She talked the same way that Carmen did too, but with a higher, lilting pitch. He spat bile onto the ground.

"My name's Rob. Robbie Cameron the Younger, from Ballachulish, in the west country. I dare not tell ye all of my fate, only that I was seized by some fire demon and trapped in one of these... things."

"Fire demon? Like, from Hell?" She sounded utterly disbelieving of his story, and Robbie chuckled, again reminded of Carmen.

There was no doubt; this woman was indeed one of Carmen's friends.

He pushed himself to his knees. He had to get on his feet, even if it hurt. He had to figure out how to get back to his brothers.

"I ken who ye are," he said, grunting through the pain.

"Ken? That means 'know' in Scottish, right?"

He let his eye rove over her strange clothes, then nodded. "Aye. You're Carmen's friend. Are ye no'?"

She stared at him in shock. "Carmen! You know Carmen?"

"I ken all about Carmen. Ye dinnae need to trouble yerself about that."

He struggled to his feet and rested his hands on his knees. His head spun, but at least he was up. That was the first step.

"She told us about her friends coming through with her," he went on, "but we never found any of them. Ye're one of them."

The woman blinked at him. "Yes, I am. I'm Elle. Please, where is she? Did she figure out a way back home?"

He shook his head. "I cannae tell ye that. I dinnae ken where we are, and I ken even less how ye can get back. All I ken is that ye're a long way from home, lass, and so am I. We're... somewhere beyond the borderline between here and there. That's all I ken."

Elle sighed with apparent defeat. "It all seems so impossible," she murmured. "Our friend, Hazel – she tried to send us to King Arthur's court. If we're not there, where are we?"

He ran his wrist across his mouth and took a step closer to her. Despite his predicament, he was still a man, and he couldn't deny how fair of face she was.

Prettier than any of the lasses back in his village. He hated to think what he looked like to her, and instinctively ran his fingers through his hair to comb it off his forehead.

"Listen to me, lass. We must move along, away from here, and find my clansmen. I'm sure Carmen is with Angus, my brother. They were, how shall I say... close."

"Close? Like, friends?"

"Aye, and a bit more."

"Lovers?"

Robbie grinned.

She shook her head. "I don't understand any of this."

He took a deep breath. The only way to get her to understand was to explain it to her.

"Ye'll no' understand it, but here she goes all the same. We got a curse on us, my brothers and me. A wizard – his name be Ross – told us to go to this certain castle to break the curse. He told Carmen she would get sent back to where she came from as soon as the curse lifted. Carmen and the others are back there. They're working to lift the curse. We must get there too. Understand?"

"I..." Elle faltered, her eyes cast away from him, on some spot in the distance that Robbie knew didn't exist. He felt for her plight, but he needed her to keep her wits. They had some journey ahead of them.

Finally, she answered, "I'm still confused as all hell, but I'm not a fool. I know that, despite how insane it all sounds, I don't have much choice but to believe you... for now. So, how do we find Carmen and your 'clansmen'?"

He looked around him one more time. "I have no idea."

"So you have no idea where we are…"

Her voice trailed off as he approached one of the columns.

"The fire demon captured me in the castle." He sighed. "The castle held something called the Phoenix Throne, and my brother Angus was meant to be King. That's all I can tell ye."

Elle regarded him for a moment. "All right. However, we need a plan for getting to the castle so…"

The two of them looked all around them at the glade and the columns and the frozen people. Naturally, their eyes migrated back to look at each other.

Elle's eyes stirred something within Robbie. Carmen had the same look in her eyes, no one could pull one over on her, but this woman struck him as different. She was more feminine, and Carmen had attacked Angus when he'd found her in the forest. Elle hadn't reacted like that. She was softer, more reserved.

A well of soft, deep emotion seemed to gleam in her eyes. Her hair, her voice, her skin, her body… his attraction to her was unmistakable.

Elle lowered her eyes before his stare, and a bloom of pink colored her cheeks, which pleased him. Perhaps the feeling was mutual?

She looked around the glade one more time. "Right, which way do we go then?"

He looked around. "What direction did ye come from?"

She pointed behind them.

"And did ye see a castle on yer travels?"

She shook her head.

"Seal slugs?"

"What?" she asked, visibly dumbfounded.

He gave a soft laugh. "Never mind. I say we go the opposite way of whence ye came. So, forward march, lass."

He was pleasantly surprised when she simply nodded and began to walk ahead of him. Indeed, she was nothing like Carmen in temperament, and Robbie knew that was a dangerous notion. Because like his brother, he couldn't help his carnal disposition. Despite everything – the curse, his fate by the hand of the fire demon, Elle being from some other land – he was just a man. And she was just a woman. It was only natural for him to desire her.

Yes, desire, he told himself. *That's all this is. She's a pretty lass, and ye haven't had a roll in the hay since the night afore ye left the village.*

With that thought strong in his mind, Robbie decided to not let himself entertain any more ideas of Elle. He had to focus on getting them to the castle.

That's all that mattered.

CHAPTER 3

From what Elle had gathered about the strange man she'd freed from the fibers, three things were certain.

One, his name was Robbie.

Two, he was Scottish – evident by his accent.

And three, he knew Carmen.

When he passed her on the path, she checked him over from behind while they walked. His kilt swung around his knees with his steady gait, his sword clinked in its scabbard to the rhythm, and the leather pouch around his waist bounced back and forth from one thigh to another.

She'd never seen such a masculine man. Everything about him screamed masculinity. Whatever he did for a living, he fought or labored a lot or both. Cuts, scrapes, and bruises marked him all over. Some had scarred over, so he must have faced danger for a long time.

The story he told about the curse and the wizard and the Phoenix Throne and everything made no sense whatsoever, but she didn't try to argue. If he were right about Carmen being here somewhere, Elle would go along with it. Besides, what choice did she have?

He glanced over his shoulder at her every now and then. She knew he had no more idea where they were going than she did, but at least she wasn't alone anymore. Facing this unknown country by herself was *not* her idea of a good time.

"What time do you think it is? I can't see the sun anywhere."

He didn't look up at the sky. "I dinnae ken. It's daytime. That's all I ken about it. This country doesnae work the same as the other place, as I'm sure ye've learned by now."

Indeed. It didn't. "So, tell me about this Phoenix Throne."

"It's a throne like any other, I suppose," he replied, "except it has a giant black dragon sitting behind it. It stares down on any poor soul who happens to come before the king."

"And it's your brother who's supposed to sit on it?"

"Well, he won't sit on it until he lifts the curse, and who can say if he'll ever do that. Perhaps we'll always wander in this strange country until the wraiths and demons and witches consume us all."

"Wraiths and witches as well as demons, huh? Boy, do you have it rough." Elle regretted the words as soon as they left her mouth. She hadn't meant for that to come out so blasé. "Sorry," she quickly added. "I'm just still adjusting to all this... magical stuff."

He didn't answer, just nodded as if he understood.

"What about th Ross character you told me about? He's a wizard, right? Can't he help?"

"Oh, he's helping us, all right. He's helping us as much as any mortal soul can help us, but it's we who'll have to lift the curse. That's clear if naught else is. He cannae lift the curse for us, as it's our family that carries it."

"You must miss your brothers. I can understand why you want to get back to them."

"Oh, I dinnae miss 'em yet — it only feels like it's been a few minutes since I seen 'em all in the living flesh. I was with them one moment, and then the next, I was here, with ye."

Elle fell silent. She hadn't been gone from her own world for too long either, only a few hours, but why did it seem like a hundred years? In the short time since Hazel had transported her to this strange place, her mind had wilted. She remembered every detail of her business and daily life, but the whole experience felt so far away from her, like if she didn't keep reminding herself about it, she'd forget entirely.

She spoke up one more time. "Don't you think we ought to find out where we're going before we just start bashing our way through these woods? We could be moving away from our destination instead of towards it."

He called over his shoulder while he walked: "And how do ye propose we find out where we're going when we don't ken where we're goin'? The only way to get there is to go there."

He chuckled over his own joke and kept on walking.

Elle fell farther behind while she considered the whole situation. He was just as strange as this country. She had no reason to believe a word he said about his brothers and the Phoenix Throne and all that. He could have made the whole thing up to convince her to come with him.

However, he couldn't have made up Carmen. He knew about Carmen and Elle and the others coming through on a magic spell. Thus, he must have told the truth about that.

Why would he make up the other stuff too? What could he possibly stand to gain by it? As sturdy and domineering as he was, he didn't impress her as a particularly controlling or manipulative type.

Clearly, he was used to giving orders and seeing them followed. He was a leader type for sure, but there was a softness to him. He honestly seemed to care at least a little about her welfare.

She walked along behind him in her own reverie when, all of a sudden, out of the dense undergrowth next to the path, a tan shape rocketed across her view. She tensed all over, but before she could react, it collided with Robbie and knocked him sideways. A resounding *thunk* echoed down the path as Elle launched herself forward. Robbie tumbled over and over across the ground entangled in the thing. It snarled and snapped ferocious teeth in his face. He wrestled its head back to stop it from biting him. He strapped his thick fingers around its throat and fought it off, but it still managed to gain the upper hand.

The thing bowled him over onto his back and pounced on top of him. It curled its hind legs under it to dig curved claws into his midsection. Elle couldn't watch any longer. If she didn't do something, it was going to kill him.

So, with a strong resolve, she jumped on the thing and grabbed it under the chin to yank its head back away from Robbie's face.

He reacted to the reprieve on sheer instinct. He heaved his legs up, planted his feet against the creature's chest, and kicked with all his might. The thing and Elle flew off him and landed on the path where the pair were just walking.

Elle landed on her back while the creature crashed against a tree trunk and slid to the ground. Elle and Robbie hopped to their feet, and both whirled around to face the thing, but it cowered in submission at the base of the tree.

Robbie approached Elle. "I'm sorry about that. I didnae mean to hurt ye. I didnae mean to... I mean, I overreacted. Are ye all right, lass?"

"I'm okay," she said, panting. "You did what you had to do to get rid of that thing."

They both turned to look at the creature that attacked him. Elle found herself staring at the strangest being she ever laid eyes on. It looked something like a wolf, with shaggy striped fur all over its body, but she could see pink skin under the hair. It walked on all fours, but not like any animal she ever saw. It looked like a person walking around on its hands and feet, not crawling.

The face looked like a cross between a person and some canine animal. It had a regular human nose, eyes, and forehead, but its mouth and lower jaw jutted out into a snout with a black nose. Furry hair covered its head, face, and neck.

In front of her eyes, the thing cringed in circles around the tree's exposed roots.

It whimpered and whined in a clear voice: "The Phoenix Throne! The Phoenix Throne!"

Robbie froze. "What do ye ken about the Phoenix Throne?"

The thing didn't answer. It kept whimpering and moaning. It inched away from the tree and crept parallel to the path.

Robbie took a step forward. "Stop! What do ye ken about the Phoenix Throne?"

Before he could say another word, the creature's foot touched the path, and it bolted into the trees, still crying in piteous tones, "The Phoenix Throne! The Phoenix Throne!"

Elle and Robbie looked at each other.

"We have to follow it," Robbie said, sternness fortifying his voice.

"You've gotta be kidding me? Uh-uh. No way am I following that thing," Elle told him, shaking her head and looking at him like he'd lost his mind.

"Ye need to trust me, lass, and do what I tell ye. And I'm telling ye we're going after it."

Before she could argue further, Robbie took off running after the thing at full speed.

"Goddammit," Elle said, although it came out as more of a hiss.

Again, she had no choice. She raced down the path after Robbie, her legs soon feeling the familiar burn of strain as she fought to keep up with him. They charged into the undergrowth after the creature and eventually caught up with it in a small ravine. The creature glanced over its shoulder briefly before it kept going. Elle muttered under her breath how ludicrous this was as she tailed Robbie down the ravine and up the other side. They waded through knee-deep rotting leaves, climbed over branches in their path, and onto a rocky outcrop at the top of the hill.

Robbie ran along the ridge and looked down on all sides for any sign of the thing.

Elle went the other way to cover more ground. All at once, she saw a branch sway down in the forest's dark heart.

"Over here!" she shouted.

She plunged into the trees and vanished before Robbie could catch up. He thrashed and cursed before he found her gaining on the creature in the shadows. Elle spotted a quick movement of stripes and fawn fur heading downhill toward a different river.

She couldn't keep this up much longer. They had to catch the thing and find out what it knew about the this supposed Phoenix Throne because that throne meant seeing Carmen again. And that was the only thing spurring Elle on.

The creature loped along the ground going much faster than any human could run on hands and feet together. It streaked between the trees so that swiftly that Elle despaired of ever catching it. All it had to do was tire them out, and it would break into the dense foliage and disappear.

Robbie appeared behind her. The trees parted up ahead, and the creature broke out of the forest onto a river bank. The water tumbled over rocks and waterfalls and into deep pools. Elle couldn't see any visible bank where a person could cross.

She pushed her way through the last thorny branches. The creature got far enough ahead of her so it could jump the river and get away. To her surprise, though, it didn't jump. It didn't go anywhere near the water. It ran along the bank parallel to the water, but it made no effort to cross.

Elle gave chase. As long as it didn't cross the river, she could catch it.

To her side, she saw Robbie emerge from the trees and appear to gauge the situation in one glance. He veered sideways to hem the creature in.

Elle ran up behind it. The creature made one wild dash for the safety of the forest. It tried to cut between Elle and Robbie. Elle danced on her left foot to herd the thing back toward Robbie. He adjusted his course at the same moment. The creature dived and weaved, but they kept up with it.

Robbie closed in from one side. The creature clearly saw its last avenue of escape fading before its eyes. It made one last wild dive to scoot past Elle. Her lungs exploded from the effort, but at the last second, she launched herself a few feet ahead of the thing. It tried to correct, but it was too late.

Their bodies met in mid-air, and Elle braced herself for the impact. The creature let out a feral shriek of terror and rage.

Elle flung her arms around the thing, and then they were airborne, freefalling back to the earth.

CHAPTER 4

Robbie planted his feet wide and glared down at the creature who attacked him on the trail. He balled his hands into fists and narrowed his eyes at the thing.

"Ye better start talking if ye ken what's good for ye. I'm in no mind to listen to any of yer moaning and groaning. Start talking, and I mean quick. What do ye ken about the Phoenix Throne? Where did ye hear about it? Tell me!"

The thing curled itself in circles at his feet. It fought the twine Robbie made out of tree fiber from the forest to tie the thing's hands and feet so it couldn't run away. It cast its pathetic eyes, first up at Robbie's smoldering face, then over Robbie's shoulder at Elle standing back out of the way.

"I don't know anything about the Phoenix Throne! I swear it," the thing whimpered.

The more it crouched and submitted at his feet, the more enraged Robbie became. He wanted to crush the life out of it and leave it for the rats to gnaw on.

"Where did ye hear that name? Ye must have heard it somewhere."

The creature nodded into the forest. "Ask Obus. He knows about the Phoenix Throne."

Robbie dropped to his knee and seized the thing by the throat. He clenched all his rage into his fingers to squeeze the life's breath out of this pathetic hound.

"I'm no' asking any Obus nor anybody else. I'm asking ye. Where did ye hear about the Phoenix Throne? Ye better tell me now afore I kill ye where ye lie."

The thing choked and spluttered. It couldn't get a sound out with him choking it like that. He knew that, but he couldn't stop himself. This thing tried to kill him. It would have succeeded if Elle hadn't intervened, and he never would have caught it if she hadn't helped him.

The creature's face bulged, and its tongue lolled out of its mouth. Robbie tightened his grip to break its neck when Elle's soft hand appeared on his shoulder.

"Stop, Robbie, please. This isn't the way to get the answers you want."

That was the first time she touched him, and it drained all the fight out of him. She needed an answer out of this creature as much as he did. They wouldn't get it anywhere else.

He flung the thing as hard as he could onto the ground. He spun away and strode across the clearing where they then dragged the thing into the trees.

Robbie stormed across the clearing and stood with his back to the creature while he got his temper under control. Why did he have to let that thing get under his skin? That stringy prison where the fire demons stuck him must have affected his thinking.

When he turned around, he beheld Elle standing with her back to him. From here, he could see the cut of her shoulders under her jacket. The seams hugged her square shoulders, and the back panel angled down her sides to her waist. The tails flared around her hips.

Dragon Quest

When he'd first laid eyes on her, he didn't think she had a single curve under that get-up. Now he saw the way her hips swooped down to her legs and around her trim buttocks. She had a body under there. She didn't try to hide it. It was right there in front of him all along.

He wanted to turn away, but he couldn't tear his eyes off of her. She squatted down next to the creature, and her silky voice caressed it the same way she caressed him when he first emerged from the fibrous cocoon.

"What's your name?"

The thing tried to roll over on its other side and present its back to her, but it wound up wincing in pain and bursting into tears instead.

She chuckled. "It's not Gollum, is it?"

Robbie's brown creased. *Gollum? What the devil is she talking about?*

"We don't want to hurt you," she went on. "Just tell us what we want to know, and we'll let you go. I promise. Scout's honor."

Robbie watched on in fascination. Whoever she was, she knew how to get what she wanted out of just about anybody. Her kindly tones worked wonders on the thing. The creature writhed around and turned its contorted countenance up to stare at her.

"Thank you, lady. Save me! Protect me!"

"You don't have to call me that. Just tell me your name so we can be friends."

"I swear I didn't know anything about the Phoenix Throne," the thing blubbered. "I only heard Obus talking about it. That's the only way I found out about it. I swear it's the truth. You have to ask Obus about it. He knows everything."

Robbie threw up his hands in disgust. "Aw, this is ridiculous!" He stormed aside and paced back and forth across the clearing.

The creature cast its eyes up at him and burst into loud wailing. "Save me, Lady! Don't let him kill me! Oh, please!"

Elle didn't turn around. She remained calm and soothing. "I believe you. Now, please, tell me your name. I really want to know. I'm Elle. You can call me that."

The thing stared up at her in visibly startled disbelief. After a long pause, it said, "Nerius. My name is Nerius, but no one has called me that for so long that I had almost forgotten it."

Her voice softened more. "All right, Nerius. Now we can be friends. Are you a male of your species?"

He nodded.

"I'm so glad you told me. Now, about Obus, can you tell us where to find him?"

"Oh, you can't find him," Nerius exclaimed. "He stays hidden in the forest. No one can find him. He finds you when he wants you. That's the way with old Obus."

Robbie muttered under his breath, "Sounds like Ross to me."

Elle turned around to face him. "We'll have to track him down. It's the next logical step."

"Oh, he is a wizard," Nerius broke in. "He's a wizard most powerful. You can't go near him. He'll destroy you."

"He would destroy you too," Elle remarked, "if he found out you eavesdropped on him and then went and blabbed what you heard all over the forest. You should be more careful."

Nerius stared up at her, then collapsed in a fit of further despondent weeping. "Oh, please don't tell him.

He's vicious, is Obus. Oh, please don't tell him I told you."

"Don't worry, Nerius," she replied. "You're our friend now. We would never do anything to get you in trouble. We'll keep you here with us, so you're safe. Then, in the morning, you can show us where to start looking for Obus."

"You can't find Obus," Nerius repeated. "You can never find him. He finds you."

"*You* found him," Elle pointed out. "Still, even if you can't find him for us, you can show us the spot where you heard him talking about it. That will help us a great deal. Then you can leave so you don't go anywhere near Obus. Okay?"

Robbie could hardly believe she was actually negotiating with this thing like that. He wanted to smash its face in. He never considered being nice to the thing to get what he wanted.

The lass is more than just a pretty face, aye.

Elle stood up and turned around to face Robbie. She walked up to him and murmured low, "Well, there you go. We'll camp here for the night and track this Obus down in the morning. Nerius can show us where he found Obus, and we'll find out what Obus knows about your brothers."

Robbie scowled. "You're no' thinking of trusting that thing, surely. He tried to kill me."

"That doesn't mean he's hostile. Look at him. Even if he were hostile, he's submissive now. What's the alternative? He's our only lead, and we can't go trekking all over these woods 'til kingdom come. We have to find out where the Phoenix Throne is so we can meet up with the others. I must find Carmen."

He turned away without answering. She was right, of course — that was the worst part. He hated that she was so right and so adept at finding out what he couldn't.

All the long, weary weeks he spent on the road with his brothers and their party in search of the witch that cursed them, Robbie played more the leader. If anything, they shared the responsibility.

Robbie's best friend, Brody Armstrong, scoffed at Angus for taking suggestions from Carmen. Now Robbie found himself faced with another strong woman with her own way of doing things. He thanked the Heavens that Brody wasn't here to see this. Robbie couldn't face him or his brothers with Elle around.

"Come on," she told him. "I'll get a fire going for us. You hunt around and see if you can find anything to eat."

"Like what exactly?" he asked. "There's naught in these woods but leaves and trees."

"I don't know. You said we were supposed to be in the Highlands. See if you can find any edible plants or something."

She walked away and left him fuming.

Edible plants! The idea!

He'd be jiggered if he ate edible plants out here. He and his brothers hunted for their meals on the road, and he could do the same thing here. He just had to find out where the game stayed hidden.

He waited until Elle strolled off into the trees collecting sticks. Then Robbie stormed up to the creature and squatted down next to it. The creature cringed in terror. Robbie narrowed his eyes at the thing to make himself as menacing and aggressive as he could.

"Ye're a meat-eater, or I'm much mistaken by ye," he muttered. "Tell me where I can find something to eat around here. If ye steer me right, ye'll share the food with us. Otherwise, we'll all go hungry tonight, and that'll make me surly, and ye wouldnae want that, I'll wager."

The thing's eyes flew open. "Oh, no no no! Not at all! If you follow that hollow down to the river, you'll see a watering hole where the deer come at evening. You can ambush as many as you want there."

Robbie got to his feet with a *humph*. Elle wasn't the only one who knew how to sweet-talk this thing.

He shrugged his shoulders straight and strode off into the trees.

CHAPTER 5

Elle sat next to Robbie by the fire. The sky grew dark overhead and eventually faded into night, although they never saw the sun all day. The sky stayed uniformly white and featureless right up to the moment it started to get dark.

The fire crackled, and Elle laid another stick on the coals. A pile of meatless bones sizzled in the blaze. Robbie wrapped up a few large hunches of meat in broad leaves.

"Ye never ken when we'll find another meal. We better plan for the long road."

Elle smiled up at him. "Where did you find the deer? I thought this forest was devoid of all life."

"A wee birdy told me where to find it." He settled his back against a tree trunk and sighed. "It's no' too bad out here, I reckon."

"No, it's a beautiful night. It would be better if we could see the stars, but at least it's not too cold."

He cocked his head at her. "Ye've spent some time on the road yerself, I'd say. Ye can handle yerself like most men I've seen."

She blushed. "I.... well, I've had some training. That's all. I'm really nothing but a desk jockey."

A shadow crossed his face. She should have known better than to use a phrase like that. He didn't have a clue what she was talking about.

"What kind of training?" he asked.

"Well, it's complicated. It was... well, it was survival training. You know, learning how to deal with emergencies and stuff – how to take care of yourself in a life-threatening situation, social upheaval, natural disasters, that sort of thing. Aw, just forget it. You're right. I've spent some time doing this stuff before, just not... somewhere as far away from home."

He studied her in the flickering orange light. "Ye must want to return to yer home. I can see that."

"Sure. We all want to. You must want to return to your home too."

He shrugged. "I have no home any longer. We've been gone so long I cannae really remember it at all. It's strange. I remember it, but I remember something like a dream. It isnae real any longer. I have no home any longer. My home is with me brothers – nowhere else. Where they are is where I belong."

She studied his chiseled features. The longer she spent with him, the more she found herself drawn to him. His presence attracted her like no other man she ever met. Now he revealed something as personal as that to her. She wanted to put her arms around him and comfort him for what he'd lost, but she didn't dare.

"What about ye, lass?" he asked. "Tell me about yer home and what ye're missing there."

She turned aside and gazed into the flames. "I don't really have a home either, now that you mention it. I have a house and a job and all that. But I don't have a home. I never did. You want to hear something really strange? I never told my closest friends I didn't have a home."

"No?" he asked. "And why not?"

"I don't know. Those girls I was with when I came here, Carmen and the others, they're the closest things I've had to friends in my life, but I never even told them. They think I had a normal family life like everybody else. They saw my mother and my father come to pick me up from school for Christmas and vacations. They saw me doing things with them and with my brother and my sister. They never saw below the surface. They never understood what really went on."

His eyes felt like they were boring into her. How much he really understood of what she said, she couldn't tell. She had to confide in him though. She had to tell him something about herself as damning and personal as he'd just told her. Something forgotten and mysterious inside her commanded her to do it.

"I was adopted," she told him. "My mother and father couldn't have children, so they adopted me. Then all of a sudden, my mother turned up pregnant with my brother. They had him and my sister within two years. They didn't really want me anymore. They raised me and everything. I'm not faulting the way they treated me or anything. They were very generous. They paid for everything. On the outside, they treated me the same as my brother and sister. On the inside, it was all different. They never showed me any unconditional affection. I never had any heartfelt talks with them about my life or what I was thinking about. I was an outsider in their house. I felt that way all my life."

He listened in silence to the secret that had weighed Elle down for years. It separated her from everyone she ever met, especially those closest to her. She no longer cared if he understood her language or not. She had to get this off her chest.

"I left home, went to college, and threw myself into building a solid career so I would never have to depend on anybody ever again. I went back to my parents' house for vacations for a few years, but after a while, I just didn't bother anymore. They stopped coming to pick me up, and the whole thing just faded away to nothing. I haven't seen them or my brother or my sister for years. We don't write or talk or anything. We're strangers. It's like they never adopted me in the first place. They were just a stopping place on the way, and now I'm alone, exactly the way I was when they first took me in."

His face softened in the firelight. He looked down at her mouth. She yearned more than anything to get close to him right now, to take refuge in his big, powerful presence.

She glanced across the fire at Nerius. The creature was slumped against a tree with his eyes closed. His head rolled sideways, and his limbs lay inert on the ground. She couldn't even see his chest moving from here.

She turned back to Robbie, and the way he was gazing at her gave her butterflies. It was like those smoldering eyes were telling her that she could do this. That she could let herself feel something for the first time, put aside the loneliness that had protected her for all these years.

What difference did it make if he knew who she really was? She was tough and impenetrable. No one ever touched the tender, sensitive, inner part of her she hid behind all the armor.

She would never see this man again once she and Carmen got back to the States. He would know her secret, and then she could walk away. She could leave her vulnerability in the distant past. She would return to her own time, to her career and her apartment and her car, and no one else would ever know the truth.

When he shifted, she flinched a little. His arm came behind her back, his warm palm resting on her neck. His touch seemed to soothe all the stiffness out of her soul, and when he guided her toward him, she didn't fight it. She rested her head on the space between his neck and shoulder, and he hugged his arm around her shoulders.

The fire warmed Elle's face, and even though she, much like Carmen, had never believed in "the one" or "true love" or "falling for someone at the drop of a hat", she dared to wonder if this, what she was feeling, was what such things felt like.

He squeezed and rubbed her neck and shoulders, then rested his lips against her hair. His chest rose and fell under her each time he breathed. She sank into his body. She smelled him and laid her hand on his chest. His body radiated warmth and comfort and pleasure into her like she'd never known in her life.

He tightened his fingers around her neck to peel her back, pushing her upright. The moment she saw his face, she knew what he wanted. He looked down at her mouth. He wanted to kiss her. She wanted the same thing – more than anything.

She cast a sidelong glance at Nerius. She expected him to be sound asleep, but when she saw him, she broke away from Robbie.

"Oh, my gosh! Look, Rob!"

She pointed at the creature lying against the tree trunk. Robbie jumped to his feet, and they both stared in horror at Nerius' fallen form. He lay exactly where he was a moment before, but his skin had sunk into his bones, his flesh having collapsed in on itself. In front of their eyes, the creature rotted away into the ground. In a few seconds, he turned into a puddle of slime against the tree roots and disintegrated into nothing.

Elle covered her mouth with her hand. "Oh my God! What happened to him?"

"Obus I suspect. The mysterious wizard must've silenced him," Robbie suggested. "The blasted lout! We might never ken the truth now."

Elle could see how vexed Robbie was, his nostrils flaring as his jaw clenched.

"It's all right. We'll figure things out," she told him, keeping her voice calm and level. "Come and sit back down."

Robbie did as she suggested, though with some reluctance.

"We'll find another way, Robbie," Elle said after a few moments.

Robbie peered over at her. "Aye. There's more than one way to skin a wizard." He chuckled to himself.

On the bright side, Elle reasoned, at least now they had the name of someone in this forest who knew something about their destination. They would find Obus; there was no other option.

Exhaustion from the day's events overwhelmed her then. She'd worked harder and expended more energy in that one day than ever before in her life. Fear and horror and excitement drained all her reserves.

As they sat side by side again, Elle knew the moment from earlier had well and truly passed. There would be no random, crazy kiss between them. And perhaps that was for the best. She couldn't go from modern America to kissing some Highlander in a magical kingdom in only a matter of hours. That was... just too mind-blowing to even consider right now. She laid her head on his shoulder though – the way she had before.

Robbie put his arm around her again, and she inhaled his musky scent.

Soon, her eyelids grew heavy and, urged on by the warmth of the flickering flames, they fluttered closed.

For the first time that day, Elle let herself relax and drift away...

CHAPTER 6

Robbie walked along the same trail as yesterday. Nerius was just as gone when they woke up the next morning. They retraced their steps to the place where Nerius attacked Robbie. Then they continued on their way like nothing ever happened.

Robbie walked in front, carrying a bundle of their extra food supplies on his shoulder. Elle followed a few steps behind. He looked back at her every few minutes to make sure she was still there, but neither of them said anything.

They walked the whole morning in silence.

What was she thinking about back there? Was she thinking she made a mistake almost kissing him by the fire? Was she wishing she'd gone ahead and done it or was she waiting for a chance to ditch him at the first opportunity?

He kept walking. He couldn't make his plans around her and whatever she might be thinking. She was a nice woman and very beautiful and attractive, but she was just a woman, after all. He had a mission to fulfill and four brothers depending on him. He couldn't leave them to fight the witch alone. If he could find a way back to them, he had to do it before he gave up.

He faced front and fixed his eyes on the path in front of him. The trail wound out of the forest into more open country, but Robbie knew better than to let appearances fool him. He'd fought too many battles against wraiths in country just like this. He wouldn't get caught unawares out here.

Elle might have come in handy fighting Nerius, but she was unarmed. He knew that the first time he laid eyes on her. If anything attacked them out here, he was on his own.

He scanned the fields for any threat, but he didn't see a thing. Nothing moved out there. Yesterday he could believe nothing was moving in this whole country. He couldn't believe that now. Something lived and moved here, and it would attack him without provocation and try to kill him, just like those wraiths did. Nerius taught him that.

The fields changed to rolling downs. They rose high overhead in grassy slopes to the heights of the sky.

Robbie pointed to the peaks. "We'll go up there and have a good look around. We'll see what this country holds – if it holds anything."

Elle didn't answer. She climbed up after him until they reached the tops. Robbie strode along the undulating ridge and surveyed the land all around. He came to the end and gazed out into the wide expanse.

"What are you looking for?" Elle asked.

"Anything familiar," he replied. "I kenned if I came up here, I might see something I'd seen afore. I kenned maybe I might catch sight of the castle or something near it. I suppose that was too much to hope for."

"Where do you want to go now?"

He scanned the whole countryside. Nothing made sense out here. He didn't recognize any direction. With no sun in the plain white sky, he couldn't even tell which direction was which. He didn't want to admit that to Elle, although he had to admit she probably already thought the same thing.

He strolled back the way he came to get another look off the other side. A patch of scrappy trees dotted the heights before the slope dropped away to the forest again. He passed through it to see if the downs continued farther on.

A few feet into the trees, the slope leveled out one more time to a small flat shelf cut into the hillside. The trees spread to the sides to create a little bowl-shaped glen lined with bluebells.

Robbie and Elle stopped to stare at the curious sight. Large toadstools, all bright-red, dotted with yellow spots, pocked the smooth grass. Winding flower paths twisted and turned between them and led to tiny doors in each mushroom stalk. Miniscule windows peeped out of the larger mushrooms' scarlet caps.

That wasn't the strangest thing about the place. All over the grass, tiny people, no taller than Robbie's shins, crowded the glen from one side to the other. They talked to each other, skipped and frolicked, and some played music while others danced and sang.

Robbie blinked in wonder at the scene. All the little people wore the same russet brown clothing and odd colored hats. Their wrinkled faces twisted in strange expressions, yet none of them looked outright dangerous – just incredibly strange. Their eyes glittered with innocent mischief.

Robbie didn't like the look of the place. He couldn't put his finger on why he didn't like it, but his instincts gave him a distinct *No* when he thought about going near the place. On the outside, it looked like something out of a child's storybook. He could squash one of these little people under his heel and walk away none the worse.

Something under the surface told him a different story.

Elle stiffened, too, and she narrowed her eyes at the little people. She noticeably didn't want to go in there either.

Good, the lass has good instincts.

What could he do? These were the closest thing to people he'd found in this empty country. He had to find out what they knew about the Phoenix Throne, the castle, and Obus.

However, he never got a chance to make a decision. The little people caught sight of him and Elle. They capered toward the newcomers, surrounded them in mobs, and took hold of their hands. The little creatures pulled them into the glen and danced around them in wild ecstasy.

Robbie exchanged glances with Elle. She looked back at him with wide eyes, but they had no choice but to let themselves be celebrated over and made much of. The music, laughter, and talking reached a fevered pitch. The little people seemed to have turned Robbie and Elle's arrival into the greatest festival they ever experienced. They formed a dancing procession between the mushrooms, and everyone joined the parade.

Robbie and Elle stood still in the middle of the pandemonium and waited for the noise to die down.

After fifteen minutes of steady mayhem, the procession worked its way around the glen until its head stopped in front of Robbie.

One of the little men addressed Robbie in a piping voice: "You are welcome to our village. I am Rufrout. You must come to my home for a meal. It's only right we welcome you with all our hospitality." He pranced to the nearest mushroom and threw open the door. He waved over his shoulder. "Come inside!"

He disappeared for an instant and re-emerged.

"Come on!"

Robbie dropped on one knee and peered through the door at a cozy little cottage all laid out with a tiny table, a fire blazing on the hearth, and dear little beds made up with quilts.

"I thank ye for yer hospitality, but I cannae fit into yer house. Ye'll just have to welcome me out here."

The joyous smile vanished off the little man's face. "Oh. Well, that's unlucky, isn't it? However, will we feed you?"

Robbie looked around. "I dinnae ken about that, but we have our own food, so ye neednae worry about us. If ye really wish to welcome us with hospitality, ye can tell us something that'll help us out on our journey."

"What do you need to know?"

"We're in search of a wizard that lives hereabouts. Perhaps ye and yer people have heard of him. His name's Obus."

The man smiled again, even bigger than before. "Oh, it's Obus you want, is it? Oh, yes, Obus is here. Finding him is never a problem. You just follow the moorland, and down the hill to the forest and you're there. Now come on. We must share a meal. We wouldn't be giving hospitality if we didn't at least share a mug of ale with you."

Robbie brightened up at the mention of ale. He looked all around the village. "Very well. Where shall I sit?"

Rufrout waved his hand. "Oh, anywhere you can fit."

He burst out laughing, and the whole village joined in the joke.

Robbie smiled and started to relax. These people were harmless and friendly. They wanted to share their bounty with him and Elle, so why shouldn't he settle in and enjoy a merry evening while he had the chance? How long had it been since he shared a quiet meal with friendly people? He and Elle could always resume their search for Obus in the morning.

Robbie made room for himself on the grass. He sat down and crossed his legs while the little people got busy. They rolled out barrels and screwed in the taps. They drew tiny mugs full and passed them around to everyone present. They just seemed to forget to serve Robbie.

The music started up again, and everyone prepared to make merry. They trundled long tables onto the grass and set them with roasted meat, tiny loaves of crunchy bread, and steamy stews.

Robbie smiled at them. He couldn't enjoy the ale or the food, but he could take pleasure in their merriment. They ate and drank, sang and danced, and people tapped their feet to the music while they feasted.

Rufrout and his fellows then rolled barrels of ale to Robbie's side and pried off the lids for him. He took hold of one and drained it in one gulp. It was by far the best ale he'd tasted in years.

Robbie glanced up at Elle. She stood in the same spot and didn't move.

"Come and sit ye down, lass," he told her. "Have something to eat and something to drink. Ye need it as much as I do."

She didn't move. She towered over the celebration going on around her feet. No one paid her any attention, but Robbie couldn't ignore her.

"I said sit ye down, lass. Ye're making a spectacle of yerself."

"You shouldn't eat their food," she told him. "They could be unfriendly. They could be putting on an act to get us to lower our guard. You shouldn't drink that ale. They could be trying to drug you."

"Drug me!" He snorted. "These are the nicest people I've seen in a long while, and I'll no' throw their hospitality in their faces like ye are. Sit down and stop talking nonsense. Ye're being rude to our hosts."

"How can you be so blind to the danger? You don't know anything about these people."

"I ken they're friendly," he returned. "Look at 'em — they're welcoming us with feasting and dancing. That's more'n I've seen anywhere else since I left home. I'll no' look a gift horse in the mouth or a barrel of ale neither." He upended another barrel. "Besides, they're helping us to find Obus, and isnae that what we came here for?"

"They could be getting ready to turn us over to him," she argued. "They could be trying to weaken us so we can't fight back when they tell him we're here."

He lost his patience with her. "If that's the way ye feel about it, then turn ye round and walk out of here the way ye came in."

She stared down at him in shock.

He turned away and set to work drinking whatever the little people put in front of him. They didn't try to give him food. He could have demolished the whole feast in a few mouthfuls, so he ate his own meat. He helped himself to the ale though. He couldn't get enough of it.

Elle stood where she was a moment longer. Then she sat down on the grass next to him.

She hugged her knees to her chest and murmured in his ear so no one else could hear, "I'll sit down, but I won't touch a drop of their food or ale. Understand? And don't ask me again."

Robbie chuckled at her fiery disposition. Perhaps she did have a bit of Carmen in her after all?

CHAPTER 7

Elle lay on her back on the grass. The cold ground seeped into her bones and chilled her through her suit. She shivered and hugged her arms around her shoulders to keep warm, but she didn't move.

The little people's feast carried on deep into the night. They lit tiny bonfires around the glen, and their energy and enthusiasm for their own party never waned until the wee hours of the morning.

Robbie ate and drank with them. He didn't spare the ale. Shortly after their argument when she refused to share these people's hospitality, she noticed the ale affecting his mind. His speech slurred, and his eyes blurred. He didn't argue with her again, and he even smiled at her.

She didn't smile back. She wanted nothing to do with these little people. They reminded her of something like elves, or maybe gnomes. Or hobbits! She couldn't figure out what they were, but their faces gave her no peace. They might be friendly on the outside, but that wicked mischief twinkling in their eyes told her a different story.

She sat by Robbie's side while he regaled the company with stories about his travels. They laughed and exclaimed over his adventures, but Elle's blood felt like it'd ran cold. He became too free with information than she considered advisable, but that was his business. She already tried to warn him, and he didn't listen.

The best she could do now was to watch, wait, and be ready for anything. The farther the night progressed, the more convinced she became that these little imps were up to something. Yes, that was the perfect name for them. They were imps, and very impish in their behavior. They were kind and generous and merry on the outside. Inside, however, she feared there was an insidious agenda.

She stared up at the featureless black sky over her head. She listened to Robbie breathing next to her. He wasn't just drunk. She'd heard too many drunk men breathing in her time. She became more and more convinced he was drugged. How long would she have to wait before these people made their move?

She opened and closed her frozen fingers to get some warmth moving through them. Should she get up and walk around? Maybe they wouldn't make a move. Maybe Robbie was right about them all along, and they were harmless and friendly.

She almost gave up waiting when the sky started to lighten.

Thank Heavens! Another day.

She gathered her resolve to sit up when she heard the first sound of movement in one of the mushrooms nearby. The clatter of frying pans banging against each other touched her ear, and a door opened. Chattering voices bubbled inside the mushroom right next to Elle's head.

She started to sit up and work the stiffness out of her limbs when she froze in horror. Doors opened all around her, and crowds and crowds of the little creatures flooded onto the paths. They all headed for her and Robbie.

She couldn't remember seeing this many last night, but maybe she was mistaken. More of the things that she ever thought could exist in one village poured out of their mushroom houses. They surrounded Robbie in masses and picked him up off the ground.

It was like a scene out of *Gulliver's Travels*.

Robbie sighed and settled deeper into sleep. He didn't sense a thing that was happening. The little people started to carry him out of the village, toward the down.

Elle got to her feet to follow them. "Excuse me, just what the hell do you think you're doing?"

Rufrout marched next to Robbie's body. He swung his little walking stick and called up to her in a cheery voice, "We're taking him to Obus."

"Obus!" Elle exclaimed. "Why?"

"Everyone who enters this territory has to be delivered to Obus," Rufrout told her simply. "That's the rules."

"My ass! I knew you damn things were up to no good. Drop him at once!"

Rufrout didn't answer. In fact, no one paid any attention to her protests. They hauled Robbie onto the down and through the trees.

Elle couldn't stand by and let them take Robbie though. So, again, finding a strong resolve, she launched forward, planting herself in their path.

"I said stop!"

The singing ceased, but the marching didn't. Rufrout glared up at her with flashing eyes. He waved his little walking stick at his comrades.

"Down the hill!"

Elle flew into action. She didn't know what came over her. Her heart felt like it was threatening to explode out of her ribs. She only knew she had to stop them. She couldn't exactly fight a bunch of people a fraction of her size, but her instincts took over, and before she knew what she was doing, she waded into their midst. She kicked every head she saw and skidded them out of the way right and left.

Robbie hit the ground and groaned. He rolled over on his side, and his eyes craned open. He stared in blank astonishment at Elle standing over him. As she continued to wade through the crowd, the imps shrieked in horror. They tried to scuttle out of the way, but she caught them and booted them into the trees. The sight would have been comic if she hadn't been so desperate to get them away from Robbie.

He heaved himself to a sitting position and held out a hand to Elle, but he toppled over on his face in the dirt. Elle whirled around, casting her flashing eyes over the "battlefield". She spotted a few imps peeking at her from behind the trees, but none dared come near her again. All at once, she caught sight of Rufrout crouched in a corner. She headed straight for him. He tried to bolt, but he couldn't get far on his toothpick legs. She caught him and lifted him up to her face level.

"I shall ask you again, and I want a different answer this time, a more honest one – why were you taking Robbie to Obus? What does Obus want from us?"

"Oh, please, please, please, Your Highness!" he sobbed. "Please don't eat me! I never meant any harm. Please don't feed me to the monster."

"You can stop calling me 'Your Highness'," she snapped, "and I'm not going to eat you. Whoever heard of such a thing! I only want to know why you were turning us over to that wizard. How does he know about us?"

"No one knows what Obus does or why," the little man squealed. "We have our orders, and those orders tell us to deliver any strangers to Obus, Your Highness. That's all I know."

Elle frowned. "So Obus doesn't know about us specifically? He never told you we were coming?"

"Oh, he knows all about you," Rufrout replied. "He told us to be on the lookout for you, and we were to deliver you forthwith, Your Highness."

"You better be telling me the truth," Elle returned.

"Oh, I am, Your Highness!" he exclaimed. "Oh, please don't feed me to the monster, Your Highness. That's all I ask."

"What monster are you talking about?"

"Obus' pet. Anyone who disobeys Obus gets fed to the monster. Everybody knows that, Your Highness."

"Look, I'm not going to feed you to any monster. Just take your people and get out of here. Don't bother us again."

She drop-punted him into the trees again, and he darted away still whimpering. She turned toward Robbie. He propped himself on his elbow and watched her, but he didn't get up. His hair hung disheveled around his face, and he looked quite hungover.

Serves him right.

Elle watched Rufrout disappear out of sight before she sank down on one knee next to Robbie.

"Not that I should care right now, but are you all right?"

He nodded, but he didn't look all right. Not by a long shot.

"I'm all right, lass. I'm just..."

He never finished the sentence. A spine-tingling shriek echoed out of the woods, and thousands of the little creatures charged out to pounce on Elle and Robbie. Before she could get to her feet, dozens upon dozens of the things attacked her from all directions. They climbed up her clothes and clawed at her eyes and hair. They weighed her down to the ground and almost subdued her.

Out of the corner of her eye, she saw them on top of Robbie. They pinned him to the ground and obscured him from view. He tried to fight them off, but in his weakened state, he couldn't get to his feet.

Elle reared under her tormentors, but she couldn't see a thing with so many bodies crowded around her head. The imps hung off her arms and clung to her legs so she couldn't move. They swarmed all over her back and head. They tripped her up, so she stumbled and crashed down on one knee.

Desperate fury broke out of her. The more they weighed her down and threatened to overcome her, the more enraged she became. She roared out her bottomless anger at the things trying to destroy her. They tried to kidnap Robbie, and now they wanted to drag her off somewhere too.

Not on my damn watch. Not again.

She shook herself like a wet dog, flinging the things off her in every direction. They hit the trees and the dirt and rocketed back at her for more. She stomped her feet hard against the ground until they fell off her pant legs.

More and more of them came at her every minute. She hated them. She'd sensed they were malicious when she first saw them, and now she knew it for certain. She vented all her spleen against them, and she didn't feel the least bit bad about it.

She threw them away as fast as she could, but she couldn't keep up with their sheer numbers. Once they got on top of Robbie, the extra imps came at her twice as hard. She had to get rid of them. She had to teach them a lesson, so they never came at her again.

She couldn't get to Robbie's sword fast enough. She quickly surveyed the forest and saw what she wanted. She scooped up a stout stick and swung it. She clubbed a dozen imps aside in one blow, cutting a vicious swathe through their numbers until she cleared a space around her.

The imps retreated into the trees en masse.

Elle stormed through the last stragglers and gave them an extra thump for good measure. Some of them hid behind the trees and stole peeks at her, but when she brandished her club at them, they disappeared and didn't show their faces again.

She paced through the fallen leaves to Robbie and batted his tormentors away in short order. She caught the last squealing imp in one hand, tossed it into the air, and batted it as hard as she could into next week to teach them all a lesson about messing with her again.

In a few minutes, not one imp remained in sight.

Elle hefted her club. A weapon felt good in her hands. She would keep it from now on, just in case anybody else tried to pull a fast one on her.

She returned to Robbie. He lay panting and beaten on the ground. Blood oozed out of his nose and from a gash near one ear. She knelt down next to him.

"Can you stand?"

He gasped for breath. "I cannae sit up. Whatever they put in that ale drained me strength. I only hope it's no' permanent, or I'm sunk."

"Don't worry – I'm sure it will wear off. We'll make camp here. I'll build a wall of small fires around us – that should hold them off for long enough."

She started to stand up, but he caught her hand. "Ye were right, Elle. I should have listened to ye. I'm a damn fool."

She smiled down at him. "Never mind. I was right, but I could have been wrong. Lie quietly now and try to rest. You need all your strength back, so don't overdo it. I'll get to work on those fires."

He looked around. "We left all our food supplies back in the village."

"I'll go back and get them," she replied. "Those things won't bother us again anytime soon. I made damn sure of that."

Elle touched his forehead, the gesture one of both comfort and something more. Despite being cross with him, for a little while, she feared she'd lose him. And the notion of being alone once again in an unknown land terrified her to the core.

When Robbie reached up to clasp her hand, she dared to only let him hold it for a moment.

Then, she broke the contact and dashed off to retrieve their supplies.

CHAPTER 8

Elle woke in the cold, clear light of another morning. Her hand tightened around her club when the first thing she noticed was Robbie.

He was gone.

She'd laid down next to him last night after collecting their supplies and building the circle of fires around them to hold off those nasty little hobbit-like urchins.

She got to her feet and walked around the forest in search of him, thinking the worst when she couldn't find him. The imps had somehow penetrated their camp while she'd been dozing and successfully kidnapped him this time.

Still holding the club, Elle gathered the last remains of the food provisions and slung the bundle over her shoulder. She set off up the hill the way she'd come. She would break a thousand more pint-sized heads if that's what it took to find Robbie.

She stormed into the imps' village and went straight to the mushroom where she knew Rufrout lived. She planted her feet wide, took aim with her club, and smashed the mushroom aside. The stalk snapped, and the toadstool went flying. It left the innards of the house in place with a tiny woman and even tinier children screaming and crying in the breeze.

The wind caught the flames on the hearth. The steam from the tea kettle blew across the glen. A little girl started up in bed and shrieked when she saw Elle wielding a club over the remains of the house.

Rufrout darted out of another room somewhere.

"You ruined my home!"

Elle propped her club on her shoulder and seized the little man. She brought him close to her face.

"What have you done with him? Where's Robbie? Did you take him to Obus the way you tried to before?"

"Who? What are you talking about?"

"You know exactly what I'm talking about," Elle snapped. "You did something to him in the night while I was asleep. Where is he? You must know."

He struggled in her grasp. "I don't know anything about anything. Don't you think I have better things to do in the middle of the night than keep track of your business after what you did to us?"

Elle strode over to the nearest toadstool and hauled back her club. "I'm gonna work my way through this village and smash every mushroom I see if you don't start talking."

"No, no!" Rufrout cried. "Don't do that! I'll tell you anything you want to know. Just don't do that. Don't harm any more of our houses."

"Tell me then. Where is Robbie?"

"We didn't do anything to him," Rufrout shrieked. "I didn't know anything happened to him. We never went near your camp after... after yesterday."

"If you didn't do something, you must know what happened to him," Elle replied. "He was asleep by our fire last night, and now he's gone."

"Obus must have taken him," Rufrout wailed. "That's the only answer. When we failed to turn you over, he must have taken the man himself. Yes. That's what happened. Nothing happens in this forest without Obus knowing about it. He must have been watching and seen us fail to take you in. We tried, but when you wouldn't drink the ale, we had no choice but to take the man. No one who shows up in this forest resists our ale. That's why we failed."

Elle lowered her club. "You're gonna show me where I can find this Obus character."

"Oh, no, I couldn't do that!" Rufrout cried. "No one can go near Obus without his permission. He would feed me to the monster for sure if I did that, and then who would take care of my family? My children would starve. My wife would die of heartbreak. Put me down. I can't take you to Obus."

"No?" Elle moved the little man close to her own mouth. She opened her jaws wide and pointed Rufrout's head into the gaping hole.

"No!" the little man screamed. "All right! All right! I'll take you there."

Elle pulled him back and smiled. "That's better."

She popped the little man in her jacket pocket, shouldered her club, and started across the down. She heard Rufrout complaining to himself, but she paid no attention. She wanted to make him suffer for what he'd done, and the more he fretted and worried over his fate, the more cooperative he would be.

She walked past her camp, but she refused to look at the remains of the fire. She didn't want to see Robbie not lying there where he should have been.

Where is he? What if Obus has done something to him?

She shook the thoughts out of her head. Wherever Robbie was, he would take care of himself. He was strong and brutish – when he had to be – and she had to take some comfort in that.

Elle realized then just how much she'd come to truly care for the man that she barely knew. She had to find him. For both their sakes. And, if the worst-case scenario was that Obus couldn't tell her where Robbie was, then at least he could tell her how to find the castle housing the Phoenix Throne and thus Carmen.

She walked down a hill on the far side of the down, the way Rufrout had told Robbie. The forest closed in with its dark shadows, but her club gave her courage. She would not hesitate to use it without mercy on anything that threatened her. Elle had barely been in this godforsaken land for twenty-four hours, and already she was no longer the woman she used to be.

What is this placing doing to me?

She walked a long way over flat country all covered in dense forest. She stopped and looked around, and Rufrout poked his head out.

"Why are we stopping?"

"Where are we going?" she asked him. "How do we find Obus?"

"Keep going," he told her. "Just keep going. We're nowhere near Obus' house."

She glared down at the little man. "You better not be trying to trick me. You know what will happen if you do."

"Oh, I would never try to trick you... again, I mean. I'll take you to Obus as long as you let me go before you confront him. Vicious and powerful is Obus, Your Highness."

"Fine. Keep your head down, but if you do steer me wrong, into the fires of Mount Doom you'll go."

He stared up at her, looking utterly confused by *The Lord of the Rings* reference, and she almost wanted to laugh. He muttered something as he slunk back down in her pocket, and she hiked onward.

Elle fell into her own thoughts the farther she went. The forest took on its old menacing atmosphere, now that she was alone. She'd never let herself admit she needed anybody, especially not an overbearing brute like Robbie.

She wished she had him with her now though. It wasn't just his company she craved; something about him drew her to him. His overbearing nature made him... near irresistible, and she both loved and hated that. She never let herself feel this way about any man, and she didn't want to feel it about him.

Why didn't she kiss him the other night when she had the chance? She might never get another chance to kiss him, and she might never feel this way for any other man as long as she lived.

What a rom-com heroine cliché you turned out to be, huh? she scolded herself.

She walked until nightfall, and Rufrout popped out one more time.

"Aren't you going to stop?"

She didn't answer.

"We have to stop for the night. You can't just keep walking. You'll get lost in the woods."

She threw herself down on a pile of leaves. "Oh, all right. We'll stop."

He hopped out of her pocket and looked around. They could barely see a few feet into the trees.

"Aren't you going to build a fire?" Rufrout asked.

"What for? We're only going to go to sleep and then wake up and start walking again. We don't need a fire."

Rufrout's face fell. He looked back and forth between Elle and the forest. In truth, her instincts were on alert. She sensed another malicious force creeping around out there. Perhaps without a circle of firelight, they would lurk until they saw a chance to strike.

Rufrout held himself together for another moment before he collapsed on the ground at Elle's side. He wrung his hands and tore at his clothes.

"Oh, what will become of me? What will become of my poor children, all alone and friendless in the world? They'll freeze in the night. They'll starve before I get home. The rain will soak their beds, and the wind will blow the food off the tables."

Elle threw up her hands. "Do you ever stop whining? Honestly, I've never met anyone so annoying in my entire life. If I make you a damn fire, will that shut you up?"

When he merely smiled and nodded, she shook her head in jest.

"You know, if you were in a movie I was watching, Rufrout, I might have actually thought you were a funny little oddball."

"Movie? Oddball?" he queried with one tiny eyebrow raised.

Elle sighed. "Never mind," she said and set to work making the little man his fire.

CHAPTER 9

Elle lay on her stomach in the rough brush and surveyed the little cottage tucked into the trees. A curl of smoke swirled out of its stone chimney, moss grew on the roof thatch, and the sun twinkled on the granite blocks forming its walls.

Then she peered up at the sky. *Is that really the sun?*

Yes, the sky cleared to a beautiful blue, and the sun sparkled out of it to create a warm summer day. The house didn't look like any wizard's house. It looked like any quaint little country cottage.

"Are you sure this is the right place?"

"Oh, very sure, Your Highness," Rufrout replied. "That's Obus' house. If he's not there, he will be soon. I'd wager he is in there though. See? The fire's going. Oh, look. You can see him moving behind the windows. He's there. All you have to do is walk up the path and knock on the door. Can I go now?"

"Are you certain this is the right place?"

"This is the place we bring outsiders when they appear in our village."

Elle smacked her lips. "I don't even want to know how many people you've done that to. You would have done it to us, too, if I hadn't stopped you."

"Can I go home now, Your Highness? You said I could leave as soon as I showed you where to find Obus. I have to get home to my family now. They'll be ever so worried, and I have to help them rebuild the house and all."

"I don't know," she muttered. "I have a good mind to keep you here until I see whether Obus really is there. You could be trying to trick me again."

He fell on his knees next to her. "Oh, please don't make me go near the cottage! Obus will punish me so!"

"Fine," she snapped. "You can go. Just remember though: I know how to find my way back to your village. If anything goes wrong, I'm coming back to find you, and I'll be very, very hungry when I do."

Rufrout didn't wait around to reply. He scampered off into the woods as fast as his tiny legs would carry him.

Elle faced the little cottage. Whatever Rufrout said, she couldn't bring herself to believe the cottage contained any danger. How could such a fearsome wizard live in such a nice cottage? How could the sun shine on its glistening flowerbeds and not any other part of this weird country?

Then she remembered an old film adaption of *The Snow Queen* from Faerie Tale Theatre she'd watched once. The character of Gerda, on her way to find her best friend, Kay, who had been snatched away by the Snow Queen, comes across a lovely little cottage surrounded by beautiful flowers. A nice woman greets her there and offers to help her, only to trick her into forgetting her memory and her quest to find Kay.

Either way, safe or dangerous, Elle wouldn't find out the true nature of the cottage by lying in the leaves.

She got to her feet, took a firm grip on her club, and strode up the garden path to the door. She raised her hand to knock, but to her surprise, the door opened from the inside instead.

Elle stared at the person across the threshold. A fat little old man with an enormous stomach grinned at her behind his white whiskers. His mustache curled at the ends in circular handlebars, a pair of gold-rimmed spectacles were perched on his rosy round cheeks.

This is the wizard? You've got to be kidding me...

He looked like a modern-day Santa Claus, minus the red suit. He wore rough brown clothes with a length of hemp cord holding his pants up, a tattered canvas waistcoat over his linen shirt, rawhide boots laced up to his knees, and carried a long knife jammed into his belt.

He beamed at her standing on his doorstep. "There you are. I was wondering when you would get here. Come right in. Tea's on."

He disappeared into the cottage and left the door open.

Elle stared inside at the rustic furnishings. It looked like a larger reproduction of Rufrout's house, only much more comfortable and inviting. The only difference was a large shelf full of books against one wall and a rocking chair in front of the fire. Oh, and she could actually fit inside.

The old man puttered around the cottage doing this and that. He mixed something in a bowl on his workbench. When he finished, he turned a mass of white dough out on the board and kneaded it into a loaf. He put it in a pan and set it in the burning coals. He hummed to himself while he cleaned up the extra flour.

He cast a sharp glance at her over his spectacles. "Are you coming in or not?"

Elle frowned, then stepped inside – what else could she do?

"Take a seat," he told her.

She sank into a rocker chair, all her resistance gone. She had to go through with this and find out where it all led.

He took the tea kettle off the fire and poured the boiling water into two stone cups. He set one in front of her and cut a slice of cake onto a rough wooden plate. He set it in her hands and sat across from her on a wooden armchair.

Elle couldn't stop staring at everything around her. What in the world was going on here? Was this the vicious, powerful mastermind Rufrout feared so much? Did the imps know all along Obus was a harmless old man drinking tea in his little house?

"Now then," Obus declared after he swallowed a swig of his tea. "I know what you've come for. You're here about the boy."

Elle blinked. "The boy?"

"The younger brother. You're here to find him. Am I right?"

She struggled through her confusion as to what he was talking about.

"You mean Robbie? Yes, I'm here to find him. Those things, the imps, they seemed to think you took him."

"I don't have him. The dragon's got him. You can get him back though. It won't be too hard."

"Come again? Dragon?"

"The dragon on the mountain. He's caught your boy and is holding him captive on the mountain. You just have to make up your mind to go up there and get him. It's as simple as that."

"Wait a minute." Elle shut her eyes against the onslaught of information. "Are you saying you didn't have anything to do with taking him?"

"Oh, those rascals are always blaming me for everything that goes wrong in this forest," Obus replied. "They probably wanted to roast you and eat you for their next feast. That's the way they do it. If anybody comes into their territory, they drug them with ale and eat them."

Elle's mind spun more. "They definitely tried to drug us, but they said they had to turn us over to you or you would feed them to your pet monster. They said you captured Robbie. They kept telling me how vicious and powerful you were."

Obus threw back his head and laughed. His eyes danced, and his cheeks glowed bright red. "They're always making up stories. They would say and do anything to stop anybody finding out what they're really up to."

"I can't believe it… Or hell, maybe I can. Nothing makes sense in this crazy place."

"Come on, lass. Eat your cake and drink your tea before it gets cold."

Elle fixed her eyes on him. He called her lass. That name struck her, right to her guts. That was the name Robbie called her. It twisted inside her and woke forgotten emotions of the connection and relationship they were forming.

Whatever else Obus was, he wasn't the dangerous wizard Rufrout made him out to be. Elle was starting to trust him.

"Do you know Nerius?" she asked.

"Oh, yes. Nerius runs errands for me sometimes."

"He told us you knew about the Phoenix Throne."

Obus' head shot up, and the happy twinkle vanished from his eyes. His face smoldered and flashed.

"I know about the Phoenix Throne, and from the sound of it, so do you."

"What do you know about it? Please, tell me what you know."

He set his plate on his knees. "You want to know about the Phoenix Throne? That boy and his brothers went to fight the witch. They had to defeat her and break the curse so the eldest could inherit the throne."

"Then it's all true." Elle sighed. "Everything Robbie said about his brothers and Carmen... They're out there fighting somewhere, and he's trying to get back to them."

"Did you really think he would lie to you about that?"

"I should have trusted him fully," she remarked. "I just couldn't believe it, but I do now. Then it must also be true that Carmen and I and the others will go back to our own time when the curse lifts."

Obus took another sip of his tea and murmured under his mustache.

Elle set her tea and cake aside. "I better go. I have to get to the castle and find the others."

"There's just one thing you have to think about," he told her.

"What's that?"

"You can't free that boy from the dragon *and* find your way to the Phoenix Throne. You have to choose."

She stared at him, wide-eyed. "I what?"

"You have to choose between freeing him from the dragon and finding your friends to return to your own time. You can't do both. You probably think you'll free him and then go with him to find your friends. Think about it. You could get killed fighting the dragon. You could fail to lift the curse. Anything could happen. You have to choose. What's really more important to you? Do you want that boy, or do you want to go back to where you belong? Granted, you might be able to do both. On the other hand, you might only be able to do one. Which is more important to you? If you can only accomplish one, which will you choose?"

Elle stared at him in shock, but she couldn't deny the truth of what he said. If anything happened to her facing one of these challenges, she would never get around to the second. She had to decide which was more important to her.

She looked all around her without seeing anything. The wide world outside stretched before her mind's eye. Robbie was in danger somewhere from some random dragon that captured him. While far away, somewhere out of sight, her friends battled untold forces to reclaim the Phoenix Throne, which was the only way she could get back to her own home and her own time.

Which did she really want? And how important was Robbie to her anyway? If she didn't free him, no one would. His brothers had no idea where he was. Elle's friends didn't know where she was either, but at least they had some people working to break this curse. What did Robbie have? Nothing. She was his only hope.

She returned her gaze to Obus who regarded her with kind, deep eyes. He already knew her choice. She felt it.

"Robbie," she told him. "I'll free him from the dragon. Then, we'll focus on finding the castle."

Obus jumped out of his chair so fast he almost knocked over his tea.

"Finding the throne is easy. You just follow that line of peaks over there." He pointed to a sharp outline of mountains lying purple and mysterious against the distant sky. "You follow those peaks, and it will lead you to the castle. You can't go wrong."

He put aside his plate and cup and busied himself around the cottage.

"You said finding the dragon and freeing Robbie would be easy too," she pointed out. "You said that right before you said I might get killed doing it. Which is it?"

"It's both. You could get killed walking through the forest. You could get killed getting out of bed in the morning. Everything has its risks. You have to choose what you're going to do, but that's neither here nor there. You're going to get that boy, so you'll need a few things to take with you."

"Like what?"

He didn't answer right away. He rummaged around in his bookshelves until he pulled out a little cloth bag. He handed it to her.

"You need this. It's an amulet that robs the dragon of his power. That's the dangerous part. You have to get close enough to the dragon to put this around its neck. Once you render the dragon powerless, you'll be able to free the boy and take him away with you. That's all you have to do. Nothing could be simpler."

Elle opened the bag and drew out a smooth stone disk dangling from a thin leather cord. The cord ran through a hole bored sideways through the disk. The stone glowed deep green against her hand.

She looked up into Obus' twinkling eyes. "Thank you, Obus. I mean that. I shall not forget your kindness."

"No bother, lass," he said with a chirp. "I know you'll find him. You'll take him home to his people. I knew you would."

"How do I find him though? Do you know where the dragon lives?"

"Of course. Everybody knows where the dragon lives. He's notorious. He lives in the smoking caldera at the top of that mountain." He pointed to the same line of rocky pinnacles he'd indicated to before.

Elle gazed up at the mountains. If Obus was right, she could get Robbie away from the dragon and then trek down the same mountain range to the castle.

This might just work out...

The amulet sizzled in her hand. She glanced down at it and back up at Obus. He smiled at her warmly. He'd given her everything she needed to continue this quest. All she needed was the strength and courage to see it through, and he couldn't give her that.

She had to find that within herself.

CHAPTER 10

Elle camped under the mountain. She lit a fire to warm herself and ate the few morsels Obus gave her for the journey. She finished them all in one meal. She would have to find some other way to feed herself on this trip.

She should have questioned Obus more about where to find game in these woods. She should have asked Robbie where he got that deer, although that wouldn't help her now. She would have to spend tomorrow and maybe another few days hunting to get enough supplies to last her up in the mountains. She certainly wouldn't find anything to eat up there.

She threw a few more sticks on the fire and leaned back against a tree to rest. She couldn't see the mountain in the dark, but it hung there in the space above her. Her life, despite the success of the spell, currently had a tinge of monotony about it. All she ever seemed to do was make campfires and then sit by them worrying about what her next step to getting home was going to be.

Why did this dragon have to capture Robbie? Had it already eaten him? Was Robbie suffering up there with every delay until Elle could free him? Hadn't there been enough drama of late?

She closed her eyes, but the mountain gave her no peace. It was like she could hear its guttural voice in her sleep, growling and rumbling, the smoking caldera blasted stinking sulfur into the atmosphere to choke her. Did she really want to go near it? Could she physically do it?

Suddenly, she was extremely homesick and wished she'd never gone to Hazel's that night. She wanted to be back in her ordinary life doing ordinary things.

However, despite her natural fear, which was indeed warranted, Robbie compelled her to buck up. He was up there somewhere, and he was her ticket to getting to the elusive Phoenix Throne. What was the point of any of this if she had to face it alone?

She never really thought that way before. She never really cared about being alone until right now. He'd changed all that.

The amulet burned a hole in her pocket. How could she get near enough to a dragon to put something around its neck?

This was a Brer Rabbit moment. She could never defeat a dragon in an all-out fight, so she concluded that she had to use trickery. She would use whatever means she could to accomplish her ends.

She closed her eyes and imagined the dragon perched up there on the caldera. The smoke and lava kept it warm, and its scales scratched over the rocks when it slithered around.

For some reason, she didn't see Robbie in her vision. Maybe the dragon had him stashed in a hole or something?

Elle must have dozed off while still pondering such thoughts because she blinked her eyes open to find it was morning. She didn't give herself time to mull the situation over again; she set off through the forest. But after a few hours of walking, she couldn't ignore her hunger any longer. She had to find something to eat, and it had to be something with a little extra she could take with her. She had a long journey ahead.

She kept moving, scanning the surroundings for any signs of life. Now that the sun shone through the thick mist, she saw more signs of animals, bugs, and birds. That was a relief, at least. Still no people though.

She hiked almost all day before she found what she was looking for: a thin trail winding through the woods. Pellets dotted the ground at odd intervals, and towards evening, she spotted a cluster of deer in the distance.

She froze in her tracks. The animal in the very rear of the group turned its head to stare at her. Then they all bounded away into the dense forest.

Elle didn't take another step. She had to hunt them, but she didn't have a weapon. She had a club and nothing else. She thought fast, but it didn't take her long to decide what to do – she needed to eat; otherwise, her hunger would drive her to insanity.

She set to work right away, stowing the club under a nearby tree and selecting a long straight stick from the forest. She ground the tip against a rock until she carved it into a sharp point. Then she climbed a tree above the deer's path and settled herself into a crook of a branch to wait.

She steeled herself for a long wait, but she was in no hurry. Her hunger gave her icy cold determination. She wouldn't take another step until she got herself some food supplies to replace the ones she took with her from the imps' village.

Night fell a lot colder than it had in the mist. Stars sparkled in the motionless sky, and Elle huddled into a ball for warmth. The deer wouldn't come out at night, but she would still be here in the early morning when they did come.

She closed her eyes and buried her head against her knees. The mountain, the dragon, the amulet — everything she had to do hovered before her eyes. It cast her into a dream...

Inner tremors vibrated through the mountain's insides. The caldera belched its hideous gases into her face. The dragon's eyes sparkled deadly intent at her. Its rough hide scraped the rocks where its tail and belly dragged across the ground...

She jerked awake to find a glimmer of light peeking through the trees. She pried her eyes open and forced herself to focus on the path below. She needed food, and in a few minutes, it should walk right past her on the trail below.

She waited for what seemed like hours. The sun rose against the mountain and filled the forest with birdsong and the click of distant insects. She started to doze off again, but she forced herself awake one more time.

A *crack* almost startled her out of her tree. She steadied herself to see a deer tiptoeing down the path toward her. She tightened her grip on her makeshift spear, praying to whatever god was listening that it would work. Her heart thundered in her temples. This was it. All the survival skills she'd learned and practiced amounted to this moment. Could she do it? Could she really *kill* an animal for food?

Her stomach screamed *Yes!* Her palms broke out in sweat, and she steadied her nerves for the blow. She eased herself closer to the edge of the branch, hanging suspended right over the path.

The deer stopped to visibly listen and look around. It swiveled its ears. Could it hear her heart beating overhead? She waited until the first big buck strode by underneath her. Then, some doe came next, with their fawns.

That was it.

Her Achilles heel.

The fawns completely melted her resolve.

The sight of the group of deer made Elle think of her parents who had abandoned her, and the parents she wished she'd had. How could she do to the fawns what had been done to her, twice – become an orphan, not by choice.

She waited until all the deer had moved on before she climbed down out of the tree. Disappointed with herself, for both wanting and not wanting to hunt the deer, she meandered a little further down the path, on the verge of breaking down.

What am I going to do? I can't save Robbie if I starve before I can save him.

She kept walking, neither slow nor fast, just blithe. She had no plan and no tenacity. She was wilting, and she hated herself for it. And then, the strangest sight beheld her...

It can't be, can it?

Before her, just off the path a little way, was a single tree in full bloom. And hanging from its branches was a green fruit.

It is! They're pears!

Elle couldn't remember the last time she'd been so excited. She dropped the spear and rushed to the tree.

Briefly, she thought of Eve and the snake in the Garden of Eden. Maybe it was a test, a trick of some evil being that dwelled in the woods. However, the one thing she did have, that she knew she could trust, was her instincts. And they told her to eat the damn fruit!

So, she did. Five in fact. Then, she picked fifteen more for the trip to the mountain and bundled them into the top of her pantsuit to take back to where she'd left the now virtually empty bag of supplies.

*****

Later that night, Elle rested by set another campfire with a full stomach and plenty of food, albeit just the one staple, for the long road ahead. She didn't quail before the mountain and its challenges now. She would find Robbie and save him from the dragon.

When she fell asleep and dreamed about the dragon, it didn't bother her as much as it did before. She stood before the caldera. The dragon's scaly hide grated against the rocks the way it always did, but she didn't cringe in horror. The reptile curled its hot body around her to protect her. Its slithering length aroused her to the depths of her flesh. It awoke deep-seated lust in her being. She ached for it, and when it caressed its scales over her skin, she moaned and writhed in ecstasy, calling out its name over and over again:

"Robbie... Robbie... Robbie!"

CHAPTER 11

Elle stood on a mountain peak and gazed across at the caldera smoking on the next jagged summit. There it was, and there was the dragon, just like Obus told her it would be. It bobbed its spiked head on its long neck and weaved back and forth. It narrowed its fiery eyes at everything in search of any threat. It scratched its belly against the hot rocks, and its long tail whipped through the air.

Elle studied the creature for a long time. She thought long and hard about how to approach it, but her ideas got all mixed up with her fevered dreams. She didn't understand her own feelings toward this lizard. She shouldn't find it appealing, but she did. She fantasized about it touching her, and her dreams aroused her beyond anything she ever thought possible.

It was sick. Wrong. And yet... she was not ashamed.

Now she saw the thing in the flesh. She gazed down on its scales flashing iridescent green and purple and blue in the sun. The caldera bubbled and rumbled in the distance. She planned to approach the dragon and see if she could trick it into giving up Robbie. Now she didn't hesitate to do it. She wanted to get close to it, to see if it produced the same effect on her in person that it did in her mind.

She watched for several hours without moving. She didn't see any sign of Robbie anywhere.

Where is the dragon keeping him? Is he dead?

She had to move and go somewhere as she'd used up all her food supplies on the journey.

The dragon made one circuit of the caldera after another. It stretched its leathery wings and beat the air, but it didn't take flight. *Why not?* It glared all around it in hawkish vigilance, but it never left the caldera.

It doesn't make sense... How can a creature that big fly down and capture Robbie without even waking me? And why capture him and not me? Or just kill us both on the spot if it was hungry or vengeful?

Elle realized only now that she was questioning everything from a logical perspective. Why hadn't she before? Why had she too readily accepted that a random dragon had stolen Robbie away?

Maybe I'm going crazy... Maybe this place has finally taken its toll on my simple, American, earthly mind?

Despite the doubts pinching her thoughts, she shouldered her pack and set off down the long pass to the other peak. The journey took all day, and she chanced to eat some icicle plants that she found clinging to some bare rock. She had no idea whether they would poison her or not, but she no longer cared. She was hungry, and the alternative was to drop from exhaustion and die anyway.

Ha. Some damn spell, Hazel. Wait until I get my hands on you...

She struggled up a steep gravel scree to the mountain's highest pinnacle. She perched on the very apex and stared down on the caldera directly below her. There was the dragon, curled up with its eyes closed. This was the moment she'd planned for. She had to make her move before it woke up.

She stowed her bundle in a hollow under a boulder, then set off down the long slope toward the reptile. Her heart pounded, but she wouldn't quit until she found out if this would actually work.

She gave a part muted laugh then. Here she was, about to face a dragon, with a "special" amulet that was meant to weaken it.

What the hell am I doing here?

For a few moments, she looked out towards the horizon and thought of home. Her life was busy and simple, but it wasn't dangerous. Or extreme.

I want to go home, she dared to utter under her breath.

But then she felt the amulet in her jacket pocket, and she was reminded that another life was at stake here. She couldn't walk away from this.

So, Elle carried on. She got halfway down the slope of slick rock when her foot slipped.

Holy crap.

She stumbled a few feet before she caught herself, but a few pebbles dislodged under her boots. They pattered down the walls ahead of her, and the worst happened.

The dragon stirred.

It raised its wicked head, and its slitted eyes fixed on her. Her nerves stretched to breaking point, and she wanted to run for cover, but she forced herself to continue climbing down, refusing to look at the thing. If she did, she might falter again, and that wasn't an option.

She climbed all the way down to the very lip of the caldera and stopped near a large rock. Only then did she close her eyes, take a deep breath, and muster the courage needed to face the dragon. She looked up at its face in wonder, then gasped.

It was the most beautiful, majestic, and terrifying sight that she'd ever beheld. It exuded death and magic and intoxicating power all in one fold. Its eyes felt like they were boring into her soul... She couldn't look away...

At that moment, it spoke in a clear voice, as low as thunder, that shook the mountain. "What are you doing here?"

Wow. It can talk? That had never crossed her mind. Just when she thought things in this "fairy tale" land couldn't get any nuttier.

She swallowed, maintaining her gutsy resolve, and looked straight into its eyes. "I came here to see you."

Its head slithered back and forth on its serpentine neck. "For what purpose?"

She surveyed the caldera. She saw no sign of Robbie.

"I had a dream about you. I had to find out if it was true, if you would be the same in person as you were in my dream."

So far, she hadn't spoken any untruth. His eyes seemed not to let her.

Wait, when did she start thinking of it as a 'he'?

The dream... The way he made me feel...

Yes, that's how she knew.

She looked up to find him scrutinizing her with his demonic, flashing eyes. Could he read her thoughts? Did he know what he did to her when he looked at her like that? God, she couldn't deal with this. She couldn't cope with the sheer power of her emotions, the emotions he elicited in her.

This isn't normal.

She had to get her mind working. She wanted to trick him, so now she better do it. First, though, she had to determine if he did have Robbie. None of this meant anything if he didn't.

She made herself smile up at the dragon. "What's your name?"

He strutted around in a circle and rustled his wings against his back. A hissing sound came out of his mouth.

"Ushne."

He dragged the sound out into a long, breathy hiss. His forked tongue darted out of his mouth at her before she realized he was answering her question.

"Ushne. I'm Elle."

He slid his head closer to her but didn't answer.

She thought hard for any way to open up a conversation with him, short of asking point blank if he was holding Robbie somewhere around here.

"You're alone up here, aren't you? Are there others of your kind in these mountains?"

"There are no others of my kind anywhere," he rumbled. "I am the only one."

"The only dragon!" she exclaimed. "I find that hard to believe."

"I have never seen another of my kind."

She stared at him in astonishment. "Have you looked? Do you fly around the countryside very often?"

He cocked his head to one side. "I never fly around the countryside. I stay here."

"If that's true, then how did you—" She broke off.

She was about to ask how he found food and capture Robbie.

What if Obus had steered her wrong? What if Obus was wicked like the imps had implied, and worked for the dragon? Maybe he directed hapless idiots to the dragon's caldera so it wouldn't have to go hunting for food. It could just eat the fools that happened upon it...

That is the one thing that would make sense in this place.

"It's warm here. Out there..." He gestured to the horizon. "It's cold."

"How do you find food then?" she blurted out.

He hooked his neck to stare back at her, then fixed her with an intense gaze. "What are *you* doing here? You didn't come to see me. No one comes to see me."

"The wizard down in the valley, Obus, he told me where to find you."

"For what purpose?"

He'd already asked her that. He must not have believed her.

Elle threw all caution to the wind. "That wizard told me you captured a young man I was... I was traveling with. He said if I came up here, I could find him and free him from you."

The dragon flared his nostrils at her and let out a puff of hot air. He dragged his long body over the rocks and stretched out next to the caldera where the rocks were hottest.

He sighed. "I don't know who this wizard of yours is, but I have no captive up here. I'm alone."

And with that, the dragon simply laid his body flat against the ground and closed his eyes.

CHAPTER 12

Elle slumped against the boulder. So it was all true. Obus either made a mistake or deliberately gave her misleading information. This dragon didn't have Robbie. Now what the hell was she going to do? Trek all the way back the way she'd come, alone? Try to find the castle by herself? And even if by some miracle, she did succeed, what would she tell Robbie's brothers when she got there?

She had no way to find him and wouldn't go back to Obus. Even if he'd made an innocent mistake, which she highly doubted, she didn't trust him.

Everything had gone to crap, and she didn't want to stay in this empty, hollow world full of mystery and magic and unknown forces. Yet the idea of returning home wasn't as strong as it was before...

The dragon's silky voice touched her ear. It vibrated through the rocks into her legs and body. He barely made any noise at all. Somehow the concepts worked their way into her brain without her hearing them in the normal way.

"Come and eat. You must be tired after climbing all that way."

"Something to eat? How?"

"Come over here and see. I think you'll be most pleased."

Not really seeing she had any other choice, Elle pushed herself off the boulder and took a step forward. She had no idea where he wanted her to go, but she would do just about anything for a mouthful of something to eat right now.

She walked forward until she stood next to his side rising like a green wall next to her. He pointed his head at a hollow under a different rock.

"In there."

She inched forward until she stood next to his head. She looked under the rock he'd indicated to and beheld a white crust of large crystals jutting out of the rock.

She glanced back at the dragon watching her. "What is it?"

"Food. Try it."

She stared at the stuff. It looked like large blocks of white quartz embedded in the rock. How could she eat that?

She squatted down and touched one of the larger formations. It crumbled under her hand and left a dusting of shiny particles on her fingers. She hesitated at first, but then thought, *screw it*, and put her fingers in her mouth. It tasted sweet, buttery, and even a little fruity.

She broke off a large crystal and took a bite. It filled her mouth with delicious creamy goodness. She crammed the whole thing in her mouth then, eating it all. Then she sat down next to the hole and ate as much as she could.

The dragon reclined on his flat rock next to the caldera and watched her eat. She sucked the powder off her fingers.

"Thank you, Ushne. That was... strangely delicious."

He purred under his breath. "There is water over here for you to drink."

He showed her another hole with a clear, fresh spring of sparkling water resting in a pool. She cupped it to her lips and washed down the food. She resumed her seat and gave a sigh of satisfaction.

"So, is that what you eat? Is that how you survive without flying anywhere?"

"No, I don't eat that food."

"What do you eat then? You couldn't survive up here if you didn't eat something."

He looked all around him like he was seeing it for the first time.

"You can lie down anywhere to sleep. The rock is warm enough to keep the chill off at night. Even when it snows, this caldera stays warm. That's why I never leave it."

She regarded him for a moment. He never told her what he ate or how he survived without flying out for food. What was he trying to hide?

The setting sun touched the rim of peaks beyond his head. The light went out of the sky, and a frigid wind blew over the caldera. A pocket of warm air hung over the bowl where the dragon lay.

Elle looked around her. She'd better find a warm spot to sleep tonight. She needed to rest her legs after driving herself up here. Now that she was here, she could relax into the job of winning his trust.

The instant that thought crossed her mind, he spoke again.

"Lie down here next to me. This is the warmest spot, and my size will protect you from the wind."

She looked up at him, but he didn't look at her. He faced away so she couldn't see his eyes. Was he suggesting what she thought he was suggesting? How could he know what she'd been thinking about him all this time?

He couldn't. It was impossible. He wasn't suggesting anything. He simply offered her a warm place to sleep, the same way he offered her something to eat. It was common decency – nothing more.

She got up and went to his side. He rested his head on the rock and didn't open his eyes as she sat down. The rock seeped warmth into her limbs and relaxed the tension and weariness from her long trip. She stretched out on the flat stone and closed her eyes.

She told herself to stay awake, to stay alert, but she must have fallen into a doze. In her dreams, she felt him slithering around her. His scales scratched against her skin, but the rough sensation only excited her more.

She jerked awake in darkness. Clear, bright stars sparkled over the mountain, but peaceful heat warmed her from below. She spread her body as flat as she could make it against the rock to soak up as much of that delicious heat as she could get.

Ushne grumbled in his sleep. His massive sides rose and fell next to her. She lay still and listened. Power and majesty vibrated off him toward her. It infected her in ways she couldn't comprehend. How could she feel this way about a serpent? She must be sick. *Very sick.*

She closed her eyes again, but she couldn't fall back to sleep. Her emotions warred against each other. Disgust for herself fought against her desire for him. She hated herself for wanting a... well, an animal. It just made no natural sense. She would never let herself touch him or let him touch her. She couldn't. She had to keep all these feelings and desires and cravings hidden where he would never find out about them.

How long she stayed awake, she couldn't know without a clock, but she fell asleep again and dreamed about him the way she did on the trail.

She woke in the gray morning light and sat by the hollow to eat.

Ushne rose from his slumber and paced around the caldera. He flexed and flapped his wings, but he never lifted off the ground. Elle watched him. Maybe he couldn't fly. Maybe he was stuck here.

If that was the case, what did he eat? She couldn't deny the fact he was trying to hide something from her. She considered it long and hard before she decided what to say to him.

"How long have you lived up here, Ushne?"

"I can't say," he replied. "I don't really remember when I came here. From what I can tell, I've always been here."

He couldn't have been here long without something to eat. Didn't he ever get hungry? She never saw him drink from the spring either. Then again, he was a dragon living in a magical world. Maybe he didn't need to eat. Maybe he lived on magic.

Yes, like everything else, magic must be at play here, and you're in way over your head, she told herself.

After she finished eating and drinking, she looked around for the thousandth time. There was nothing more to do. Should she leave? If Robbie wasn't here, why stay? She needed to move on and get to the Phoenix Throne and find Carmen. Robbie would have to...

No. She still couldn't leave. Something compelled her to stay — the same desire to trick Ushne into revealing himself. She wanted to crack the puzzle of what he was and how he'd managed to survive up here. Somehow, she felt as if it was important in her quest — which sounded ridiculous yet tugged at her instincts all the same.

"Tell me about yourself," she said. "Can you really not remember where you came from? Do you really believe you're the only one of your kind? I find that hard to believe."

He crooked his neck around to stare at her. "You tell me about yourself. Where did you come from, and where are the rest of your people?"

She regarded him for a moment before she answered. She couldn't unburden herself to him the way she did to Robbie. Robbie alone knew her secret. She couldn't expose herself to this animal. Still, she wanted to talk to him. Maybe if she told him something about herself, he would reciprocate.

"I come from another world. A friend of mine, a budding witch, cast a magic spell, and she and I and three other of our friends came through some kind of time warp to this world. She tried to send us to King Arthur's court, but I guess she made a mistake. I was traveling with a young man, but he disappeared. That wizard told me I could find him here. That's all I can really tell you."

He chuckled deep in his throat. "So it's a man you want?"

"It's not a man I want," she shot back. "It was just that one particular man I wanted to get back. He was on his way somewhere important, and there he thought that I could find my way back home. His brothers and one of my friends were fighting a witch to break a curse on their family. They thought that if they broke the curse, my friends and I would get sent back. That's why we were traveling together."

His eyes flashed fire. "He means a lot more to you than that, or you wouldn't have come up here looking for him. Tell the truth."

Elle was taken aback by that. How did the dragon know of her desire for Robbie?

"He does mean more to me than that, but he's not here, so I guess I'll have to go there alone," she replied simply.

"You won't go there alone. That's why you stayed. You don't want to be alone."

She cocked her head. "Do you have some ability to tell when someone is telling the truth? Do you have some inborn sense that shows you what's going on inside a person's heart? Is that how you know so much about what I'm doing and why I'm doing it?"

"I have no inborn sense of anything. I can see it in your face when you talk about him. You don't want to travel without him."

She looked away. "I never said that."

"Now that you know he's not here, you want to stay with me. Isn't that so?"

Elle faltered. "Look, even though you're a dragon, which, where I come from, is utterly impossible, you're the only… thing I've got to talk to at the moment, even if you won't tell me anything about yourself."

"I told you," he replied. "I cannot tell you anything about myself because I don't know anything about myself. I would tell you if I did."

"I find it amazing that you don't remember how you got here. What's the last thing you remember?"

"I don't remember anything. Living in this caldera is the only thing I do remember."

"You don't remember anything at all? You just appeared here?"

"That's right."

"And you have no idea how long you were here before I came?"

"No," he replied. "I was here, and then you came."

She cocked her head the other way. When had she heard that before? Something weird was going on here. He couldn't have just appeared here right before she showed up. That was impossible – or was it?

What if something zapped him here? What if something put him here the same way the fire demons put Robbie in that column? What could have the power to do that?

There seemed to be a lot of zapping going on. She got zapped to this crazy world. Robbie got zapped into that column, and Ushne got zapped here.

She got up and paced around the caldera. "What do you do up here all day? Don't you get bored for something to do?"

He eyed her. "What would you like to do?"

"Maybe you could fly me to the castle where I was going. Maybe you could practice your flying. Would you like to do that?"

"I have never practiced my flying. I never had anywhere to go."

"Now you do," she told him. "Would you like to try it? It would save me a long walk getting there."

He turned away and didn't answer.

What is wrong with him?

"Don't you know how to fly? Are you unsure if you can?"

"I can fly. I am sure I can."

"Why don't you want to try it then? Do you want to live in this caldera for the rest of your life?"

"I can think of worse places to live. It's warm here."

She gave up. He made no sense. Maybe his brain didn't work the same. It couldn't. After all, he was a damn reptile. All he really cared about in the world was staying warm and fed. This caldera must be his idea of Heaven, and Elle knew she was hopelessly getting nowhere.

Something had to give with the beast.

CHAPTER 13

Elle had finally made up her mind.

She was leaving.

She would hike down the mountain again, take a supply of the crystalline food to keep her energy levels up, and then follow the line of peaks and ridges until she found the castle where Carmen and the other Cameron brothers fought a supposed witch for the Phoenix Throne – or however the story went. It was still hard for Elle to fathom. Her life in this place had all the makings of a fantasy novel, and a part of her, at times, honestly struggled to take it seriously.

However, her resolve and logical mindset was determined to not despair in the fact she was about to be alone again.

She would find a way back to modern-day America and forget this bizarre world ever existed.

Yes, that will be so nice, she mused, looking forward to such a moment.

So, in the early hours of the next night, Elle made her move. She'd earlier scouted a good bearing to leave from, and now, quietly but quickly, headed for the spot high on the peak where she'd hidden her bundle of tools and club.

She ran for her life to get away from Ushne, the amulet from Obus hanging around her neck and bouncing as she went. She had to put as much distance between herself and the dragon as she could. Although she had to admit that she'd grown fond of the gentle beast, and her feelings towards it were still utterly strange, Elle felt she had no choice but to leave without telling him. Perhaps it was the disappointment in his gargantuan dark eyes that would've made her falter. After all, now he too would be alone.

Come on, Elle, listen to yourself. It's not human; it's just a damn dragon. Don't get emotional. Not now. Not when more important things are at stake.

What she didn't count on, or rather, had forgotten, was a dragon's acute sense of any change to its surroundings.

A flurry of whistling air sounded above her, and Ushne rocketed into sight so fast that Elle barely saw him. He slithered forward and curved around in front of her to block her path with his mighty bulk.

"Stop, Elle," he rumbled.

Elle, at once, stopped running, her chest burning from the sprint.

"I'm sorry, Ushne, but I must leave," she said, panting. "I have to—"

"Don't go," he boomed.

She gave him a wan smile. "Look, you are a gentle beast, and I appreciate both your hospitality and company, but I have to find my friends. And what I'm starting to feel for you is... well, quite bluntly, messed up."

"Messed up? I don't understand your meaning."

"Wrong. My feelings are not normal. I only usually feel this with a human man, not a—"

"A what? A man?"

Elle saw something shift in his eyes when he'd asked that. Like there was some vague recognition of something. Something she still didn't *quite* understand.

"I never realized I was alone until you came," Ushne then murmured. "I thought I had everything I needed. Now, for some reason, I can't let you go. I need you. Come – come back to the caldera and lie down with me. I don't want to be alone again."

One benefit of being human, of staying logical, was the freedom of choice. Whatever magic was encouraging her to stay with him, to give in to the sexual pull she felt for the beast, Elle still had the ability to denounce it. Not because the feelings weren't real, but because this wasn't her. She didn't fall in love with dragons and stay with them on high mountain peaks in magical lands that she wasn't born from.

Instead, Elle made up the space between her and Ushne. She held her hands up, and he understood her meaning, bending his neck down so she could hold his large rough-skinned head in both palms.

"You are not alone, dear dragon," she said, her voice as tender as it would be if she were speaking to a lover. "Out there..." She gestured to their surroundings and the infinite horizon. "... the whole world is waiting for you. As it does for me. It's time you let yourself be free."

Reaching up on tiptoes, Elle then tilted her head up to kiss Ushne's scaly snout. He closed his eyes, as if savoring her touch.

"Take care, friend," she whispered, and released his face.

What she did next, she had never intended to do. But at that moment, an inner voice told her that it was the one mercy she could grant the beast.

Elle took the amulet hanging around her neck, and while Ushne's eyes were still shut, she thrust it against the skin over his heart.

Immediately, she took several steps back, a warm but sad smile etched on her lips.

Ushne's eyes flew open, and he recoiled as he stared at her.

"What did you do?" he demanded, the betrayal visible in his big, desolate eyes.

He went to move towards her, but then wavered.

His whole body began to shake violently.

"Elle, what have you—"

The dragon didn't get the chance to speak again. Instead, he bellowed in pain.

Elle gasped as she was forced to leap further away as he lost all control of his limbs.

"Ushne!" Panic speared her along with guilt.

In horror, she watched his body contort and convulse as if it were imploding in on itself.

He's dying... But the amulet was only supposed to weaken him. No. What have I done?

Elle felt utterly helpless; however, in mere moments, the dragon wilted onto the ground, and the gleaming green of his scales faded to soft white-pink.

Her eyes widened at the sight she now beheld in the aftermath.

It's not possible... It can't be...

Ushne was no longer a dragon.

He was a man.

A man she recognized all too well.

"Robbie?" his name barely left her lips.

He groaned and tried to move, the soreness of such a task evident as he struggled to even get onto his knees.

Elle rushed to him, and noticed the amulet hanging around his neck.

"You… you were the dragon," she whispered. "I understand now… My feelings… Why I felt so close to you…"

She almost wanted to laugh with relief. It wasn't the makings of bestiality between them at all. She wasn't perverted, and neither was Ushne. It was real and right because he'd been human all along. Well, half human.

Robbie blinked once and craned his neck around to look at her. "Aye. I remember it now."

"What do you remember?"

"Everything that happened."

"What happened? How did you get up here?"

"I was asleep – by the fire with ye. The next thing I kenned, I awoke to unbearable pain. It ripped through my whole body, Elle, but I couldn't scream. Then, wings broke through the skin of my back and green scales covered me. I launched into the air on instinct and flew here. I dinnae ken how I did it. I just did. And once I got here, I couldnae think of naught but that I was a dragon. It'll not make sense to ye, lass, but that was the way of it."

Elle sat back on her heels. "It's okay, I believe you. In fact, given everything, your story makes complete sense. Why did you call yourself Ushne though?"

"I didnae ken who or what I was," he replied. "I couldnae tell ye. Ye asked my name, and that's what I said. The reason why evades me."

"Obus said the dragon took you. I guess that's what he meant."

Robbie closed his eyes, and let out a shaky breath. When he opened them again, there was a gleam to them. "I'm so glad to see ye, lass. It's good to be me again."

She had to smile. "Ditto."

"Ditto? Is that another one of the strange sayings from yer world?"

She chuckled. "Yes. What it means is that I agree and feel the same way. I thought I'd lost you."

Managing to sit upright without swaying, he reached out to take one of her hands. He rubbed his thumb over it, his touch sending warm shivers through her.

"Let's get out of here, aye?" he said and looked down toward his nether regions. "Otherwise I'll freeze my balls off."

Elle laughed, louder this time, and helped him to get to his feet. She tried not to glance down at his... impressive package... but it was hard given the context.

"We should return to the caldera and stay here the night," she suggested. "It's warm here, and there's food and water. We've got a long way to walk over rough country to get back to anywhere we could find food and build a fire, and you definitely need the rest after... the transformation."

That had sounded so weird for Elle to say out loud, but that's precisely what had happened. He had transformed from being a dragon into a human.

Robbie didn't put up an argument, which she was thankful for. Usually, he was stubborn as all hell.

When they reached the caldera, she collected their supplies and helped him get dressed. She brought him some of the crystalline food and water.

By the time he finished eating, the sky had lightened, and Robbie was eager to get going.

"It's time, lass," he said.

"Are you sure?" she asked, still uncertain about him having enough strength to make the trek back down the mountainside.

"Aye. I'm fine. I promise ye." He gave a small smile and lifted his hand to touch her cheek. "Thanks for caring about a lout like me. I daresay I don't deserve it most of the time."

Elle felt warm shivers travel through her again. It re-stirred her secret desire for him, and the lust she had felt for him, Ushne, in her dream.

She dared to cover his hand with hers, keeping it on her face, relishing the warm roughness of it.

"Robbie, I…" The words had come out breathy, and she subconsciously ran her tongue over her lips as she stared up at him.

Before she could collect herself and finish her sentence, his free arm encircled her waist, pulling her against him.

"I cannae resist this any longer, Elle," he whispered, lowering his mouth towards her. "I have to taste ye."

Elle didn't flinch when his lips pressed against hers. She melted in his arms, letting the kiss deepen and become fiercer. Her stomach felt like it had turned to Jell-O, her knees threatening to give way like she was a damn cliché in some romance novel.

But that's how Robbie made her feel.

Desired.

Special.

The heroine that belonged to the hero.

Her hands lifted to rake through his hair as she kissed him back with as much intensity as he was giving her. He hoisted her up onto his hips, her legs wrapped around his waist, as he carried her over to the nearest wall of the caldera.

When he finally broke the kiss, Elle mourned the loss of contact, but then moaned as he began to kiss her neck, biting gently down on her skin.

"I want ye so bad, lass," Robbie murmured, his yearning for her laced in his voice. "When ye ran away from me, when I was that dragon, I knew then ye were mine. And I would never let ye go."

Elle knew it was all insane. She barely knew him – he was just some Scottish ruffian she'd met in this strange, foreign and dangerous mystical land, and yet now, home meant nothing to her.

Robbie was all she wanted.

Needed.

She dared to imagine that this was what fate had planned for her from the second she was born.

She was always meant to travel through time, meet this man, and give herself to him completely.

No, you can't do this.

The rational part of Elle was rearing its head, begging her to stop, to re-center herself before things escalated any further.

He's a freakin' dragon for God's sake, her inner voice implored. *Are you out of your mind? This is not your home. HE is not your home.*

Elle gripped his shoulders and pushed them back.

"Wait, we can't do this," she said and lowered her legs, so they were no longer wrapped around him.

She waited for him to step back, but he didn't. He stayed right where he was, as close to her as possible, with obvious confusion marring his handsome face.

"What's wrong?" he asked. "I know ye feel the same way, Elle."

She closed her eyes, willing herself to stay strong, to not embrace him again, and let him take her right then and there.

It was a bittersweet feeling — being so turned on and sure of something yet equally feeling like she wasn't ready.

"It's — I —" Words failed her, and when he tried to kiss her again, she shoved him away.

"Please, I need some time," she said, her tone adamant.

Anger seemed to flare in his eyes, and he nodded. But not in agreement.

"I will not touch ye again, lass. Ye have my word on that."

"Robbie, don't be like that. It's not that I don't want you." She sounded weak, but it was the truth.

"Then what is it? Is it the dragon thing? I disgust ye now?"

"No, not at all," she replied, crinkling her brow. "I mean, it should, technically, but it doesn't."

He continued to stare at her in puzzlement.

"It's all just… too much for me, that's all. I need to take a breath. Surely, you must understand that?"

"Aye." He nodded again, then turned his gaze to the boundless blue of the sky that stretched into the distance. "And what I said stands — I will not touch ye again." He paused to look at her again, the hint of a smile tweaking his lips. "Not until ye come to me. Not until ye beg me to take ye, and truly make ye mine."

Elle had a great deal to say to that. Only, again, words failed her, and stunned, she watched as he scooped up their supplies and began to walk towards the edge of the caldera for the trek down.

Until you go to him? Until you beg him to take you? Who on earth does this guy think he is? Chris Hemsworth or something?

For the first time since Robbie had changed back into a human, Elle wanted Ushne back. At least, in dragon form, his ego had been suppressed.

One thing she knew for certain, though, was that Robbie Cameron was kidding himself if he thought she would ever "beg for it". Elle was a single, empowered, modern-day, successful career woman.

If anyone was going to beg, it was going to be him.

CHAPTER 14

Robbie was livid as he led the way out of the caldera and down the mountain slope. And the stiff bulge under his kilt wasn't helping the situation. When Elle rejected him like that it had cut him in a way he'd never thought possible. He had never been that man. A man with a weakness for a pretty face. A man who let whimsical notions flood his mind. Yet, somehow, she had cast a spell over him. He needed her like nothing else. The idea of her leaving him, and going back to her time where another man might claim her was... untenable.

The memory of their wild kiss... her thighs wrapped around him... her soft skin beneath his lips... how she'd moaned from his touch, pressing herself against him... it gave his mind no rest. He couldn't stop thinking about it.

The dragon within him felt it too.

He glanced back at her and her beauty stabbed him in the guts. He had to fight this weakness. He had to focus. He had to get to the castle and rejoin his brothers. Then, he had to find a way to send her back to her own time. That's what she wanted. Yes, that's why she rejected him. She didn't want to fall for him because then it would be too hard to leave.

Aye, lass, I do understand now.

It didn't take too long for them to reach a trail on flatter ground. It was only then that Elle broke the silence that had hung over them ever since the caldera.

"You know, there is a way to get to the castle a lot quicker," she said, a comical undercurrent in her voice.

Robbie stopped walking but didn't turn around to face her. "And what would that be then?"

"Fly, of course."

"Are ye daft? By what means?"

"You can't be serious, Robbie?" She marched up to him, forcing him to meet her gaze.

He pretended to still be confused.

She gestured to the amulet hanging around his neck, but still, he remained indifferent to her meaning.

"Okay, I'll spell it out for you then," she said sharply, crossing her arms in an apparent show of intimidation.

He inwardly chuckled at the attempt.

"It's a simple matter of you taking off that amulet. You turn back into a dragon, and then fly us to the castle."

He shook his head, knowing he couldn't ignore her this time. "I'm not taking it off. I dinnae want to turn into that thing again – ever."

She raised her eyebrows in visible surprise. "So you would rather walk to the castle? That could take weeks. Your brothers could be in danger. They might need you, and the sooner you get there, the better. I need to find Carmen."

"I said no," he snapped.

"Why not? You are a dragon, Robbie. It's okay to embrace it. This could be a good thing for both of us."

It recoiled at that. "It would be a good thing for ye, ye mean."

The furrow in her brow deepened. "What do you mean by that exactly?"

The minute the words had fallen out of his mouth, he spun away from her at his own callous behavior. Why did he have to go and say that? He meant to keep such a fear to himself. Again, he couldn't bear to face her. He couldn't see the look of hurt on her face. She'd hiked for days to find him at the caldera. She'd found Obus and got the amulet to save him from his own dragon self, and she never gave up. Well, almost, but that had been justifiable.

Why did he have to degrade her sacrifice and loyalty? He didn't deserve a woman like her. He was still a brute. She needed a man much better than he was, and she wouldn't find it here in this world.

When he didn't answer her, he heard Elle walk into the forest ahead of them. He hated himself. He ought to let her walk out of his life forever. That would be the unselfish thing to do.

No, the unselfish thing to do would be to take the amulet off, change into a dragon, and fly her to the damn castle. That would be the gallant thing to do.

Yet he couldn't bring himself to do it.

Why?

He knew why. He didn't want to admit it, not even to himself, but the secret squirmed there in his heart. He was afraid. Afraid of becoming the dragon again. He didn't want her loving the dragon more than she did his human self. He wanted her to love *him*, and that might never happen. As a dragon, he'd been kinder to her, and he was convinced that was why she had let him kiss her.

Besides, what if he couldn't change back into a man? What if he somehow got stuck as dragon? He couldn't live in that form forever. And what would his brothers do when they found out? What if he was the only one of the five like this? He would be shunned and, again, alone.

His heart pounded in his chest. He never wanted any of this, and now he had no choice but to suffer through it. He ached to go back to the time when he lived with his father and brothers at their ancestral home, before the wraiths came and the five of them had to leave.

He would never get those days back. He would never again experience the innocent enjoyment of fishing in streams or getting into trouble with Brody and hiding in the cattle shed from his father's wrath.

He had nothing left – nothing but Elle. She was the only person now who cared about him in some way, and she wanted to get to the castle so that she could find Carmen and go home. A decent man would repay her kindness by helping her do that.

Thus, Robbie walked after her. He didn't give himself a chance to change his mind. He had to get Elle to the castle. Nothing else mattered.

He put aside any notions of something happening between them. Nothing would happen. He had a task, and he would do it. He would forget the way he felt about her. He had to.

When her slim figure came into view, and he closed the distance between them, he didn't try to talk to her or apologize for his behavior. That would only soften both of their resolves, and reawaken his weakness for her.

They walked all day without a word, and when evening came, he lit a fire and they sat in silence next to it. He didn't dare look at her face, in fear the beauty of it would sway him to go back on his oath to help her, and instead, lead her in the opposite direction so he could have her all to himself.

"I'm sorry, Rob. She was gazing into the flames. "It's your choice to transform again. Not mine."

Desire stirred in him at her endearing choice of name. Rob.

"I shouldn't have mentioned taking the amulet off. I won't mention it again. I'm just glad to have you back. I don't care how long it takes us to walk to the castle. I don't care about you changing into a dragon."

He chanced to look at her then, shocked by her words. "Ye don't?"

"Of course not. I didn't know what to do when... when I found out you weren't at the caldera. I thought I would give up. Now you're here. I don't care about anything else."

He let his head sink into his hands. "Oh, Elle."

"What's wrong? What did I say?"

"How can ye be so good all the time?" he said, exasperated, peering back at her. "How can ye forgive me like that? Don't ye ken what it does to me?"

"What it does to you? What am I supposed to do — not forgive you? Keep up this silent treatment? Would you rather I stayed mad at you?"

"Aye," he replied. "I would rather ye stayed mad at me forever."

"I don't understand. You're not making any sense."

"Why did ye have to come and find me on that mountain? Ye should have left me there to rot."

"How can you say that?" Her voice cracked. "How could I leave you there? Obus told me that I had to choose between saving myself and saving you, and I chose you. I was the only person who knew where you were. If I hadn't come, no one else would have. I couldn't live with that."

He buried his face in his hands again. He couldn't deal with this woman. She was too fine and good and noble for him.

"When we reach the castle, ye will go your way and I will go mine. I'll get ye to Carmen, and after that..." He couldn't finish the sentence, and cursed himself for faltering.

Stop being so weak.

She stared at him with anguish. "Just like that? You want to forget what happened between us?"

"Aye. Ye don't belong here, and what's more, ye don't belong with a brute of a lout like me. I'll only hurt ye."

That last bit was a lie. He would *never* hurt her. He would do the opposite; he would worship her like a queen.

"I don't believe that. I don't think you're capable of hurting me. You're lying." There was venom in her voice.

"Ye foolish, lass. I hurt ye today, didn't I?"

She blinked up at him. "No, that's different. That was—"

"Leave it be, Elle," he said, but it came out as more of a growl.

"You... you don't desire me?"

He chuckled at such a senseless question. He'd never yearned for a woman so much in his entire life.

"Ye want something other than I can ever be. It's better if we forget what happened on that caldera."

She stood up and crossed her arms in defiance again as she glared down at him. It only made him want to yank her back down to him, so he could make love to her by the fire.

"I won't beg you to show me attention, Rob. I won't beg you to kiss me or touch me or screw me. If you want to be a stubborn asshole, that's fine by me."

Screw? Asshole? What bleedin' kind of language is that?

Robbie had never heard such words. To be honest, they didn't suit her pretty mouth. They sounded rather vile.

"I don't ken what some of that meant, but I caution ye to not speak that way to me again."

"You don't own me, Robbie Cameron. I shall do and say I please, savvy?"

Savvy?

She was just trying to rile him up now with her foreign tongue because she knew he had no damn idea of the meaning behind it.

He refused to let her goad him and rose to his feet.

Sure enough, she retreated away from him, which was his intention. Although he would never truly hurt her, he needed Elle to loathe him. That would make the whole situation much easier for him to handle.

"Curb yer tongue, lass, or I'll make ye."

Her trepidation seemed to disappear then, which hadn't been his intention, and was replaced with a fiery disposition. She took a step towards him, her eyes sharp and narrowed.

"I dare you," she said with a wry smile.

That tried the last of his patience.

"The sooner we get to the castle, the better, as then I won't have to put up with ye. It's not natural for a lass to act in such a way. A woman should know her place in a man's presence."

That earned him a mighty slap to the face that, astonishingly, stung. She had a fair wallop to her. He'd expected a reaction but to hit him...

On reflex, he grabbed her, lifted her up, and flung her over his shoulder as if she were as light as a feather.

"Put me down this instant," Elle shouted, struggling in his grip.

"Ye need to learn some manners," Robbie countered and walked her over to a large rock not too far from the fire.

He sat down and held her place with little effort needed. She was as fiery as a demoness in his grasp, and strong, but not strong enough.

Seeing no other choice, or risk going back on his threat and looking weak, he pulled down her strange breeches to reveal her buttocks. But what lay beneath took his breath away. Her flesh there was not bare. A line of red string rested in between her two creamy cheeks.

What manner of undergarment is this?

Robbie had never seen such a thing on a woman, and the string became slightly thicker as it continued upwards to wrap around her hips.

"Let me go this instant! What the hell are you doing?" Elle shouted.

Robbie found that his mind was torn in two directions. It was all too common for Highland men to spank their lovers and wives when they spoke out of turn. Men were considered the more dominant of the species, although Robbie had never agreed with that. Stronger, yes — that was irrefutable. However, women were people in their own right, too, and suddenly, he didn't know if he had the merit to hit a woman like his forefathers had done for generations.

So, instead, he brought his hand down only to pause just before he slapped her skin. Then, he merely gave it three, light taps. It was enough to settle her but not hurt or humiliate her beyond forgiveness.

With her still exposed to him in such a way, naturally, Robbie felt his manhood stirring and thickening. How much he wanted to peel back those cheeks and mount himself just past them, where her sweet center lay. He had to suppress a moan as his mind went to unseemly places.

At once, Elle shifted forcefully and wrenched herself away from him to cover herself back up.

"You're nothing but an asshole, Robbie Cameron," she snapped. "Was that your idea of a joke? Because news flash – it wasn't funny. It was ridiculous!"

Without bothering to look at him, she strode away.

Guilt pierced him then as he realized that he'd overlooked one pertinent fact. Even though he hadn't hurt Elle, back in her time, perhaps men were different. Perhaps they didn't punish their women for such outspokenness, or if they did, they were reprimanded themselves.

I'm such a fool...

CHAPTER 15

Elle was in shock. Had Rob really just done that? Almost "spanked" her for her apparent insolence?

Even though, despite trying to deny it, his light taps on her exposed cheeks had aroused her, it was still a little humiliating. In other contexts, it would've been funny, and led to further "bedroom activities", but here, in an enchanted land, that wasn't the case.

Elle had some idea of why Robbie did it. She'd read enough Highland romances to know the way the "hero" responds to the "heroine" defying him. But still, this wasn't some great love story; this was reality.

She had refused to look at him afterward and still hadn't. She was too afraid to, because if she did, and he looked guilty, she would be tempted to break her silent treatment. Why? She had no damn idea. He deserved it, yet she could already feel her slight aversion for him waning. Was she losing the essence of what made her an empowered woman due to a mere handsome, alpha male rogue?

Is that what falling in love does? Strips you of who you are a little? Leaving you vulnerable and exposed to that person? You know better than to feel this way, Elle.

It was clear to her that their quarreling partly stemmed from Rob's refusal to admit that the dragon was a part of him. That is why he'd said that absurd statement about her preferring him in his dragon form. That couldn't be further from the truth. She was attracted to *him* — his hazel eyes, his lean but muscular body, the husky tone of his voice, and even the manly way he carried himself and spoke.

Dammit.

There it was again — the familiar fluttering in her stomach whenever she thought of the both of them intimately. She still wanted him, desperately, and she was disappointed in herself for it.

And hey, truth be told, she wouldn't object to an actual spanking, especially if he were in the driver's seat again.

Dammit! No, Elle. He's a jerk. Period.

Needing some space, she had left the fire and walked out a little way into the surrounding forest. Above her, in between breaks in the canopy, the sky had darkened to a deep pastel gray, hinting the beginnings of sundown. The forest was quiet, serene, and her thoughts drifted to how very different it was from the woods back home. She couldn't quite explain it, but here, the natural beauty of the landscape was so much more prevalent. It made her feel… exhilarated, as if she wanted to seek adventure and she didn't care how much further it took her away from home.

After about an hour of wandering aimlessly, Elle knew it was time to head back. As much as it annoyed her, her destiny right now was tangled up with Rob's. They still had to get to the castle to find the Phoenix Throne, his brothers, and Carmen. However, things couldn't go on like this forever – they couldn't keep arguing and hurting each other with words – or light spanks on butt cheeks.

Again, something had to give with the rugged Highlander.

All at once, she heard footsteps coming toward her through the woods. She stood still and didn't turn around. She already knew what it was, and it was no creature to fear or run from.

"Elle?" His voice held no harshness to it. It was gentle, much like Ushne's.

How she missed the dragon at that moment.

"What do you want?" she replied, her tone indifferent, emotionless.

"It's not safe for ye to be out here alone. Come back to the fire."

"I'm fine," she snapped over her shoulder.

He stepped closer to her, still speaking in a low manner. "Please. I'm… sorry for what happened. I was never going to hurt ye. I don't hit lasses; I am not that manner of man."

When he came up behind her, only standing mere inches away, she fought the erotic shudders that rushed through her limbs as his warm breath cuffed against her neck.

"Come back to the fire, lass. Dinnae stand out here in the cold."

"Why should I?" she asked, her tone curt as she fought against her yearning for him.

"Because I want you to ."

"Are you sure about that?"

"Aye."

She stayed there a moment longer. She didn't want to give in, but she already knew she would. When she turned to face him, in the dying light, she saw the remorse in his eyes and the sincerity.

He really did want her to return to the camp with him.

With partial reluctance, Elle nodded. "But for the record, I'm only coming back because I'll freeze my ass off otherwise."

Rob had the good sense not to speak again, and so she followed him back to the fire's welcoming glow. They sat down, but on opposite sides of the hearth. Elle wrapped a blanket around her to beat back the encroaching cold, and eventually, her eyes naturally strayed to the Highlander across the way. In the space where his shirt dipped forward, she saw the amulet, the flickering light of the flames glinting off it.

What would happen if he took it off? Would he turn back into a dragon? Or was Ushne a one-off, some kind of spell or curse that had befallen him?

Perhaps they would never know.

"Do ye still want me to take it off?" His voice startled her.

Her gaze shot up to find him staring at her.

"No," she replied. "I meant what I said – it's not my choice to make. Despite everything, I like you for how you are now."

Elle felt like she had betrayed herself. The second he had been nice to her, out in the forest, she'd gone and practically forgiven him for, well, kind of, assaulting her.

"Are ye sure?"

"Yes," she replied with conviction. "I don't want you to take it off until you're ready to be both man and dragon."

He broke eye contact and sighed, his gaze going to the burning embers that separated them.

"Rob," she added when he didn't speak again.

He peered over at her once more.

"You broke your word."

He bore a confused expression, so she went on.

"You said you wouldn't touch me unless I 'begged' for it. Yet, technically, you did with that light spanking business." She couldn't help the small smile that snuck onto her face.

She was relieved when he emitted a small chuckle.

"Aye, so I did, lass, and I am more the fool for it."

"Damn straight," she agreed.

After a few minutes, she decided to lay down to try and get some sleep. But before she did, she sat up and addressed him again.

"Rob?"

"Aye?"

"I know you didn't mean to offend me, and perhaps it's just part of your culture, but don't hit me again, not even lightly. Where I come from, that's not acceptable unless its consensual. Understand?"

Elle didn't wait for a response; she merely cocooned herself in the blanket, laid back down, and turned her back on him.

*****

She woke up the next morning to find Robbie in the same position. It was like he hadn't moved, but he was gazing at her.

For how long? she wondered.

He waited until she sat up before he stretched and got to his feet. "We should get moving to make use of as much daylight as possible."

"Okay," she replied, unraveling herself from her sheath.

"I say we go along the flat land. That'll make it easier going."

"Fine with me."

Once they ate and were all packed up, Elle and Robbie set off. Not only did the country get gentler slope-wise, but the new understanding between them had seemed to lift the weight of tension from both their shoulders.

They talked the route over as they went, and followed deer trails to open countryside. They found rolling fields beneath a vast azure sky and kept the mountains on their left-hand side. The ridge of peaks Obus had pointed out to Elle cut across the cloudless firmament, jutting up into the distance.

Robbie surveyed the landscape. "This is an easy walk compared to the time my brothers and I had finding the castle. No wraiths are jumping out at us at every turn. No witches or sea monsters stopping us from crossing every river we come to. Aye, I could get used to this."

"Tell me more about your journey to the castle," she said as they continued onward.

"There's naught to tell about it that I haven't already told ye," he replied. "There was killing and dying and shrieking and bleeding. That's all I care to tell ye. I've no doubt there's been naught but the same since my brothers entered the castle and lost me."

"You must still be really worried about them."

"I fear it's not just me that's fallen. It's no pretty sight, this fight. I can tell ye that. That's why I'm in a hurry to get back to them. They'll be desperate for any hand to help."

She didn't say what was really on her mind. If the fight to free the castle and reclaim the Phoenix Throne was so desperate, his brothers would need him fighting as a dragon. Heck, maybe they were all dragons. If so, they could conquer anything that way, but only if they were willing to take their dragon forms.

"Makes ye wonder, though, doesn't it?" he seemed to muse aloud. "Makes ye wonder what I couldae accomplished if I'd been a dragon fighting the wraiths."

Elle gasped in agreement. "That's what I was just thinking! Only I didn't want to say it, and I thought that perhaps your brothers might have the same... condition."

He cocked his head. "I have wondered that too. Maybe you're right about it being a good thing. I dinnae like to think what they'll say when they find out, but that's a matter for another day. Or perhaps they've already discovered such a peculiarity."

She opened her mouth and closed it. She could think of so many things she wanted to say and ask, but she didn't want to offend him accidentally.

"Go on. Say it. You'll no' bother me with the saying of it." He winked at her, knowing somehow that she was holding her tongue.

"Well, what if we come across something out here, and you have to change into a dragon to fight it? What if you can't get the amulet off in time?"

He stopped in his tracks and faced her.

"All right, lass. Ye've been after me all this time to take the thing off. Here – I'll do it."

He grasped the amulet between his palms.

"Stop, wait a minute!" she exclaimed. "That's not what I meant."

However, before she could stop him, he'd wrenched it over his head and into her hands.

For a heart-stopping moment, they stared at each other and waited.

Nothing happened.

Elle blinked, first at him and then at the amulet.

A minute passed. Then another.

Still nothing. He was the same old Rob.

He *humphed* and resumed walking, and she hurried to catch up with him.

"Do you feel any different? Do you feel like you could change if you wanted to?" she asked.

"Nae. I feel no different. I dinnae ken how it happened afore, and I dinnae ken how to do it now."

He strode across the fields and down a wooden bank to the river beyond.

Elle walked at his side and kept stealing glances at him. As he no longer wore the amulet, theoretically, he could change at any moment. He might change in his sleep again. He might fly off somewhere with no memory of how he got there, and she wouldn't be able to find him.

A thousand nightmare scenarios swarmed in her mind. She wasn't traveling with a man anymore; she was traveling with a dragon.

"Rob, here!"

Elle stepped in front of him, forcing him to halt his gait. She slipped the amulet back around his neck but kept her hands on his chest. She could feel the bulk of his muscles under her fingertips and longed to feel the skin beneath the fabric of his shirt. His masculine scent wafted over her, and she secretly drank it in like it was oxygen.

Elle looked up at Robbie and gave him a warm smile. "Just in case – I don't want you suddenly flying off on me. I couldn't handle another expedition to find a mysterious wizard and then another hike up a mountain peak."

He gave a soft, amused exhale and nodded.

"I promise ye this, lass. I won't leave yer side until we've safely made it to the castle. I swear that on my life and the lives of all my brothers."

When he offered her a small smile in return and then moved past her to continue their journey, Elle's heart felt as if it had leaped into her throat.

His promise was a double-edged sword.

Yes, he wouldn't leave her, but his oath was only temporary. As soon as they reached the castle, he would bid her farewell, and she and Carmen would leave this land to return to their time.

Where they belonged.

Elle would never see Robbie again.

CHAPTER 16

Elle and Robbie followed a river that cut through the mountains toward their destination. The sun shone down on them, bright and warm. Robbie enjoyed the pleasant journey. They took a leisurely pace and appreciated the natural beauty around them.

Soon, the river entered a country populated by people. Farms and fields full of livestock lined the river, and within an hour, they came to a bridge crossing the water between two well-maintained roads.

"Well, here we go," Robbie murmured. "We may as well follow this and see what kind of people live here. We cannae do any worse than traveling on our own." He glanced at Elle. "Unless ye think we ought not to make ourselves known. After all, we don't want a reprise of what happened with those imps."

Robbie saw a wave of uncertainty wash over Elle's face as if she were thinking back to all those horrid little beasts had done.

"We might as well," she finally replied. "Whoever lives here knows how to manage the place. Look at the cows — they're fat and healthy. There are certainly no imps here."

They both chuckled at that.

They climbed onto the road and left the mountains behind, keeping them in sight so they could still find their bearings toward the castle.

In the meantime, Robbie appreciated traveling by road instead of breaking a path through heath and forest. The road relaxed him.

In a few hours, they made it to the first village, and his heart went out to it. Simple cottages full of ordinary country people lined the roads and dotted the farms.

People greeted the pair on their way past. The women wore plain dresses and aprons, and the men wore kilts. Although he didn't recognize their tartan, he understood these people.

"Let's stick to these roads as much as we can," Elle suggested. "We probably won't have to hunt for our food in this country either. It's too bad we don't have any money. We could get lodgings and take a bath. Hmm... I would give anything for that."

He laughed. "Ye wannae take a bath?"

"What's so funny about that? I haven't had one since... wow, I forget. I should find new clothes too – this pantsuit is filthy."

The smile on Robbie's face weakened then, and guilt overcame him. He still couldn't fathom how he had been so brash to remove her breeches yesterday and almost properly spanking her. He would keep his promise to the end of days; he would never do such a thing again.

Shaking off the thought, he managed another grin. "I can just imagine ye in a big bath full of soap."

She narrowed her eyes. "What are you suggesting, Robbie Cameron?"

"Oh, nothing at all. Ye have a dirty mind, lass." He laughed with heart.

They left the village and returned to the open farmland, where he and Elle sat down under a spreading oak tree next to the road. It was well past midday, so they ate some food and drank some water from a nearby spring.

Robbie leaned back against the tree. "Ye wouldnae think a country like this could exist in the same world as wraiths and dragons and those little demons and such. It doesnae seem like the same world."

"Maybe it isn't," Elle suggested. "Maybe we crossed some barrier, and we're back in the Highlands."

"I was thinking the same. Whoever these people may be, they're Highlanders like me and my brothers. I wonder who they belong to. I dinnae recognize their tartan. They must be a different clan altogether."

"You could ask somebody? They must be thinking the same thing about you."

"Everyone kens the Camerons. All of them ken I'm a Cameron."

The sound of drumming horses' hooves abruptly rumbled down the road. A company of mounted horsemen then cantered into view with banners flying and their weapons gleaming on their pommels. The horses wore plate mail, and the first few men in the cavalcade wore glistening golden decorations pinned to the plaids across their chests.

Robbie got to his feet to watch them pass. Each rider's long hair waved in the breeze, and their eyes skipped over the countryside as if in search of any danger.

The company rode up a small rise in the road, and Robbie got his first good look at the man leading the procession. He sat tall and straight in his saddle, and he wore a jeweled sword at his waist. His mount snorted and tossed its head. A circlet of gold adorned his head, and a golden emblem hung on a chain around his neck.

He reined his horse when he spotted Robbie.

The rest of the company slowed behind him until the whole cavalcade stopped in front of the oak tree.

The man in charge eyed Robbie. "Ye're a Cameron, are ye no'?"

Robbie bowed. "I am. Robbie Cameron, the Younger."

"If ye'll do me the honor, ye'll come with me and mine to my castle. We have a matter of business to discuss with ye."

"And what business would that be?" Robbie countered, staying on guard. "Ye'll forgive me if I dinnae come until I kens what it's all about."

The man closed his eyes and lowered his head. "Of course. It concerns the Phoenix Throne."

"The Phoenix Throne! What may ye and yers ken about it?"

"Ye'll ken when ye come to the castle. We must ask ye for yer help, and ye'll understand all when ye come."

Robbie glanced at Elle, but she only offered him a blank expression.

"Ye bring yer companion with ye," the man told him.

"All right," Robbie replied. "I'll come with ye to find out about the Phoenix Throne, but I'll no' promise any help nor naught else 'til I hear what ye have to say."

"Of course. I'm Prince Alan, of the House of Munro."

Robbie frowned. "Munro?"

Prince Alan snapped his fingers, and an unridden horse appeared from the back of the company.

"Ye can ride this. You'll no' face any danger with us."

The Prince reined his horse around, and the rest of the band followed his lead.

Robbie hesitated for a moment.

Elle murmured in his ear, "What's wrong? Do you not trust them?"

"No, 'tis all right," he murmured back. "We'll go and see what's what."

Elle nodded, but when he turned to look at her, he saw that wave of uncertainty breach across her face again.

"If ye sense anything out of sorts, any danger, ye tell me, understand?" he said.

She nodded again and managed a weak smile.

"Good." Robbie seized the horse's bridle. "Now, ye mount up behind me."

He swung up into the saddle and offered her his hand. Elle took hold of it, and he hauled her up behind him. When her arms went around his waist, he fought the feeling that it caused within him. He felt his manhood stirring, yearning for her hands to go lower.

Not now, he scolded himself. *Remember what's important.*

Prince Alan and the rest of the company galloped off the way they'd come.

Robbie touched his heels to the horse's flanks, and the animal shot off down the road after its friends.

The horsemen flew down the open road, their armor and weapons clattering as they went. The excitement of riding alongside other men fortified Robbie. He wasn't a wandering ghost anymore; he was on his way to a castle in the company of a prince to do some royal business — whatever that might be.

The road wound around a wood, and then the castle came in sight. It rose crisp and sturdy on a hill in the distance. Iron-gray granite formed its walls, and people flowed in and out over the open drawbridge. Life and activity surrounded the place, and birds wheeled through the sky overhead.

Prince Alan rode over the drawbridge, and the company drew to a halt in the courtyard. Grooms and boys rushed out to take the horses, and pages helped the men out of their armor. The place seethed with noise and bustle. Chickens and sheep got underfoot and rushed away cackling and bleating.

Robbie slid off the horse and helped Elle to the ground, as Prince Alan approached them.

"Come along with me, both of ye, and meet my father. He's anxious to meet ye."

He crossed the courtyard to a flight of steep granite steps leading up to an immense grand door and pushed it open. Several knights who'd ridden with him followed after Robbie and Elle as they accompanied the prince inside.

Prince Alan led the way across a towering entrance room, up another flight of sweeping stairs, and into an enormous hall. This castle resembled an enchanted castle, but with no apparent magic in sight.

People dressed in the finest of clothes packed the hall, and a king sat on a magnificent golden throne at the far end. A platform raised the throne above the admirers clustered all around the room.

The crowd parted to let Prince Alan through, and he strode all the way down the hall to the throne.

Robbie squared his shoulders and followed a step behind him. Talking to the King must be the business

Alan wanted Robbie to perform. Robbie never shrank from talking to any man, and he wouldn't do so now.

Prince Alan stopped at the foot of the throne.

The atmosphere struck Robbie as so different from the castle he'd left behind him, and he found some ease with that. No black dragon glared down at him. The King was a regular man with twinkling blue eyes. He resembled Prince Alan, only older.

"Robbie Cameron, the Younger," Prince Alan introduced him, then turned to peer at Elle. "I'm afraid I failed to ask yer name, lass."

"Elle Watson," Robbie replied for her. "Now we're here, may I ken the business ye wish to discuss with me?"

The King waved to an empty chair next to him on the platform. "Sit ye down here, lad. We'll discuss that in good time. Ye must make yerself comfortable first."

Robbie didn't want to make himself comfortable until he knew what they wanted from him, but he had no choice. No king had ever invited him to sit at his right hand before.

He glanced at Elle briefly before climbing the steps to sit down next to the King.

"Yer companion, too," the King said.

Elle hesitated a moment, then took the chair next to Robbie, but she never said a word.

The crowd broke into excited murmurings and went back to milling around the room.

The King leaned closer to Robbie and murmured into his ear, "We must finish this affair of state. We'll adjourn to the dining hall after this and share a meal. Then we'll be free to talk in private."

Robbie said nothing. He trusted Elle to tell him if she got any sense of danger here, but he already knew she wouldn't. These were regular people who had something to say to him about the Phoenix Throne. He had to get through a state dinner and maybe some other festivities.

Then, he would find out what was going on.

Chapter 17

A steward in a gold-trimmed kilt and sash held the door open to a large bedroom.

"This is yer room, sir."

Elle and Robbie peered into a chamber lined with rich brocades and an enormous bed that occupied almost the entire room.

"This is a grand bedchamber, aye, but 'tis not necessary. A bunk will do me just fine," Robbie said.

"King Farlane wishes for ye to reside here, sir, and so it shall be."

Robbie took a deep breath. "All right. Well, when ye put it like that, I suppose I'll just have to stomach it."

He strode into the room, an impish smile set on his face.

Elle went to follow Robbie when the steward cleared his throat. "Yer room is across the hall, milady. If you dinnae mind…"

His tone told Elle that on the contrary, *he* did mind.

The steward crossed the passage and opened the door to an identical bedroom.

"Ye'll stay here until the King sends for ye, milady."

Elle frowned but entered the chamber. She gazed back through the open door at Robbie.

This is all so weird, she thought yet didn't sense any danger. She was going to keep her wits about her though.

The second the steward's footsteps faded down the stone passage, Elle darted across the hall to Robbie's room and shut the door behind her.

"Well, what do you make of this?"

He paced around the room and looked at everything. His window had a view of the courtyard below.

"I dinnae make naught of any of it. I suppose they wish to talk to me about something. I'll find out soon enough, aye."

"They seem friendly enough too, and that was some feast. Is that normal for people here – in your world?"

"Aye, 'tis what any other king or laird would serve. However, there's one thing I ken for certain. They're no' from Clan Munro."

An edge of panic crawled under Elle's skin. "How do you know that?"

"They're no' wearing the Munro tartan, for one thing. I kenned a few Munros in my time, and these arenae them."

"So, who are they then?

Robbie's gaze tapered. "That's what I need to find out, lass."

He resumed examining the bedchamber. "It's a very nice castle anyway. Ye'll be certain to get that bath..."

Her head shot up, but when she saw him grinning, she scowled, "You jerk!"

His expression told her that he had no idea what "jerk" meant but took it lightly as he suddenly scooped her up around the waist in both arms and tackled her onto the bed, laughing.

She pretended to struggle and wrestle under his weight, but he overpowered her easily.

He pinned her arms to the bed, and Elle felt the familiar tug of desire for him, making her moist in her most intimate place.

He leaned his head down closer to hers. "I'll give ye a bath."

She pretended to be insulted and smacked him on the arm before trying to escape his grip again. But her efforts were still utterly futile.

Eventually, she stilled as she tried to catch her breath. Robbie stared down at her, his hazel eyes enticing her to reach up and kiss him again.

"Robbie, I—"

A loud series of knocks on the door stole away their attention, shattering the moment.

"Yes?" Robbie called out, still not moving from his position over Elle.

"It's Prince Alan. My father, the King, wishes to see ye in his private audience hall. And the lass – I assume she is presently in yer company?"

Both Elle and Robbie had to suppress childish giggles.

"Of course," Robbie replied, visibly fighting to keep his tone even and free of a snicker. "Just give us a moment, Prince Alan."

With only moderate hast, Robbie climbed off the bed, allowing Elle her freedom.

She straightened out her pantsuit and hair, catching the mischievous flicker in Robbie's eyes as he watched her. She had been about to tell him, in a moment of weakness where her need for him had peaked, that she regretted rejecting him on the caldera. She wanted him more than any man she'd ever known.

She wanted to *feel* him against her, inside of her.

"Come along then," Robbie said with a wink. "After all, it'd be rude to keep a king waiting. Unless there was just cause, that is."

Elle faltered. She understood his meaning perfectly and was about to step towards him when he strode towards the door.

Get a grip on yourself! Have you already forgotten what's really important here? Getting to the castle. Finding Carmen. Going back home. You can't encourage these feelings for the Highlander.

Inwardly agreeing with herself, Elle walked after Robbie, and they both followed Prince Alan back down the hall.

Robbie shot her a significant smirk behind the Prince's back, which didn't help her desire for him that hadn't even weakened a little.

Prince Alan led the pair into a different room where the King waited for them. Elle braced herself for what they were about to hear and prayed it would lead them to the Phoenix Throne.

The King, Prince Alan, Robbie, and Elle stood in a square. The rest of the room was empty. They had complete privacy.

Prince Alan spoke first: "We have a wizard with us. His name is Abraline. He told us of yer coming into our country. That's how we kenned to come and find ye the way we did."

Robbie nodded. "That's no' here nor there. Now tell me what ye ken about the Phoenix Throne. My brothers and me were trying to get it back when I wound up here. My older brother, Angus, was meant to be the King."

"That's what we must tell ye," Alan replied. "A strange people have taken the Throne. The Urlus took the country, and an Urlu King sits on the Throne in yer brother's place."

Elle saw the change in Robbie's face, and despair washed over her own.

"What did ye say?" he asked, a deep crease marring his brow.

"They've overrun the country. They occupied the castle and pushed yer brothers out. Yer brothers are dispossessed, and Angus was burnt in a fire. They cannae take back the throne for the Urlus control everything."

Robbie's hands balled into fists, the whites of his knuckles pressing up against the skin.

Elle wanted nothing but to take his hand and hold it – let him know that she was there, to support him.

"Then we need to send aid," Robbie said, clenching his jaw.

"That's why we brought ye here to tell ye," Prince Alan continued. "We're making war against the Urlus. We need ye with us. Ye're the only one strong enough to fight them."

Robbie frowned again. "How do ye figure that?"

"Ye're a dragon," Alan replied simply. "Ye can defeat the Urlus. Ye're damn near the only one that can."

Both Elle and Robbie were taken aback by the prince's revelation.

Robbie glared at him. "How do ye ken about that?" His tone brooked no pleasantness.

"Abraline divined it," Alan told him. "I reckon all the wizards in the country ken about it. Ye can get your throne back, Robbie Cameron. Yer brother, Angus, alas is gone. So ye're now the next rightful king. Ye must sit on the throne to break the curse and send the Urlus back where they belong. Will ye help us?"

Robbie's face contorted in rage. "I'll help ye. I'll use all the power I can muster to destroy 'em. Ye can count on that."

Without waiting for another response, Robbie stormed out of the room, leaving Elle alone with Prince Alan and the King.

"And ye, lass," the King said. "What part do ye play in all of this?"

Elle didn't know how to answer that. Well, she did, but it was too complicated. Plus, for the first time since meeting the prince, then arriving at the castle, her instincts had changed. She couldn't explain it, but something felt... off. She no longer wanted to trust them as quickly.

So, she lied.

"I'm his woman," she told the King. "Nothing more."

"Aye, that much was clear," the prince said with an air of amusement.

Elle wanted to fire a witty comeback at him but knew it wouldn't be appropriate so held her tongue.

"Please, if you would excuse me, I must go after him," she said.

When they nodded in understanding, she surprised herself by curtseying then raced after Robbie.

He must have returned to his bedchamber because he was nowhere in sight along any of the halls.

As she hurried back to their quarters, the severity of what the prince said echoed in her mind. Angus, Robbie's brother, and, apparently, Carmen's supposed lover, was dead, and the throne lost to these Urlu people. She worried about Carmen's safety. Had she been injured too?

Nothing made sense but one thing was evident to Elle – with the Munro clan, or whoever they were, fighting alongside them, she and Robbie stood a chance to reclaim the castle and the throne, which also meant getting Carmen and Robbie's remaining brothers back.

Another realization resonated within her then.

King. Robbie will become the new king. Now, that was indeed a bombshell.

When Elle finally reached Robbie's chamber, it was empty.

Where the hell is he?

Having no choice but to simply keep walking onward down the hall, she came to a set of stairs and climbed them. They led to a rooftop, and when she stepped out into the open air, she saw Robbie standing on the edge of the parapet.

He had one foot propped up against the wall, and looked deep in thought as he peered down at the ground far below.

Elle slowly walked up behind him. She wanted to talk to him, comfort him, but hesitated. What could she say to a man who probably felt as if he'd lost everything, again?

He showed no sign of being aware of her presence. Maybe he wanted to be alone. However, this was not the time for masculine egotism.

Her hand gently touched his. "Rob."

To her surprise, he started talking really fast, though it seemed more to himself than her.

"I'll drive 'em into the furnace if I have to. I'll destroy every last one, even if they beg for mercy."

"Rob, please, calm down. I think you're putting too much faith in the people here. They could be mistaken," she told him. "Angus could still be alive somewhere. You of all people should know that everything is not always what it seems in this world."

He shook his head. "Ye heard the prince. Their wizard kenned about me. Whatever the wizard saw, he must have seen about Angus, too."

Elle emitted a soft sigh, knowing that if she countered his logic, he might not take it so well.

"Why don't you just come back downstairs with me. Maybe you could give me that bath."

She blushed at her own courage. She'd finally admitted it out loud; her unrelenting desire for him and how she wanted them both to act on it again without further hesitation.

But Robbie acted as if he hadn't heard her.

"I must go speak to Prince Alan and the King about their preparations for the war. We must fight these Urlus until we destroy them. I'll no' be able to rest until I do."

She inwardly reeled from him but hid her disappointment.

"Okay. I'll leave you to it then," she said, forcing out a smile.

She started to turn away when he caught her arm.

"Elle."

She faced him again. "What is it?"

"I… I want to, but I cannae. Do ye understand? My brother's dead, and I have no notion where the others may be. I cannae—"

He didn't have to finish. She did understand. He couldn't feel anything for her beyond his burning drive for revenge. They couldn't be together until he fulfilled his mission. But she already mourned for what could never be. Nothing had changed. As soon as they reached the castle, and Robbie took back the throne, they would go their separate ways.

They would never have that bath together.

Elle returned to her chamber and shut the door. It was the nicest room she'd ever laid eyes on, much less stayed in, and someone had lit the hearth. It was crazy being here – she was too used to sleeping on bare dirt by a campfire, or on the flat rock of a caldera.

She plopped down on the enormous bed and looked around.

So this is how the royals live.

If Robbie became King, this would be his backdrop forever. He would be matched with a woman just as noble and make her his Queen. And Elle... she would be back in America, running her investment firm, pretending that it had all just been a vivid dream.

A small knock on the door severed her thoughts.

"Yes," she called out.

The door opened, and a pretty blonde maid entered the room.

"Beggin' yer pardon, milady," the maid said as she laid what looked like an elegant dress on the chair by the bed. "The King has sent this for ye. He said ye may like a change of clothes."

Elle gazed down at her modern-day America attire. It might be a good idea to fit in more. "Tell the King thank you," Elle replied. "Oh, and would I be able to have a bath? I'm quite dirty from the journey here."

The maid bobbed a curtsy. "Of course, milady. I will fetch another servant to bring it in for ye."

"That would be perfect. Thank you."

The maid scurried out, and soon two different servants brought in a wooden tub and filled it with steaming water. Elle couldn't wait to get naked and sink into the water. The hardships of the last few days had bruised and battered her. Now, she could rest and relax.

When the servants left, she peeled off her pantsuit, threw it away, and climbed into the tub. She dipped herself under the water, right up to her ears, and closed her eyes.

Straight away, her mind drifted to Robbie. Right now, he was probably back with Prince Alan and the King, making plans to besiege the castle and conquer the Urlus. It was despondent in a way – a few simple words from two men they'd only met that day had changed everything. Elle no longer felt the closeness with Robbie that had been growing since she freed him from the fibers imprisoning him.

She'd tried to open him up to the idea of using Ushne, his dragon form, to transport them to the castle. Now, he planned to use Ushne to destroy the people inhabiting it.

The joke is on you. You knew falling for him would be a mistake, her invoice voice whispered, and ironically, the Bee Gees song, "I Started A Joke", played in her head.

"Oh if I'd only seen..." she sang quietly, "... that the joke was on me..."

CHAPTER 18

Robbie and Prince Alan rode side by side through the forest beyond the castle. In the week since he'd come to this castle, Robbie had risen to be the King's right hand and spent most of his time with Prince Alan. They'd planned their assault on the Urlus, and when they finished all their battle preparations and logistical conferences, they rode out hunting together in the clear autumn air.

Alan showed him where to hunt deer in the forest and fitted Robbie with a suit of armor and all the weapons he needed.

The two men galloped over the fields and plunged into the dense woods. They turned up a herd of deer and flanked them. They shot down four big bucks, and their pages and squires carried the carcasses back to the castle while Alan and Robbie rode on for pleasure.

Alan reined to a halt in a sunny glade by a stream. He dismounted to get a drink of water, but instead of remounting and riding on, he pulled his horse's bridle off.

"What in the world are ye doing?" Robbie asked. "We must get back afore it gets too late. Yer father wants us both at the council of his generals."

"He can wait," Alan replied. "Besides, ye're almost a king the same as he is. He wouldnae dream to criticize ye for taking yer time out here."

Robbie shifted in his saddle. "I'm no' king as yet, lad. Ye're more a king than I."

Alan snorted. "I'll never be a king, and certainly no king as powerful as ye are. Come on. Get ye down from there and rest."

"I'm no' tired enough to rest."

Alan didn't listen. He unsaddled his horse and turned the animal loose on the grass. He sat down by the stream and leaned back to look up at the sky.

"What're ye doing now, ye daft lad?" Robbie asked. "Dinnae tell me ye're going to sleep out here. They'll be looking for us at the castle."

"Let them look," Alan shot back. "Do ye ken how long it'll be afore we get a chance to sit and enjoy the sun once this war starts? If ye're smart, ye'll take the chance now."

Robbie looked around. It was a nice enough spot, but he didn't feel right just sitting around doing nothing. He ought to be doing something to get ready for the war.

Alan read his mind. "Ye cannae speed it along by fretting over it. It'll happen when Father says so and no' afore that time. Sit ye down, and dinnae make me tell ye again."

Robbie sighed. Alan was right. The army wouldn't move out to attack the Urlus for another week at least.

He got down and unsaddled his horse too. The animal snorted, tossed its head, then joined its companion to graze.

Robbie sat down next to Alan. Now that he'd let himself relax, the sun and the water's gentle trickling made him sleepy.

Alan chuckled. "Good lad."

"Ye and yer father have been good to me and Elle," Robbie told him. "We're grateful for that."

Alan shrugged. "Ye're the ones doing us a service. We wouldnae stand a chance against the Urlus without ye."

Robbie faced the river and closed his eyes. "Ye're like my own brother now. Ye're the only one who kens about... about *that* – besides Elle."

"About what? About ye being a dragon and all? Wheesht, lad, that isnae naught ye need bother about."

"I never wanted it – I just wanted to be a normal man like any other. Now ye make it out to be some kind of honor or something when it's naught but a curse."

"It's no curse, lad. Ye're the best we got to fight the Urlus. We wouldnae dare face 'em without ye. Ye must understand it as an advantage and a blessing."

"Ye sound like Elle. That's what she says."

Alan cocked his head. "Is Elle... Is she yer betrothed?"

"My betrothed?"

"If we succeed, ye'll be King. Ye'll need a queen. Did ye no' consider that? Will ye make her yer Queen?"

Robbie stared at the sun shimmering on the water. *Marry Elle?* That was another whimsical notion that he couldn't afford to let himself indulge in. Their fates weren't aligned for such a thing.

Of late, the war against the Urlus had occupied all of his attention. He hadn't spent much time with Elle. He had no idea what she did with herself every day while he hunted and planned with Alan.

What a rude, ungrateful haggis ye are – to throw her away the moment someone else came along.

However, she never voiced the slightest objection to him spending time with Alan or planning this war. She never spoke against his plans to avenge Angus or assume the Phoenix Throne himself. Robbie should value her input more. He should give her more consideration. Even now, it might be too late. He may have offended her beyond redemption.

Even in the midst of all those thoughts, he couldn't think of marrying her. She was too different to make a good queen for this land. She was strange and strong and foreign, unlike the soft, more subdued women Robbie knew who wore dresses, not manly breeches.

Robbie had never quite understood what Angus saw in Carmen. Yet now he had his own strange woman to think about. Maybe he wouldn't have to consider her at all. The moment the curse lifted, Elle and Carmen and the other girls who were about somewhere would return to their own time.

He shook himself alert, but Alan wasn't looking at him. The Prince was inspecting some stain on his kilt like he'd never asked Robbie that question in the first place.

They sat in silence for a while, then caught their horses and rode back to the castle.

Alan jumped down in the courtyard and handed his reins to a groom.

"Meet me in the forum, and we'll send out the declarations to the country people about supplying food and wagons for the campaign," he told Robbie.

"Ye handle the forum," Robbie told him. "I've something I must do first. It may take me the rest of the day."

Alan cocked his head and frowned.

Robbie didn't wait around to explain. He headed indoors and climbed the stairs to his chamber. He stopped outside the door and looked up and down the hall to make sure no one saw him. Then, he stepped across and knocked on Elle's door.

Her voice answered him from inside, "Come in."

He let himself in and shut the door behind him. She was sitting reading a book in a chair by the window. She rose to meet him. She wore a full-length gown like the rest of the women in the castle. Pearl and silver thread shone in the sun with her hair swept off her face into a twisted coiffure decorated with gems.

She wasn't an inch taller, but she looked every inch a queen in that dress. His heart wrenched at the sight of her. How could he have kept away from her for all these days? How could he shun her company in favor of Alan?

He crossed the room to stand in front of her. Her clear face shone up at him the way it always did. Her eyes seemed to read him to the depths of his soul. She'd known his secret before anybody else, and she accepted him. She didn't need him to win any war for her, and she cared for him anyway.

What a fool he was to spurn the gift he'd found in her. He couldn't bear the thought of his own behavior toward her. He fell on his knees in front of her and threw his arms around her waist. He clutched her to him for all he was worth. He couldn't lose her, no matter what happened in the battle against the Urlus.

For a moment, she stood stunned and still. Robbie buried his face in her stomach. He couldn't stand the thought that she might reject him the way he'd rejected her. He closed his eyes and waited for her to do something, anything, to show him that she still cared.

Little by little, she softened in his arms. Her slim hand came to rest on his neck. She squeezed him and petted his hair out of the way. She stroked his skin until he dared to look up at her blessed face.

The sun shone behind her and gave her hair a blazing halo of heavenly light. Before he could say a word, she leaned down and kissed him. Ecstasy and hope flooded over him. She kissed him! She still cared.

His lips felt like they were melting into the goddess-softness of hers. He never imagined kissing her could feel this good. Up on the caldera, it had been intense, but this kiss was something much more.

Robbie could barely contain the surging energy within him. He slipped his hand up her back and pressed her down toward him. She sagged against him, and when he opened his eyes to gaze up at her, he beheld an expression of matchless desire.

She wanted him.

And this time, he would not allow her to fight her desire.

He stood up. "Turn around, lass, I want to see all of ye under that dress," he said, running his tongue over his bottom lip.

She smiled coquettishly but spun to face away from him.

Robbie made quick work of freeing her from the dress and undergarments, having had such experience *many* times before back home.

When he gently turned her to face him again, his breath hitched in his throat.

Her form was perfect. It was neither too thin nor too muscled. Her breasts were round, pert, and ripe-looking with taut red buds he longed to suckle on.

"Ye're the bonniest thing I have ever seen," he murmured, and saw a faint blush rise to her cheeks.

The coyness only heightened his desire, and he captured her in his arms. She made no protest as he carried her to the bed and laid her down on the brocade coverlet.

She stared up at him with an air of affection he hadn't seen before, and still showed not even a hint of resistance.

This was the moment they'd both been waiting for...

CHAPTER 19

As Elle gazed up at the smolderingly handsome Highlander, she knew he was everything that she'd ever wanted. The same fiery magnetism that hypnotized her at the caldera burned in his eyes.

Every touch flooded her with seething passion.

He propped himself on his elbow above her, his hair hanging around his face. She didn't have to ask why he'd stayed away so long; she'd passed far beyond those petty questions.

Her body longed for him, and judging by his face and eyes, he wouldn't hold back either.

Elle's bare breasts heaved as his hand circled her waist. His touch spoke volumes to her flesh, and she responded in turn, lifting her hands to rake them through his hair.

When they kissed again, he clutched her to him with more vigor, his erection pressing out through the material of his kilt to tease her thigh.

"God help me, Elle. I must have ye," Robbie said when his lips released hers.

"Then take me," Elle replied and laid back, inviting him to take his fill.

She reached up to cup his face in her hands, her palms caressing the roughness of his beard.

Robbie needed no further affirmation.

His strong hands began to stroke every inch of her body, sometimes gentle, sometimes firm.

A small gasp escaped her lips when he palmed one breast, the taut nipple peaking further. Her body bucked at the sensation, her need for him reaching breaking point. And then he did something she didn't expect...

He lowered his mouth to the skin just beneath her breasts, then lightly kissed his way down, and further still.

When he found her most intimate place and laved it with his tongue, Elle cried out.

A guy hadn't gone down on her in months; she'd almost forgotten how mind-blowing it felt.

The things Robbie was doing with his tongue told her straight away that he was no novice of oral sex, and she relished in the thought that every other girl before her had not managed to woo him enough to take him as her own, a husband.

Right now, he was only hers.

It didn't take long for her to undo for him, the nerves of her sex building quickly and intensely.

Her thighs shook as her orgasm peaked and she held her breath as she rode it to its highest point, then relaxed in the waves of the comedown.

Robbie looked up at her, a huge grin splitting his face.

"Rob," she said, her voice coming out desperate.

"Aye?"

"Make me yours."

His grin widened still, and then he was above her again.

Taking advantage of the position, Elle reached down under his kilt to the hard mass standing at attention for her.

He groaned when her hand closed around it, clenching his jaw, his hazel eyes now showing how vulnerable she was making him.

"You're big," she whispered, her tone purposely provocative.

"Aye, ye approve then?"

She chuckled. "Absolutely."

She pushed his whole kilt up to expose him fully, reveling in the sight of his beautiful rod. She couldn't wait any longer and hastily tugged off his kilt, as Robbie shirked the rest of his clothes.

Now they were equal; flesh against flesh.

Robbie drew her up off the bed, then spun them around so that he was sitting upright and she was on his lap. He cradled her in his arms and kissed her as they rocked together, her aching sex brushing against the tip of his shaft.

Ever so gently, he lifted her hips, and she understood the intimation, positioning herself perfectly so that when he let go, she sank onto him.

They moaned in unison at the feeling the act created, staring into each other's eyes with devoted hunger as Elle slowly rode him.

The way they moved together, in complete sync, was like their bodies were crafted for each other, like their meeting was a deliberate intervention of a higher power.

Dragon Quest

Soon, Elle felt the oh so familiar swelling sensation of another orgasm, only this one was more profound, more laden with meaning.

She'd never experienced sex quite like this, and she never wanted to experience it with anyone again.

She wanted Robbie.

And him alone.

She closed her eyes, and found herself back on the rock next to the caldera. But it was Ushne filling her body and soul with the greatest pleasure she'd ever known.

His eyes burned above her, and she opened her body wider to receive him. His presence filled her with unstoppable rapture as she gushed around his piston driving her upwards to the infinite blue sky.

He was her dragon.

He commanded her to belong to him, to yield to him when he looked at her.

Her breath snagged. Every rocking movement of his hips pushed her further to the edge. She would collapse any second now – she would have if Robbie wasn't holding her up and demanding her eyes never leave his.

"Come on, lass. Come on," he both ordered and begged.

"Rob..." Her words came out breathy. "I'm... I'm going to...."

"That's it," he urged. "Surrender yerself to me, *my* lass."

That broke the last of Elle's resolve.

A cry tore out of her as her climax came in one mighty upsurge.

Robbie plunged his rock-hard shaft upward, as far into her as it would go, but she'd already catapulted over the precipice into intoxicated bliss.

He came, too, in a maddening rhythm, hooking his powerful biceps around her waist. He groaned, deep and loud, as she bucked, emptying his seed into her.

In the aftermath, they held each other for several minutes, catching their breaths, then both toppled backward onto the bed.

"That was..." Robbie began but couldn't finish the sentence.

"I know," Elle said, panting. "I've never—"

"Experienced it quite like that afore," he completed for her.

She tilted her head to look at him and gave a seductive nod while biting her lip.

"Hmm, don't do that," he warned.

"Why?"

"Because I'll take ye again, and it will not be so gentle."

Rebirthed excitement stirred within Elle.

Rough sex doggy-style had always been one of her guilty pleasures.

"Try me," she said and flipped over onto her stomach, insinuating he take her from that position.

"Aye, ye're a right wild lass. But then again, I always knew that."

A carnal growl sounded in Robbie's throat, his manhood stiffening again, ready to claim her for a second time.

He climbed off the bed and walked to the very end of it, as Elle shifted down to meet him. She presented herself with eagerness, knowing he had an incredible view of her most exposed and cherished area.

When he gripped her hips and pulled her ass firmly closer to his pointed shaft, Elle squeaked out of delight at what he was about to do.

He gave no warning before he thrust into her.

Hard and deep.

She cried out, the pain and pleasure undistinguishable.

"Robbie, oh, Robbie," she moaned as he plundered in and out of her.

"Yes, Elle, say my name, my bonnie lass," Robbie said through gritted teeth.

He drove into her with greater severity.

Like a wild beast.

No, a dragon, Elle thought, feeling herself getting wetter still.

"Spank me," she begged, thinking back to when they'd been on the road, and he'd so brazenly grabbed her.

"What?" he asked, sounding uncertain.

"I want you to spank me, Robbie."

"Are ye sure, I mean, I don't want to—"

"I'm asking you to – this time. But I don't want light taps. I want you to mean it. Please."

Robbie grunted like he'd heard the 'call of the wild'.

THWACK!

Elle flinched in delight.

"Again!" she cried.

THWACK!

"Again!"

THWACK!

She smiled with satisfaction when he started panting behind her and countered his every thrust by pushing back, allowing him to penetrate deeper. Every time her cheeks slapped against thighs, she whimpered, which made him quicken his pace all the more.

Elle's eyelids fluttered as her body kept responding. She flexed her abdomen in rhythm with his movement, wildly throwing her head back and forth.

"Robbie," she said, gasping, the syllables hurled at him with the intoning of 'RR-OOBB-IIEE', ending with a final scream of just 'E'.

A tsunami of nerves cascaded over her like her insides was nothing but mush.

His reaction was a final burst of strength and agility as he, too, shouted out his mirth, coming inside of her with as much full-force as he'd done just minutes earlier.

They collapsed back onto the bed, side by side, sweating and panting for breath.

Elle stared up at the wooden beamed ceiling, her body still tingling and gushing as his semen slowly trickled down her thighs.

"I'm done fer," Robbie said, his eyes also directed upwards.

She chuckled. "How so?"

"Ye, Elle. I'll never find another lass like ye. I know it, deep in my bones."

Elle inwardly faltered, their blissful respite suddenly tainted.

Even if he meant it, they could never be. Not once he defeated the Urlus and took back the Phoenix Throne.

This, here, this moment, was the peak of their relationship.

"Please tell me, my lass, that ye feel the same way?"

He shifted on the bed, turning on his side to gaze at her.

Elle forced herself to look at him, tears threatening to brim in her eyes as she surveyed his disheveled hair, flushed cheeks, and earnest, hazel eyes.

She could stare at him forever and never tire of it.

"Ditto," she finally murmured.

A wicked smile lit up his face, having clearly remembered her explanation of the word.

Robbie pulled her into his arms with almost too much excessiveness and held her for what felt like hours, pressing a kiss to her forehead now and then like she was something infinitely precious.

Something beloved to him.

How long they actually lay there didn't matter. Nothing mattered.

Nothing except the two of them and the time they had left together.

CHAPTER 20

Robbie woke in darkness with Elle's warm body nestled against him. He closed his eyes and drank in her warmth and softness, her sweet aroma covering him all over.

He wanted her again, now, but he wouldn't dare wake her. She needed rest after his delicious assaults on her last night. After the fifth time, he'd finally let her fall asleep in his arms. How many more times would he be able to take her before he had to leave for the war?

Elle stirred in his arms, blinking her eyes open.

"You're awake," she said, the undertow of slumber lacing her voice.

"Aye, lass. I am."

"You should sleep in more. It's barely dawn, and it's been a long night."

He chuckled. "Indeed, and so should ye. Ye'll need your strength for when I'm gone."

She stiffened against him. "Gone? What do you mean?"

"When I go to war. Ye'll be safe here."

"I'm going with you!" she exclaimed, breaking away from him and sitting up. "I'm not staying behind if that's what you think."

"Ye cannae go to war, lass," he murmured. "Ye ken that as well as I."

"No, I damn well don't. Have you forgotten who I am? Where I come from? I have to get to the castle as much as you do."

He opened his mouth to answer, then stopped. He'd never considered that she would want to go now that the Urlus possessed the castle.

"Listen to me, lass," he told her. "If the Urlus have taken the castle, the curse cannae be lifted."

"It will be. It has to be," she countered, an edge of fear in her tone. "When you defeat the Urlus and take back the throne."

"Ye cannae go. Ye must stay here where ye'll be safe. When it's all over—"

"What? What will happen when it's all over? Tell me."

He took a deep breath.

He had to say it.

"Ye'll come and join me. Ye'll be my Queen, and ye'll stay with me there."

Elle went still and quiet.

"What is it, lass? Do ye no' wish to be my Queen? Is that it? Go on and tell me."

Her voice quavered. "I... This world isn't for me. I came here by mistake, and all I know for certain is that I must find my friends and go home."

Despair pierced him like the sharp blade of a dagger.

"I can never be your Queen, even if I wanted to be," she went on. "You belong with a woman from your own people. Besides—"

"Besides?"

She let out a shaky breath, then opened her eyes and faced him in the dark.

"We're not the same... species. You're... you're part dragon. I'm human. We could never have children, and isn't that the Queen's job?"

Robbie inwardly flinched. "So that's it, is it? Ye dinnae want to be saddled with a dragon. I shouldae kenned it would come to that."

"Come on, Rob. You know it isn't that. I would give anything to be with you. I just spent the most amazing night of my life with you. Don't you know I want you more than anything?"

"What is it then? Why cannae ye see beyond that to just ye and me together? Why does it have to be anything else?"

"I don't want it to be. It's just..."

"What?"

She hung her head. "Don't ask me that when you already know the answer."

He heard his voice rising, but he couldn't stop it. "How could I ken the answer when ye havenae told me? Would ye stay here and be my Queen if ye could?"

Her eyes met his again. "Yes, but it never will happen. Me staying here while you fight the Urlus won't change that. The curse will lift, and I know I'll vanish back to my own world no matter where you are. We'll... we'll never see each other again."

"Is that why ye want to come to the war with me? Ye want to be there when it happens? Is that it?"

"Oh, Rob." She groaned. "What's the point in us loving each other so much if it can never be? What's the point in hurting each other like this?"

"Is that what last night was to ye? Did it hurt ye? That's just bloody splendid."

She tried to put her arms around him. "Don't say that. You know I love you."

"Then stay here. I'll find Ross, and I'll find a way to keep ye here with me."

"I don't want to stay here. I want to find Carmen and—"

"Carmen!" he shouted. "Ye want to find Carmen? Ye want to go back? Ye've wanted to go back all along. Ye never wanted to stay here with me."

"Be reasonable. How could I want to stay here? I never thought it was possible."

"It is possible!" he cried. "Ye ken it could be. How in the name of Heaven can there be wizards and such like running around all over the place if it isnae possible? One of them must ken a way to keep ye here if ye really wanted it."

She put out a hand to him. "Rob, please..."

He jumped out of bed and snatched his shirt off the floor followed by his kilt.

"Go on. Go find something to send ye back. I've no doubt this Abraline will do it. I've no doubt these Munros, or whatever clan they are, won't bat an eyelash when ye tell them ye dinnae care to be saddled with any kind of dragon oddity. Go on and be damned."

He pulled on his kilt and set to work buckling his belt, even though his mind was reeling.

What the devil is wrong with ye? Why are ye pushing her away like this, just when ye need her the most?

Elle leaped out of bed to go after him. "Don't walk away, Rob. I would give anything to stay here with you."

He fought her off for a moment when she grabbed his arm, but she held on so tight he had to struggle to free himself.

Finally, he yanked his arm free and hurled her down onto the bed. She cried out in surprise, and he stared down at her in horror.

What was he turning into, that he could push her like that? He loved her. And more than anything he'd ever loved and desired in his whole life.

She stared up at him from the pillow. Her wide eyes caught a glimmer of light from the window, and he read her face plain as day. She didn't recognize him. She just gave him a night of rapture and went and treated her like that.

He slumped down by the bed before her and hung his head. "Forgive me."

He didn't expect her forgiveness. Not this time. How could any woman take such insults and keep loving a man?

When she spoke, the steady determination that kept her going all this time made her answer smooth and sure.

"I want to be there," she murmured. "I want to be there when it happens. If you get ripped away from me, if I get whisked away back to my own time, I want to be with you when it happens. I want to feel you there with me. I want to see your face and feel your hand and hold you right up to the very end. I want to spend every minute with you that I can."

No man deserved a woman as fine as her, and when she slid off the bed and into his arms, he pressed his lips against her ear. He could barely get the words out.

"All right, lass. All right. We'll go to the castle together."

After a few minutes of just holding each other, they finally broke apart, and Robbie finished getting dressed.

Elle followed suit but did not change back into a dress. Instead, she walked over to the wardrobe and took out the clothes he'd first met her in.

Robbie watched her. "Have ye been hiding those all this time?"

She shot him a wicked grin. "Yep. The maids and everybody looked horrified that I wanted to keep them, so I thought I'd give the other clothes a try. Now that I'm going with you, I'm putting these back on. They're more practical for the road."

He shook his head. "Whatever ye want to do is fine with me. Come on. We have something to do afore the army leaves."

He headed out the door.

The castle still slept in silence as their heels clipped along the stone passage.

"Where are we going?" Elle asked, having to hurry to keep up with him. But time was of the essence.

He cast a wary look over his shoulder. "There's something I have to do, and I dinnae trust anyone but ye to come along. I dinnae wish to turn up on the battlefield without doing this here first."

He found his way out to the courtyard, and they slipped over the drawbridge into the open country. Mist shrouded the land all around and cast a spooky atmosphere over the country.

Robbie headed down the road toward the woods.

"How far are we going? Do you really think we ought to walk there?" Elle asked.

"We have to walk. We dinnae want to frighten the horses."

She kept quiet after that. He didn't want to tell her what he planned to do, but he needed her for this. He had to do it, and he needed her resolve to help him.

He found the woods where he'd hunted with Alan so many times. He crossed it to a certain field that he knew on the other side. All the cows were in the barn.

He pressed into the field and gauged the distance around him.

Aye, this will work.

Elle frowned. "Well? What are we doing here?"

He didn't give himself an instant to hesitate. He closed his eyes and forced his life energy out through his skin. He flung himself outward as hard as he could. He spread his arms, and his mind sank under a black tide of forgotten power.

His chest erupted out of him. His arms extended far beyond his body. Wings sprouted from his back, and his neck craned back to an unimaginable length. Before he could think twice, he changed into the huge iridescent dragon he was at the caldera.

Elle gazed up at him in awe. "Ushne!"

He curved his head around to look at her. His voice rumbled out of somewhere deep inside this huge body of his. "Get on my back."

He stooped low, and she stepped on his elbow. She swung her leg over his neck and settled into the hollow between his neck and shoulders. He flexed his wings and took to the air. He soared over the fields and forests to the mountains far away.

Elle clung to his neck with her legs. He pumped his wings, and the power of his flight carried him into the sky where the rising sun painted the clouds crimson and gold.

Robbie had never experienced anything so exhilarating as that first flight. He narrowed his eyes against the wind whipping over his scales. It whistled all around his head as his sleek body cut the chilly air. He worked his muscles harder. He could fly faster than he ever thought possible.

Elle bent low over his neck and let out a wild whoop of excitement. The sound spurred him to fly faster. No matter how hard he flapped his wings, he could always fly faster.

He put hundreds of miles behind him, the landscape rippling away below him, and he didn't feel a thing.

He never would have dared to fly this fast if Elle hadn't come with him. Now that he knew she was enjoying herself, he pushed himself faster and farther than ever. The air rushing past made a breathy sound in his ears, *ushne ushne ushne*. So that's where that name came from. It spoke out of the forgotten depths of his dragon soul.

He flew beyond the mountains and to the blue sea in the distance. Islands dotted the coasts. He banked and soared down the shore. Storms kicked the waves up, and spray splashed in his face. He zoomed around in a circle, and Elle shrieked with glee. He chuckled low in his throat.

Despite what the future held – whether the curse would be broken or he found his brothers or Elle found Carmen, or if Robbie would be forced to watch his love be ripped away from him for all eternity – at that moment, they were together.

Bound.

Exultant.
And free.

CHAPTER 21

Elle and Robbie walked into the forum hand in hand.

Alan turned around and narrowed his eyes at them. "What's she doin' here?"

"She's coming with us," Robbie replied.

"She cannae come with us," Alan countered. "We're on our way to war. It's no place for a woman. Ye should ken that, lad."

Robbie stiffened. "I'm no lad, lad. I'm a man if anyone in this room is, and it's my apparent throne we're fighting for. I'll be the one to decide whether she comes or no', and I say she comes. I'll no' leave her behind. If she's no' coming, then neither am I."

Alan glared at him, and the King scowled. "Ye're a man of war, and ye ken best how to get yer own throne, and we'll no' tell ye otherwise. If ye care anything about yer companion, ye'll leave her where she'll be safe. She's best to stay behind with the women, and that's all there is to it. If ye insist on bringing her along, it's on yer own head."

"It is," Robbie replied, "and I say she comes. Now, if ye care at all to make our plans, ye'll go ahead with that and leave the subject where it lies."

Alan and the King exchanged glances.

"Ye bring her or no', as ye please," Alan returned. "However, ye cannae think to include her in our plans."

"And why not?" Robbie asked.

"She's... a woman, and a foreign one at that."

"I'm a foreigner myself," Robbie countered.

"Ye're the rightful King," Alan corrected him, "and ye're the only one who can fight the Urlus. Ye have to come. As for sharing our plans with a foreign woman that dinnae belong on the battlefield in the first place, ye cannae include her in this forum."

"She'll be included," Robbie declared. "That's my last word."

The King and the Prince looked at each other one more time, but neither said a word.

Elle had watched the exchange with both fear and elation. Rob seemed to get more confident with every moment that passed. That short flight he took outside had strengthened him for what he needed to do.

How long had he really held himself back from changing? He must have known all along he could do it. He just had to overcome the mental block stopping him from transforming.

The same mental block had held him back from her. It made him fight against his feelings, but now that he'd embraced his love and dragon self, he'd let go of all his resistance.

They were together for good – that is, right up until the moment they wouldn't be.

The King and Alan didn't argue with him, but they didn't discuss any war plans either. Not in front of Elle. That much was still abundantly clear.

Robbie surveyed the two of them one more time. "No? Very well."

He took Elle by the hand and spun on his heel to march out of the room.

Elle's heart pounded. He couldn't walk out. He'd invested weeks of planning into this war. He needed the army to attack the Urlus. He couldn't win on his own.

He got halfway across the room before Alan raced to his side.

"Stop where ye are, Rob. Ye cannae walk away from us."

Robbie didn't stop. "No? Watch me."

Alan darted in front of him and held out his hand. "Please, Rob. Ye ken we cannae do this naught but together. Come back and talk about it with us."

"If ye wish to talk about anything to me, ye'll talk about it with Elle as well. Ye'll ken that right now, or ye'll see the back of me this very morning. We traveled a long way afore ye asked me to come here and help ye, and if ye dinnae want to do that any longer, then good morning to ye and yers. We'll carry on the way we were afore, and I'll see how the land lies when I get to the castle and find my brothers."

Elle didn't say a word. Adrenaline burned in her guts.

Will this work?

She only hoped and prayed that Rob knew what he was doing. She didn't mind hitting the road with him the way they did before. However, she didn't so much look forward to facing the Urlus and trying to get the Phoenix Throne back with just the two of them. They might never find his brothers. They could be wandering this backward country forever.

"All right, mon. Ye win. She can stay," Alan finally said.

"I ken she can stay," Robbie replied. "It's ye who'll come or go as ye wish."

He turned around to face the King. "Do ye wish to confer this morning or no'?"

The King bowed his head in silent acceptance.

"We need to plan the main assault." Alan motioned for Robbie to follow him back into the forum.

Elle let go of Robbie's hand and took an empty seat between two higher-ranking looking soldiers also in attendance.

When Robbie returned to the King's side, Alan unrolled a large map. "We'll set up our blockade here. Our forces will assault the castle here, and the main body of the Urlus will come out and face off on this plane here. Once we engage them, that's when ye'll strike."

"Ye tell me what ye want me to do," Robbie replied. "I'll go along with yer strategy. I'm only one man."

"Ye'll no' strike them as a man. Once their forces lock with us, ye'll swoop over and lay waste of them with yer fire. That's the way we'll drive them back and take the castle."

Robbie narrowed his eyes at him. He didn't say it out loud, but Elle read his thoughts.

His fire?

Alan must mean the dragon's fiery breath. He wanted Robbie to incinerate the Urlu forces. They wouldn't stand a chance against a full-sized dragon. So that's why they invited him along in the first place.

Of course. Makes sense.

Robbie nodded. "All right. I'll do it. Anything else?"

"Once ye devastate the Urlu forces, their king will come out of the castle and challenge ye. Ye'll fight him one to one. That's their way. Once ye defeat him, ye'll have the throne."

Robbie stared down at the map. He showed no sign of suspicion, but Elle couldn't relax.

Fight the King of the Urlus one on one? Can he even do that? If he loses, he will never get the throne. The castle will remain under its curse, and you will…

The truth hit her like the hard slam of a touchdown.

She would stay here, possibly forever. She might meet up with Carmen and the others, but they would never return to their own time.

Elle's thoughts and emotions tangled into one confused knot of conflicting loyalties and desires. Did she really want to stay here forever – with Robbie?

Alan and the King appeared to study him for any hint of protest, but Robbie only nodded.

He raised his head to lock eyes with them. "Very well. Prepare to march."

Robbie stood then and gestured for Elle to follow him out of the hall. He marched down the passage to his room, threw back the door, and ushered her inside.

She eyed him. "I sure hope you know what you're doing."

He put his arm around her waist and pulled her into his embrace. "I do. I'll take them, and when I get that throne, that's when we'll see what's what."

She wanted to say more, but he silenced her with a kiss. He picked her up in his arms, and she breathed into his mouth, "Rob…"

He broke away from her lips. "I'm yers, lass, both Robbie Cameron and Ushne. Always."

Elle's smile threatened to split her face, and she giggled when he toppled them over and onto the bed.

She wrapped her arms and legs around him, and before long, they had picked up right where they'd left off after round five the previous night.

CHAPTER 22

The long column of the King's knights, yeomen, cannon, cavalry, archers, and siege machines rumbled down the roads on their way to the castle where Robbie had parted ways from his brothers. He rode next to Alan at the head of the column. The clatter of several thousand wagon wheels, armor, spears, sabers, and cook wagons echoed over the countryside.

Elle learned fast how to ride a horse, but she stayed well back with the wagons to keep out of the soldiers' way. Alan insisted Robbie ride out front with him to show the troops a united front, and Robbie acquiesced to this, though he sensed it was a clever piece of flattery to get his presence to inspire the troops on their mission. They could see Robbie leading the campaign. His presence had to give them the impression they were invincible. They had a dragon to spring upon the enemy at the most crucial juncture of the battle. That should inspire anybody to victory.

Robbie went along with the plan to make himself a figurehead – or was he a scapegoat?

He always camped with Elle at night though. He found her in the column, and they sat together around a campfire the way they used to. Whether Alan tried to manipulate Robbie with flattery or not, Elle was still the only person that had seen him as a dragon. She saw, rode on his back on his maiden flight, and loved him. She was the only person who also knew the name Ushne. It was their secret.

Unfortunately, he didn't make love to her on the campaign. He didn't want to take her on some rough, cold ground with several thousand soldiers listening. She was too precious for that. He wanted to take her in silk sheets in his own castle, where he ruled and dominated and conquered. Nothing else would do for the woman he loved.

He closed his eyes into the sunshine and let his thoughts drift back to their time in the King's court. He would carry those memories forever, no matter what happened on the battlefield.

Alan chuckled at his side. "Ye'll wipe the floor with 'em, mon. I cannae wait to see their faces when ye come blasting over the mountain and down on top of them."

Robbie didn't answer. Wiping the floor with the Urlus was the last thing on his mind right now. He was a million miles away in a sunlit bedroom with Elle stretched out naked at his side. She'd shuddered each time he ran his fingertips across her breast, her breath catching in her throat when he trailed his hand down her belly to her quivering fissure.

Mmm, yes... those thoughts always made the dreary days of this march pass easily.

When would he touch her like that again? She never said so, but she still worried about what would happen when their campaign succeeded. He refused to think about it. He couldn't lose her. Once he became King and sat on the Phoenix Throne, he would find a way to keep her. He would find a wizard or a sorceress or something who could overturn whatever magic would take her away when the curse lifted.

Robbie turned in his saddle and scanned the column, but he couldn't see her. She was back there somewhere, behind the foot soldiers and the archers, stuck close to the noncombatants where she belonged. That alone made him feel better about taking her on this campaign. She might be close when it happened, but she wouldn't be in the thick of battle.

Robbie turned to face the front again when he spotted Alan scrutinizing him.

"Ye're thinking about yer woman, are ye no'?"

"Aye. Why shouldnae I think about her?"

"Ye cannae take her as yer Queen. Ye must ken that by now."

"No?" Robbie squinted at him. "And why no'?"

"She's no' the same kind as ye. She's a different variety. She's no' a dragon like ye are. Ye ken that, mon. I shouldnae have to tell ye."

Robbie snorted. "I'll be the one to decide who I take as my Queen, and I'll be the one to decide what to do about Elle."

"Ye'd never be able to have an heir with her," Alan replied. "Ye ken that as well as I do. Ye're incompatible."

"Ye dinnae ken that," Robbie countered. "Ye ken naught about it – unless ye're no' telling me something ye should have."

Alan looked away. "I dinnae ken naught about it."

"Then for the love of Heaven, keep yer peace, and dinnae talk to me about Elle. It concerns ye no'."

Alan lowered his voice to a murmur. "Every man in this column means to lay down his life for ye and yer throne. If ye really intend to throw the throne away by taking a queen ye can never produce an heir with, then it concerns everyone here. Why should we give our lives and our arms to ye if ye plan to throw it all away like that?"

Robbie shot him a fierce glare, but he didn't answer. So he wasn't just a figurehead at the front of this column; he was a byword and a target of rumors and whispered conjectures. The whole column talked about him and Elle behind his back. They all thought he was throwing away the Phoenix Throne by having her by his side.

Alan reined his horse closer to Robbie's mount.

"Ye must put Elle away, mon. It's the only way ye'll regain yer throne."

The minute he got the words out, Alan spurred his horse away so Robbie couldn't answer.

Robbie kept his place at the head of the column for the rest of the day, but his thoughts gave him no peace. It was a fair question, he had to admit that: what was the point of him sitting on the Phoenix Throne with a barren queen by his side? Why should all these men fight and die for him if he was going to do something like that? Why should Angus and all the men who died getting the brothers to the castle in the first place sacrifice their lives for that?

Even knowing that Robbie couldn't turn his back on her. She was the only woman he wanted. He would never put her away – never.

Toward evening, Alan called a halt, and the soldiers dismounted and pitched camp. They lit fires, and the cooks got a meal going for the men.

Robbie turned his mount and trotted down the column in search of Elle. He looked for her fire, but he couldn't find it anywhere.

He hunted up and down the column. When he still didn't find her, he started to worry. Did something happen to her during the day? Did she get lost or separated from the main body of the army?

He reined his horse back to the front. He would find Alan and report Elle missing. Alan would know where she was. Then again, Alan just told Robbie to get rid of her. Maybe Alan had something to do with Elle's disappearance.

No, that was too far-fetched. Robbie couldn't believe Alan or the King had anything to do with her disappearing. Besides, she hadn't disappeared; he just couldn't find her.

He had to stay calm, but he couldn't keep his heart steady. He couldn't lose Elle now, after everything they'd gone through.

He had to find her.

The crash of metal against metal caught his attention. That was strange. Who could be fighting at a time like this when the whole column was readying to go to sleep for the night?

He rode toward the sound and spotted two figures fencing between the trees by the roadside. Their silhouettes stood out against the gloom, but Robbie would recognize one anywhere.

It was Elle, sparring with one of the knights.

Robbie jumped off his horse. He approached the spot as the two combatants separated.

"What do ye think ye're doing?" he asked her.

She grinned in the flush of excitement. "I'm learning how to sword fight."

"Why?" he demanded. "I told ye ye're no' going to fight in this war. It's too dangerous. It's no place for ye, especially when all us soldiers plan to do yer fightin' for ye."

"I just want to learn. That's all. Whether I fight or not doesn't really matter. It's a skill I wanted to learn a long time ago, and now I have a chance. Simon's going to teach me how to throw the javelin next."

She smiled at the knight retreating into the trees.

Robbie glared at the man. "I told ye I dinnae want ye fighting. I only agreed to let ye come on this campaign on condition ye'd be safe. If I'd kenned ye'd take up swordplay and whatever else, I never wouldae let ye come."

The grin evaporated off her face. "Let's get one thing clear right now, although this shouldn't be news to you. You don't let me do anything. I decide what I do and when. *I* decided to come on this campaign, and *I* decide if I learn sword fighting or whatever else. You don't decide those things for me. Got that?"

His temper flared. "Ye're the most unaccountable woman I ever had the misfortune to meet. When are ye going tae learn ye cannae just throw your weight around wherever ye please? We're going to war, lass. We're no' out for a lark. Men will bleed and die afore this thing is through, and I for one dinnae wish to see it happen to ye. Perhaps ye do want it to happen to ye. I dinnae ken. Perhaps ye're just as daft in the head as I always suspected."

She glared at him one more time. Then she laughed in his face. She hefted her saber and walked past him.

"That's pretty funny. Come on – it's time we got the fire going, and I'm hungry. Look – the cooks are already starting down the line. We don't want to miss out."

Robbie stared after her figure fading into the shadows. He couldn't move a muscle. What was he going to do with this woman? He couldn't bend her to his will by dominating her and telling her what to do. She confounded him at every turn.

Even so, he couldn't stay mad at her. He needed her, and he needed her confounding and unaccountable. That was her secret power over him. He couldn't understand her. He had to accept her just as she was.

His guts ached at the thought of her fighting in this war. If anything happened to her, he was finished. He didn't want the Phoenix Throne or anything else if he couldn't have her.

He didn't want to go find her. He didn't want to face her after she just made a joke of his boorish demands. She saw right through him. She held him in the palm of her hand, and she knew it.

He looked right and left, unsure what to do with himself. He turned to go... when a shadowy shape emerged from the trees.

Its familiar voice touched his ear. "Ye see what I mean? Ye can never make her yer Queen. It'd never work."

Robbie closed his eyes. "Leave it alone, lad. I cannae listen to any more of yer talk about her."

Alan didn't leave it alone. "She'll fight in the war. She wouldnae study swordplay if she didnae mean to use it in the battle. Leave her to it. Let her fight, and ye'll no' have to put her away. She'll put herself away, and ye'll be free to choose another queen of yer own kind."

"My own kind?" Robbie asked, renewed fury welling up in him. Aye, the Prince had some damn balls, demeaning Elle so incessantly. "And what is my 'own kind'? I dinnae ken any others of my kind."

"Ye're no' the only one," Alan told him. "Ye'll find others when ye take yer throne, but ye'll no' be King with her by yer side. Ye must get rid of her – either send her away or let her fight and die."

Robbie shook his head, feeling his mind being torn in opposite directions. He wanted to slice the prince's belly open for his poisonous words, yet he couldn't argue with the man. For some reason, he'd come to trust him, but couldn't nail down at that moment why. Some inner voice told him that Alan meant well, despite his tarnishing of Elle. He wanted what was best for Robbie and the realm. That was the only reason for his impetuous words.

Thus, what if Alan was right? What if Robbie had to take a different queen? Would it be better for all if Elle just disappeared? And aye, what more convenient way to make that happen than for her to accidentally get killed in the war?

She had no battle experience. Sure, she could handle herself in a small bout. Robbie had seen that for himself. Fighting with a sword and javelin on the battlefield though?

That was a different story.

CHAPTER 23

Elle sat astride her horse on a ridge overlooking a sunny valley. Fields of waving grain, livestock, and dark forest stretched as far as the eye could see. A few herdsmen inched along the ground between their flocks.

There, in the middle of the whole scene, sat a huge castle of gleaming stone. The sun played on its bright white walls, and colored flags flapped from its towers.

"That's the place," Prince Alan told Robbie.

Robbie frowned. "It looks different. It looked black when I saw it afore."

"Must have been a trick of the light," Alan replied. "Ye see? That's the plane where we'll attack. We'll set up our tent city back here."

He turned back to where the wagons had unloaded in a hollow behind the ridge. No one in the castle could see the army amassing on their southern boundary. Tents popped up, and the teamsters set up their tents and cooking fires.

Robbie and Elle stayed where they were.

Robbie murmured under his breath. "Something's missin'."

"What do you mean?" Elle asked.

"I cannae say from up here, but we're missing something, something important. I ought to fly over and see."

"If you flew over, they would see you," she countered. "We would lose the element of surprise. The whole idea is that they don't know you're coming."

"Right." He let out a heavy sigh. "I suppose we'll just have to go for it and see what happens."

She peered up at him. "Do you really think we're missing something that important?"

He shook his head and turned away. "It's naught. It's just a queer feeling I have. Maybe it's just nerves afore the battle."

He walked away into the camp sprouting up all over the hollow behind the ridge, but Elle stayed where she was. In the long weeks traveling with Robbie before they came to stay with this clan who still called themselves Munros, they'd both learned to trust each other's instincts. If one sensed danger, the other took it seriously.

Elle sensed no danger from that castle. In fact, it looked inviting and majestic to her – a lot more majestic than the King's castle she loved so much. Robbie didn't like it though. He'd never suggested flying anywhere. Now he wanted to reconnoiter the battlefield just in case they'd missed something in their long conferences.

When she turned back, she saw him talking to Alan, but as the day wore on, he didn't fly. He stayed in camp, but he never mentioned his misgivings again. He had put on an enthusiastic face.

Later in the afternoon, the knights, soldiers, and archers formed up for review on the field. Alan and Robbie inspected them, and Alan visibly pretended not to see Elle in her new armor, her sword and her javelin at her side, lined up with the infantry.

Robbie scowled at her but said nothing.

He didn't mention it in their camp that night either.

*****

A crier ran through the camp at first light. "Form up! All divisions, form up."

Elle launched herself to her feet and seized the breastplate her new friend Simon had given her.

Robbie put out his hand to stop her. "Wait, Elle."

"I told you not to try to stop me," she replied. "I'm going out there. All these people want to help you win back your throne, and so do I."

"I willnae try to stop ye," he told her. "Just listen to me for a moment."

She drew herself up to her full height in front of him. "I'm listening."

He took a deep breath. "Stay near me out there. All right? If ye must go out there and fight, stay close to me."

"So you can protect me, you mean? That kind of defeats the purpose of me fighting, doesn't it?"

He shook his head and came near to lower his voice. "It's no' that. I ken ye can fight if anyone can. It's just…"

She regarded him with her head tilted to one side. What was he trying to tell her?

He shook his head again, but that didn't help him get the words out. "Something's gonna happen out there. I cannae say what it is, but it's coming."

"Do you mean the battle?"

"No, it's no' the battle. It's something else, something... It's not exactly dangerous – not to me, anyway. I... I must be the only one of this whole army that it isnae dangerous to."

She frowned. "You're not making any sense."

"I ken it, Elle. I ken I'm making no sense. I cannae make sense of it myself. I only ken it's there. It's waitin' for this army out there on the plane. I dinnae like to see ye fight in the army, but I ken ye'll be no safer back here than ye'd be on the plane. Not a man of this army will be safe out there but me. That's all I ken about it."

She studied him for another minute. "All right. Rob. I'll take you at your word. Where will you be?"

"I dinnae ken." His voice cracked from the strain. "If ye stay back here, ye'll be alone when I fly out there to attack the Urlus. I dinnae ken what to do."

His eyes darted all over the place, and he wrung his hands in confusion. Elle had never seen him like this.

She laid a hand on his arm. "All right. Take it easy. You're the one who'll be able to come to me if anything happens. Okay? You'll fly overhead when you attack the enemy. You'll be able to see me and find me if you need to. Will that satisfy you?"

Her words didn't settle him down. He shifted from one foot to the other.

Elle threw her arms around his neck.

"Ushne. Ushne," she whispered.

Her voice calmed him instantly. He put his arms around her waist and hid his eyes against her neck. Whatever danger he saw out there, it must be pretty serious. Just for an instant, she considered staying behind and not going out to the battle after all. The next minute, she discarded the notion. Staying behind wouldn't protect her from whatever it was. She would be just as alone when he flew out to assault the Urlu forces.

He raised his face to kiss her.

"You come find me, Ushne," she murmured. "You come to me when you're ready. If you tell me to go, I'll go. Okay?"

He closed his eyes, rested his forehead against hers, and nodded.

At that moment, the crier came past again. "Form up! All divisions, form up!"

Elle tore herself away. "I better go. I'll see you down there. Take care of yourself. When it happens, you tell me, and we'll go."

He stood back and watched her buckle on her armor and her scabbard.

She gave him one last kiss and hurried away to join the troops. She didn't want to miss this, but something major bothered him. This was his moment of triumph, but whatever it was disturbed him so he couldn't function.

The divisions formed up just behind the ridge where they couldn't be seen from below. Prince Alan rode his horse back and forth in front of the divisions. The knights' chargers and the cavalry's mounts stamped and snorted. Armor clanged all down the ranks. Most of the men wore black paint smeared across their faces to give them a demonic appearance.

Elle took her place next to Simon with the infantry.

Prince Alan wheeled his horse around to face the army. "Our clan has waited generations for this moment to drive the stinking hordes from our land. Now is your moment, men. Ye'll stamp them into the ground, and the vermin will never raise their heads to disturb us again. Are ye ready?"

A great cheer rose out of the crowd. The men raised their weapons on high and shook their armor to a deafening roar.

Horses squealed and reared in their excitement to attack.

Out of the camp, Robbie appeared. He walked through the grass to Alan's side. His kilt kicked around his knees, and his shins brushed the long grass stems. He was nothing but an ordinary man, but his presence quieted the troops in an instant.

Alan's horse shied and strained at its bit. Robbie didn't have to take his dragon form to intimidate anybody; even animals sensed the beast within him.

Peace seemed to settle over the army. The sight of him standing there told them what they needed to do.

Alan spoke in a soft voice, but everyone heard it. "Take your positions. Ready the first assault."

The army rushed to the ridge.

Horses brushed their sides against each other.

Armored bodies jostled Elle into her place. Her heart pounded against her ribs, but she wouldn't back down at this moment for anything. She wanted to fight. She wanted to test herself against hardened men of combat and win the day.

Alan's voice boomed over the lines from behind. "Ready, first wave! First wave, fire!"

At his word, the siege machines set up on the ridge unleashed their first bombardment.

Missiles soared over the plane and struck the castle.

Alan laughed behind the ranks. "That'll wake 'em up if naught else will do."

The siege machines unloaded shot after shot. Projectiles pounded down on the castle and struck its walls. A thin wail of screaming voices drifted on the wind. The drawbridge creaked upward and slammed into place.

The next instant, a heavy missile smashed against the closed drawbridge, obliterating the wood to splinters. The portcullis came down at the same time and got caught on a twisted plank sticking out of the drawbridge. The hole gaped open.

Elle looked through the gap into the courtyard beyond. Nothing protected the castle from invasion.

Alan called out, louder this time, "Ready, second wave! Second wave, forward."

At his word, Simon jumped off the ridge. Black dye discolored his face, turning him into a raging fury. He planted his feet wide and swung his sword above his head.

"Forward, brothers!"

The infantry lunged forward in a body. Thousands of men charged down the mountain heading for the castle.

Battle fever infected Elle like never before. She ran down the slope toward that broken drawbridge. All of Robbie's warnings vaporized out of her mind.

The siege machines pounded their constant fire on the castle in all directions. Walls crumbled to expose rooms and courtyards and stables behind them. The closer she got, Elle saw individual people rushing everywhere behind the walls.

She brandished her saber and ran for all she was worth. She bumped into other armored soldiers, but no one stopped running. The noise and confusion only fueled her burning rage to fight.

The army got halfway across the field before the Urlus reacted. Out of the yawning hole in the drawbridge, armed men streamed out to meet the oncoming foe. They charged the army in the same headlong rush for blood. They crashed into the enemy forces, and the two armies were locked in mortal combat.

In seconds, men with axes hacked the broken drawbridge away. Others threw boards across the moat, and horsemen in plate mail charged onto the field. A deafening ruckus boomed across the plane, and cavalry and knights galloped down the mountain to meet them.

Out of nowhere, a ferocious man with a bushy brown beard under his helmet rushed at Elle, roaring loud enough to wake the dead. He raised his sword over his head to cleave her in half.

The next thing she knew, all her awareness dwindled to a pinprick. She lost all cognizance of anything around her. All her energy and attention focused on this man. She raised her saber to block his stroke, all her strength and power trained on keeping her alive for the next few seconds.

CHAPTER 24

Robbie watched the battle from the ridge. The infantry, knights, and cavalry of the King's army engaged mounted fighters and foot soldiers from inside the castle. The longer the two armies grappled for every inch of space on the field, the more troops poured out of the castle to defend it.

The siege machines bombarded the castle in a constant drumbeat of pounding missiles. Towers crumbled, and plumes of dust billowed into the clear air.

Alan's charger trotted down the line. "Fourth wave, ready! Fourth wave, deploy!"

The archers, the last division of the army, set off running down the hill. They formed ranks behind the front line, and the archers dropped to their knees behind the army.

The next minute, a hail of arrows peppered the warriors streaming out of the castle. They struck down dozens of Urlus at a stroke.

However, the Urlus never wavered. They fought with all their power to defend their castle. Robbie hadn't expected the scene before him. He didn't think they would let him walk in and take the throne without a struggle, yet this battle clearly was a passionate cause for both sides.

He was also vexed by Elle? He still couldn't believe he'd just allowed her to do as she pleased. A woman in battle? The notion was absurd. He wanted to take wing, swoop down, and get her out of there. Perhaps he never should have gotten mixed up with the Prince and King, but it was too late now. He could never take the castle alone, but something about this situation didn't sit right in his mind. His mind still felt as if it were being tugged in two directions.

And where were his brothers? Were they captives inside that castle? Were they wandering the countryside again? Were they on their way back home, now that they'd lost Angus?

Alan came trotting back. His horse pranced right and left. He fought the reins to keep the animal under control.

"Get ye ready, Rob! It's time."

Robbie climbed up the ridge to gaze out over the scene again. He knew the plan. All he had to do was fly down there and unload his fiery breath on the enemy. He could finally exact his revenge on these Urlus for what they had done to his family, his brother, the rightful King.

He would do it for Angus.

Alan slapped him on the shoulder from behind. "Go on. Ye can do it."

Robbie took a deep breath. He almost changed when a flock of black specks burst out of the castle into the air. They erupted from behind the shattered walls and took wing. They rocketed over the landscape going a mile a minute. In a few seconds, they raced over the battlefield and up the mountain to the spot where Alan and Robbie watched.

Robbie ducked his head, but not before he saw them in all their horrible glory.

They were dragons — hundreds of them of every imaginable color. They zoomed on their papery wings and swooped low to whizz at the soldiers once again. The air hummed off their scales, and their wings sent blasts of air into Robbie's face.

He stared in stunned shock. In front of his eyes, more and more took flight from inside the castle. They stooped at the King's troops and let loose their jets of flame upon the enemy.

The whole sight was like something out of a dream. Robbie always imagined himself flying over the Urlus and incinerating them with his own fire. He never once imagined they would do the same thing back.

Alan yelled in his ear, "Get ye up there afore it's too late! Go on! What're ye waiting for?"

Robbie glanced at him. He didn't recognize the man he once considered a friend.

"What the devil's going on? Ye never told me they were dragons too."

"Did ye think we needed ye to fight an army of men?" Alan shouted back. "Get up there! This is what we needed ye for. We need ye to fight them. Ye're the only one that can!"

"I cannae fight 'em all! Are ye daft? I am but one dragon."

Alan moved closer to Robbie's face. "Do ye mean to stand up here like a coward and watch those things destroy our army? Get ye up there if ye ken what's right. Ye'll no' win the Phoenix Throne any other way."

Robbie faced the battlefield. His head spun in a thousand directions. Elle was down there. One of those dragons could hit her, and there was nothing he could do to stop it. He had to get out there and fight them. He had to find her and get her out before it was too late.

At the same time, a queer thought weaseled its way into his brain. These were dragons like himself. They lived in a castle, and some of them fought as men against men. That must mean they could change back and forth at will, the same as he could. These were his own kind, so why was he fighting them?

He didn't let himself think twice.

He had to find Elle.

Nothing else mattered.

He launched himself off the ridge into the air. The wind and gravity caught him and tore his clothes away from his skin. The cold pierced his bones.

The next instant, he spread his wings and as Ushne plunged towards the battlefield. He slashed any dragon he saw with his tail and hammered them with his fire. He'd never used his fiery breath before, but it came out of him easier than he thought. He released his revenge on these dragon people who killed his brother and dispossessed his family. Yet all the while, a feeling niggled under his skin, telling him that all this wasn't right. Yet he couldn't stop. It was like some force was controlling him.

Dragons screeched and plummeted out of the sky all around him. He darted from one to the next. He slashed their wings off and whipped his tail around them to break their necks. He didn't bother to look at them. He killed without discrimination in his headlong rush to destroy them all.

Ushne streaked over the castle and blasted the courtyards and ruined chambers with devastating fire. He even got a sick thrill from seeing women and children running for cover at his approach.

Is this what ye're becoming? A beast without a soul? a voice questioned in his mind, only then to be overridden by a surge for vengeance.

He banked and raced back over the fields of battle. Both armies cringed at his approach, and even the dragons hesitated to engage him. They skirted the battlefield and attacked the periphery, but they wouldn't come near the main field with him patrolling there. It had become all too evident to Ushne that despite them too being dragons, he was far stronger, larger, and swifter.

He scanned the ground for Elle and finally spotted her locked in a deathly struggle with some Urlu soldier. Their swords clashed, and the man shoved her back to menace her one more time.

Ushne narrowed his eyes and bent his wings to dive at the man when a shout went up from somewhere to his left.

"The King! The King is coming!"

Ushne didn't have to hear any more to know what they were talking about. King Farlane would never get mixed up in this battle. They could only be talking about one person.

Alan had told him the King of the Urlus would come out to fight him. Ushne had to beat him to take the throne and break the curse.

He turned around and beheld a huge black dragon rising out of the castle. The spikes along its head, neck, and back gleamed in the sun. Its sheer size changed the atmosphere, causing the air to prickle down Ushne's scales.

Ushne turned all the way around to face the menace. He hovered over Elle. If he won and broke the curse, she would vanish off the battlefield, and he would never see her again. The alternative was dying here himself. Then she would be trapped in this world alone.

He didn't have time to think about that. The black dragon gained the atmospheric heights and trained its glittering eyes on him. That dragon dwarfed even Rob. The smaller dragons fluttering all over the place didn't dare come close. They knew what was coming.

Everybody did.

Ushne narrowed his eyes at the creature who killed his brother. He didn't care if these Urlus were the same as him. He would kill this monster before he budged off this battlefield.

He sensed Elle watching him from the ground. This was the moment of truth. She knew it as well as he did. They would be together, or they would never see each other again. That's all there was to it.

Ushne flexed his wings and put on speed to meet his adversary.

The Dragon King lowered his head between his shoulders and pumped his own wings. He screamed out of the sky coming at Ushne on the wind.

The two dragons collided mid-air. Their long necks and tails lashed around their bodies to bind them together. Ushne slashed his jaws at the black devil, but the black dragon put up just as fierce a fight.

Their heads darted in and out. They slashed and cut and dove, retreated, and attacked again. Their screams and roaring echoed across the valley. Ushne pushed his strength to the limit, but the Urlu King still gained the upper hand.

With the two of them locked together, they couldn't fly. They plummeted toward the earth and would have crashed back into the castle, but the Urlu King whipped his tail around Ushne's body.

At the last second, he tore himself away. That wicked tail ripped around Ushne's chest and spun him out into thin air.

He screamed from the pain of it.

The Urlu King jerked away and flapped up into the clouds. Ushne flopped in the air, and every sinew ached so he could barely extend his wings. He had to act fast.

He put out his wings and swooped above the castle into the air just in time to see the King rocketing back at him at full speed.

Ushne flapped a few times to gain some altitude, but the King came in too fast. The black dragon collided with a mighty force that sent Ushne careening through in the air. In the confusion of getting his wings and tail straightened out to make another concerted effort to defend himself, he was turned around in the air above the castle. He righted himself, but when he looked right and left, he saw no sign of the King.

Out of nowhere, the huge black menace crashed into him once again, even mightier than before. One of Ushne's wings bent back at a sickening angle, and agony ripped through him. His wing now hung useless, and although he tried to stay airborne, it was futile.

He plunged towards the ground.

CHAPTER 25

Elle fought her opponent back, stealing a brief reprieve to peer up and see Ushne's green form drop out of the sky.

She darted forward. "Ushne! No!"

The dragon hit the ground so hard that the earth underneath her moved.

The Urlu man tackled her from behind and pinned her to the ground, bursting the wind out of her lungs. The man pounced on her and sat on her back. She felt him rear back to drive his saber into her from behind, but she couldn't take her eyes off the dragon splayed on the ground in front of her.

Ushne writhed in circles in a desperate attempt to get his feet under him. The Dragon King eyed his pathetic efforts from on high, but the moment Ushne made sense of his flailing limbs and wings, the King landed on him with all his claws extended.

Ushne fell under the King's talons. The enormous black creature held him down and cut ribbons into his scaly skin with his claws. Ushne fought, but couldn't do much on his back.

Elle watched in horror. She couldn't lie here while Ushne met his end.

She cast a quick glance over her shoulder to see her opponent raise his sword for the killing stroke.

Rage exploded out of her. *I'm not dying today, pal!*

She flipped over just in time to block him from lopping her head off and scrambled to her feet.

Their swords met in a shower of sparks again.

The man bared his teeth, and although Elle had learned great skill with the sword of late, she couldn't help the one weakness she couldn't master fully; as a woman, she just couldn't match his natural male strength.

But she had to defeat him so she could help Ushne.

She summoned all her strength and gave one more violent heave. His sword jittered down her blade, and his lock on her gave way.

She let go of her sword. In one desperate dive, she caught hold of his thigh and pulled upward, causing his legs to buckle. He cursed when his head hit the ground, but Elle already had her sword poised an inch from his neck.

Behind her, Ushne's screeches pierced the air. He needed her.

The Urlu soldier's eyes burned; sweat streamed down his contorted face. He stalked toward her with his sword ready. She had to do this. She had to kill him, right? Yet why she was hesitating.

She thought fast, and in seconds, the solution came to her.

She slashed her blade across the mans' legs, sinking the tip into one of his knees to hit the bone. He wouldn't be able to get up and walk, but she'd spared his life.

And he should be damn grateful for that.

Elle didn't wait any longer. She whirled around to see Ushne still struggling under the overpowering bulk of the Dragon King. The black shadow curved its wings around Ushne and hid him from view. Only his head and the green tip of his tail remained visible. Blood stained his scales, and his screeches were getting quieter, telling her that Ushne was on the verge of complete defeat.

Hang on, my love.

Elle raced toward the two dragons. She dropped her sword and reached under her neck armor. Before the battle, Rob had given her the amulet for safekeeping, and now she withdrew it, ripping it off her neck.

"Ushne!" she shouted.

She ran at him with the amulet extended in front of her. If she could only reach him in time, she could press the amulet into the King's heart. He would lose his power, and Ushne would be saved.

Ushne turned his head. Their eyes met. He saw the amulet, and his eyes widened in sudden understanding.

The Dragon King saw her at the same moment. Without letting go of his fallen enemy, he brought his spiked tail around and whipped it at Elle. He flicked her off her feet and sent her catapulting backward.

Ushne roared.

Elle hit the ground, stunned, the amulet flying out of her hand. Her head snapped back, and stars exploded in front of her eyes. She tried to sit up, but her head swam. In the cloudy focus, she saw Ushne rear off the ground in a furious rage.

He threw the King off, his damaged wing having mended a little, and the two dragons faced off once again. Their eyes narrowed to burning slits. Smoke and sulfur billowed from their nostrils, and they rustled their wings in menacing threat. They circled back and forth. Their heads wove to and fro, and they darted in to snap their jaws at each other.

Elle watched in amazement. All the weeks of preparation came down to this moment.

Ushne had to defeat the Urlu King if he wanted to reclaim the Phoenix Throne for his clan.

He now matched the Dragon King in fighting power. He blocked each of the King's threatening bites, but neither landed a blow. They feinted and struck, retreated, and closed again in a catastrophic explosion of one armored hide against the other.

This time, the King had to work hard to overcome Ushne. Ushne wrestled him to the ground more than once, and at one point, wrapped his tail around the King's neck, choking the breath out of him. He clamped his teeth into the King's shoulder and drew a spine-chilling screech from the slightly larger dragon.

The King thrashed to free himself but to no avail.

Ushne spread his wings and clenched his talons around the King's body. He cinched his tail tighter and stopped the cries in the King's throat.

Another instant and he would triumph.

Only, at that very moment, an instinctive feeling surged within Elle.

This isn't right. This battle was never right.

"Ushne, don't," she shouted.

Ushne's large eyes found hers, and he grunted out steam as if to ask her what the hell she was on about?

However, the Dragon King took advantage of his foe's hesitation.

He brought his own tail around and struck Ushne a stinging blow across the face.

Ushne's head whipped back.

The tail struck again.

In the interval before Ushne could recover, the King freed himself, and that was all the reprieve he needed to turn the tables.

The King's tail howled through the air for another blow, but he didn't hit Ushne. He looped the tip around Ushne's neck and jerked him sideways.

Elle floundered to her feet. She searched the grass around her for the amulet.

Where are you! Dammit!

She had to get it on the King's heart before he killed Ushne.

Finally, she spotted a glint in the emerald blades, and she snatched the amulet up. She staggered forward, but she couldn't get near enough to the two dragons. Tails, wings, and claws slashed every which way.

She dashed forward, but a black tail cut across her path. She jumped over it just in time, but Ushne's tail got in her way next. She had to fall back to avoid getting herself crushed.

Again, the King noticed her approach. He tried to lunge at her, but Ushne yanked him back away. They wrestled with each other some more, but neither could gain an advantage.

At last, the King let out a roar. He slithered his head around and feinted an attack. When Ushne ducked to miss the blow, the King swooped in low under his wing and clamped his teeth down hard on the tender joint where the wing met Ushne's green body.

Ushne shrieked in pain.

The King rose up to his full height and landed all his weight on Ushne's chest. He then struck a mighty blow to Ushne's face, leaving the green dragon limp, unconscious.

The King turned and took a menacing step toward Elle.

Elle stopped in her tracks, the amulet dangling from her fingers. Her blood screamed in her veins. She could do this. Even if it killed her, it was worth the sacrifice. She would've saved so many, including the man she had fallen in love with.

Nothing else mattered now.

She eyed her quarry in clear, calm determination. She had the only weapon she needed to defeat the Urlu King. He knew she meant something to Ushne; she could feel it. He wanted to destroy Ushne by killing Elle.

However, that same driving hate would deliver him into her hands.

So, she waited for him.

He slowed his pace coming closer, lowering his head, so his eyes hovered in front of her face.

That's it. Come on...

The Dragon King eyed her, almost suspiciously, but she couldn't allow him to try and guess what she was about to do. Sucking in a deep breath, Elle then rushed at him, letting out her own inner war cry.

Her intention worked; the King straightened in height, one claw raised high in the air. He brought it down, aiming to crush her, but Elle was ready. She propelled her body sideways, her feet sliding along the grass, only narrowly missing the edge of one of the King's claws.

Being a giant, his speed wasn't quite quick enough to spot what she was doing next.

With one last burst of speed and strength, Elle ran towards his massive chest, leaped into the air and shoved the amulet against his heart.

Instantly, the king backhanded her with one arm, sending her sprawling meters through the air.

She grunted and wheezed as her body hit the ground. Again, she was stunned for a few moments, her vision hazy. But soon, she knew that the extent of her injuries was small. A lot of bruising, but nothing broken.

That was close. Too close, Elle, she quipped.

She managed to get on her knees, desperate to see if the amulet's power had worked. But like with Ushne, nothing had happened yet.

And the King looked upon her with furious eyes.

He went to step towards her, but then faltered when a screech tore through the landscape.

Ushne rose from behind the black dragon, his wings spread. He slammed his head into the soft spot under the King's chin, and the black dragon collapsed.

Ushne writhed and seethed in all his lethal power. He roared his challenge to the whole battlefield. He bent his smoldering eyes on the form at his feet. He took aim at the King's throat again, ready to rip the life out of him... when the enormous black form gave a deep groan that sounded like it was caused by something else.

The King started to change, his eyes widening in agony.

He began to shake violently, jolting and bucking, contorting and convulsing.

The glistening scales slowly retracted, sinking away.

Ushne stepped further away, still staring down at the form that the beast had now taken.

The King was now a naked, muscular man with sandy-blond hair and a circlet of gold around his forehead.

The man's eyelids fluttered, and he gazed up at Ushne towering over him.

Ushne folded his wings against his back and stood upright. He swallowed the pain bursting within him, slightly letting himself transform back into his human form.

Robbie Cameron knelt over the fallen King, a grin spread across both men's faces.

"Well, I wasn't expecting this." Robbie chuckled. "But it's damn good to see ye... brother."

CHAPTER 26

The two brothers stared at each other in wonder.

Angus opened his mouth, barely managing to say, "Rob?"

Robbie's face twisted with the emotion welling up inside of him. He'd thought his brother was dead, and here he was. What's more is that he'd almost killed Angus, and Angus him.

Robbie squeezed Angus' shoulder, then pulled his brother off the ground, flinging his arms around him. Tears ran down Robbie's face.

He had his brother back.

Robbie pushed Angus back to gaze at his brother again. He couldn't stop smiling through his tears. Everything made sense now. All the uncertainty and misgivings he'd entertained since he first met Alan on the road congealed in one unshakeable understanding. He knew who his friends were and he knew who his enemies were. By some means, the Prince had cast some strange power over Robbie, trying to make him murder his own kind. His family. That explained how his mind always felt as if it were being pulled in two directions.

He slapped Angus once on the shoulder. "Come on. Let's get rid of these pests once and for all."

Dragon Quest

Angus laughed out loud. "Aye. Let's." He turned around and called across the battlefield. "Now, Urlus!"

At his word, every Urlu who was still in human form on the ground changed into a dragon. One and all, they took wing and streaked across the field toward the ridge where King Farlane's forces were camped.

Angus turned back to face Robbie. "Ye ready, brother?"

"Aye, as ready as one can ever be."

In the blink of an eye, Angus launched himself into the air. He spread his wings, and the black Dragon King joined his people pursuing the opposing clan into the mountains.

Robbie rounded on Elle. "Now, Elle!"

He bent forward from the waist, and again biting back the pain, he transformed into Ushne. He stooped low to the ground and crooked his leg so she could climb on his back. He didn't want to take any more chances of her getting caught in the crossfire.

The minute she settled on him, he took flight. He didn't have to tell her to hold on. She lay down low on his neck and hugged him as tight as she could. He bent his wings and raced across the battlefield after his brother and his people.

His people!

He now knew that he'd known it all along, in his deepest being, but it'd been blocked by Alan's magic. Now it was all true.

Angus was King. He sat on the Phoenix Throne, and Prince Alan and King Farlane would pay for their deception.

Thousands of dragons whizzed back and forth across the battlefield and rained fire on their enemies. King

Farlane's forces scattered in confusion. They couldn't fight the dragons from the ground.

Robbie's heart raced. The exhilaration of flight couldn't match the sheer elation of finding his brother alive and well after thinking Angus was dead. Dragons soared all around him. They fought together against a common foe. Robbie had found his place. His long quest had come to an end, and joy lifted his wings to the heavens.

Only one minor detail remained to be attended to. He had to punish Prince Alan and King Farlane for tricking him and almost killing Angus for real. All the vindictive revenge he once felt toward the Urlus was now turned against his former friends.

The Urlus attacked King Farlane's forces all over the field. Angus tilted this way and that. He blasted companies of knights to smithereens and scorched the infantry in swathes.

Robbie soared past him for the ridge. The one man he wanted to confront still waited for him up there.

Robbie couldn't rest until he'd dealt with that man and that man alone.

He zoomed up the mountain. Elle pressed her face against his scales. She didn't dare raise her head; he was going so fast. He swooped up the slope and hung suspended over the ridge.

There sat Alan on his horse. Robbie fixed his eyes on his prey and opened his mouth to unleash a wicked blast of blazing fire.

At that moment, the fabric of reality shimmered and bent. Lightning cracked out of the sky, and thunder rumbled from the faraway corners of the world. Alan and his horse smeared in front of Robbie's eyes. They almost disappeared, and when they reformed, he didn't recognize them.

The horse's lips curled back from gnashing, curved fangs, and its head contorted into a disgusting caricature of a skeleton. The animal reared and floated off the ground toward Robbie.

Alan let go of the reins and threw back his arms. The sword in his hand changed to a lightning bolt, and he threw it at Robbie.

Robbie caught one glimpse of the man's face, but he wasn't a man anymore. A horrible ghoul, half skeleton, half slobbering monster, glared out from under Alan's helmet. The whole picture of horse and rider shivered and blinked somewhere between this world and a hazy layer of being behind a curtain of confusion.

The next moment, the lightning bolt ripped out of the ghoul's hand and hissed toward Robbie. It cut across his shoulder and sliced off his scales like they were never there.

Pain and terror rocketed through Robbie.

The ghoul pulled back his arm one more time, and another lightning bolt materialized in his hand.

Robbie turned tail and fled back down the mountain, but he had nowhere to run. The whole of King Farlane's army — or whatever it was — had transformed at the same time their leader had. The clear blue sky turned iron gray, and every man fighting on the ground rippled and changed into an eyeless, formless ghoul.

Robbie raced down the slope to the plane. He only dared look back once to see Alan gaining on him. After that, he bent all his concentration on flying as fast as he could. He knew in the marrow of his bones he could never outfly the thing.

One streak of lightning after another scorched past him. One of them ripped through his good wing, but he kept flying through the pain. He couldn't let himself get shot down. Elle was on his back.

He had to save her if he did nothing else.

He cast his eye all over the battlefield for any avenue of escape. Every ghoul on the field turned on its dragon pursuers and fired lightning at them. Dragons screeched and began to plunge towards the earth all over the field.

Robbie caught sight of Angus locked in combat with one of the ghouls. Angus shot a stream of fire at it, and the ghoul threw a lightning bolt at him, the two forces meeting in mid-air. The lightning drove the fire back into Angus' throat and damn near blew him out of the sky.

Robbie banked and headed to his brother's aid, but no one could fight the things. Robbie stooped at the ghoul, even as Alan came up behind to destroy him. Robbie flew straight through the ghoul attacking Angus, but he didn't dare stop. He wheeled in the air and headed for the castle.

That was their only hope.

King Farlane's army might harbor this mysterious power, but they couldn't use it against the castle. They couldn't fight Angus on their own. That was clear. They had to use their human form, and they had to get someone else to defeat the King. Maybe they couldn't enter the castle for some reason...?

Angus must have had the same idea. In the few moments Robbie won for him, he turned around and headed for home. He screeched out to the remaining Urlus, and they all flew back to the castle.

Angus circled overhead while his people landed in the courtyards below. He and Robbie dodged and distracted the ghouls to give the people cover.

Robbie surveyed the battle scene, his eyes coming to rest on Alan. The Ghoul Prince still rode his disembodied horse.

As soon as the Urlus got into the air space above the castle, the ghouls retreated. They flew in circles around the castle walls, but they couldn't attack the castle itself.

Angus and Robbie pulled back to the safety of their stronghold, Elle still on Robbie's back. He didn't care about anything else right now. He didn't care if this battle turned out to be a disastrous defeat. He had her, and he had his brothers.

He didn't need anything else.

One by one, the Urlus landed and disappeared into their citadel.

Angus nodded to Robbie, and Robbie descended to the courtyard. He set Elle down and then resumed his human form. He looked around at the castle he'd left so many long weeks ago. It looked different now. People and fowls and horses crisscrossed his field of view. Voices floated out of doorways and windows.

The place breathed life, even as the Urlus mourned the dragon men they had lost.

CHAPTER 27

Elle sat by a darkened window in a lonely keep. A black night smothered the castle's windows so she couldn't see beyond the glow of lamps. She hugged her knees to her chest and shuddered.

A door opened behind her and closed again. Footsteps crossed the floor and stopped next to her.

"Here. I brought you something to eat. Robbie says you haven't eaten since this morning."

Elle jumped to her feet when she recognized the voice.

"Carmen!"

Elle threw herself at her friend, almost spilling the bowl of soup in Carmen's right hand.

"Hang on a minute," Carmen teased and broke away to put the bowl down on a nearby wooden table. "Okay, now let's hug!"

The two women embraced, gripping each other tightly as if they hadn't seen each other in years.

"Are you okay?" Elle asked when they finally parted.

"Yes, and you? Robbie told me you were fighting in the battle!"

"Yes, it turns out that with proper training, I'm not too bad at wielding a sword. I was like Èowyn in *The Return of the King*."

Both women chuckled at the lame *The Lord of the Rings* reference.

After a little while, Elle sighed. "They're still out there though. They're up on the ridge waiting for us."

Carmen sat down on the window seat in front of her. "I know. The sentries saw their fires. They're camped up there. I suppose they'll be making another assault in the morning."

"We can't defeat them. They'll keep attacking until they destroy us."

Carmen paused, stood up again. "You should get something to eat. Then we can go downstairs. Angus and Robbie and the others are holding a council of war to decide what to do."

"I'm not hungry."

Carmen sighed and sat back down. "Well, I'm really happy to see you. I didn't think I would ever see you again."

"Ditto."

Carmen laughed. "Angus is over the moon about Robbie being alive too. We all thought he was dead. I..." She touched her finger to the corner of her eye. "I couldn't live with myself. I blamed myself for him falling into that sinkhole, and I know Angus blamed himself too. We couldn't pull him back."

"You shouldn't blame yourself," Elle replied. "You did the best you could under the circumstances. I just don't understand how you can still be here. The curse is lifted, so you should have been sent back. We both should have."

"I know, but we weren't. I'm just glad to still be here. I don't know what I would have done if I had been sent back. This is where I belong. I want to stay here."

Elle stared at her. "You do?"

"Of course. I love Angus more than anything. I never want to leave. Now, Hazel, on the other hand, she might be a different story..."

"Hazel?" Elle frowned, confused. "What about Hazel? Is she here?"

"She's been here all along. She says she doesn't want to go back, but she's not happy here either. She doesn't really know how to deal with the Urlus. She can't stand them in their dragon form, and she can't relate to them in their human form when she knows they're really dragons. She only ever talks to me and Ewan because we're human. Ewan is Angus' best friend. Do you know all this already? Tell me to shut up if you do."

"I don't know anything about it. Rob and I were so busy getting here that we never really talked about the personal details about his family or clan. He said I didn't really need to know all that, and I guess he was right."

Carmen put her head to one side. "You and Robbie – you're..."

Elle twiddled her fingers and looked at the floor. "Uh..."

Carmen squeezed her arm, beaming madly. "I can't believe it. I'm so happy for you. What are the odds? You and I accidentally being zapped here and falling in love with two incredibly handsome, although at times arrogant, Scottish Highlanders?"

Elle stole a glance at her. "I'm not sure I'm happy about it. I mean, how can I be with him when I could get sent back at any second? I don't want to love him if we can never be together."

"That's the way I used to feel, but I don't feel that way anymore. I'm happy for every day with Angus. If I get sent back, it's all the more important for me to cherish the time I have with him. I don't want to waste a single day."

"I feel the same way, but still — how can you really give yourself to him when you're not an Urlu?"

"I am an Urlu," Carmen declared. "I'm as Urlu as the rest of them. Ask Ewan. He feels the same way. I can't change into a dragon, but I'm still an Urlu. This is my country too now, and I'll defend it with my life. Ewan is Angus' Captain of the Guard. He organizes all the defenses. He's down with the troops right now seeing that everybody gets the medical care they need."

Elle peeked at Carmen's glowing face. She'd never seen Carmen so happy before. This hardened cop from the rough side of town finally found her place in the world.

"Yeah, but, I mean... Don't you worry about... You can never give Angus an heir. You're two different species. Won't it cause problems when it comes to someone taking over the throne?"

Carmen pressed Elle's hand between both of hers. "It's not a problem. Humans and Urlus are biologically compatible; otherwise, they wouldn't be able to take on both forms. If you want to stay here with Robbie, you can. You can even have children with him — as crazy as that sounds given we've known these men for such a short time compared to how we'd date back in the States. You can have everything with him you could ever have with a human man. You could have so much more with him. Believe me."

"But how do you know? How can you be certain you're compatible? How do you know that's not just wishful thinking?"

"Because..." Carmen replied, biting her lip. "I'm pregnant."

Elle gasped. "What? No way!"

Carmen's cheeks glowed. "Yes way. I just found out. But shhh, nobody else knows yet."

Elle stared straight ahead, but she no longer saw Carmen sitting in front of her. This was incredible. She could... She could marry Robbie and have children with him? And Elle could too with Robbie if she wanted to. But...

Oh, it's just all so confusing and zany to think about!

"Come downstairs," Carmen urged, breaking Elle out of her anxious thoughts.

"Soon – I just need to sit here a little longer. I need to take all this in."

"Do you want me to stay with you?"

"Yes, please. You understand this situation so much better than I do."

"Only because I've been living it since I showed up here. When I first got here, it was just as confusing for me."

"Then tell me everything from the start. I need to make more logical sense of this incredible world."

Carmen smiled and nodded, then started to tell Elle everything that had occurred since being transported to Urlu.

"So, to conclude, we thought the witch put a curse on the Cameron family, but it turned out Hazel's spell created the curse in the first place. The witch set the Phoenix Throne on fire and pushed Angus into it. He burned up, and the Dragon King rose from the ashes. That's what the name means," Carmen finished.

Elle looked out the window at nothing and sighed. "That's what must have happened to Rob."

"What do you mean?"

"He changed. He was drugged and groggy, and he changed into Ushne in his sleep without realizing it. It must have happened at the same time Angus got the throne. He said he didn't know how it happened. He said he never knew before that he could change. It must have happened around the same time Angus got his dragon form."

"Of course!" Carmen exclaimed. "They all got it at the same time. The curse robbed them of their ability to change. After Angus got the throne, they could all do it. They all had to learn how to change, how to fly and everything."

Elle nodded at the window. It all made sense, yet she still couldn't get her brain to comprehend it fully. So many convolutions surrounded their journey. King Farlane and Prince Alan had tricked Robbie into attacking his own people. They got him to fight his own brother, to dispossess him of his rightful throne.

Why?

Carmen patted her hand. "Are you sure you're okay? I've never seen you like this."

Elle peered into her face. "It's all over, you know? Everything I thought I knew about myself – it's all gone. I built my whole identity on my career, and now it's gone. There's nothing more important in the world than... well, the people in this castle, and now we're in danger. It's gonna take me a while to figure it all out."

Carmen stood up. "It's all right. You've got all the time in the world. It took me some time to get used to it, too, but you will. Just let it happen and accept the happiness it can bring you. That's how I deal with it. I'll leave you alone now. Just try to eat some soup, okay?"

She turned to go, but Elle called her back. "Wait! Show me where Hazel's room is."

"You want to see Hazel?"

"I guess I better. I always sort of took care of her. Maybe she'll come out of her shell more now that she knows I'm here?"

Carmen sucked in a deep breath, then blew the air out again. "Let's hope so."

The two women set off down the passage.

"Hopefully, she will warm up a little having you around," Carmen said. "She needs as many friends as she can get as really she depends on me for all her social contact. I take her outside the castle every day, just to get some fresh air. Other than that, she stays in her room."

Elle gave a weak smile. "I can understand that. But if we're going to be here for a while, it only makes sense that she settles in and gets used to it."

Carmen stopped in front of a door. "This is her room."

"Are you coming in?"

"I better not. You talk to her. And hey, maybe if she understands about you and Robbie, she'll change her attitude toward the Urlus."

"We can only hope."

"I'll see you downstairs," Carmen said and walked down the passage.

Elle raised her hand but then hesitated to knock on the door. Instead, something urged her to she press the latch and swing the door open.

She beheld Hazel in a long gown, her red hair tied back behind her neck, kneeling on the floor next to a bed with a curious collection of articles spread out in a circle around her. There was a bound-up stick of dried sage smoldered in a dish, a bowl of clear fluid sat at her side and some Tarot cards that formed a star pattern around her.

Hazel swayed back and forth. Her arms waved from side to side, and she chanted something under her breath.

Elle didn't have time to register what Hazel was saying before a blinding flash hit her in the face.

A shockwave of air knocked her back.

When her gaze refocused, she halted on the threshold and faltered. In front of Hazel was a hole, open in space.

Elle drew back as the hole widened and ghouls flooded into the room.

The howling hollow skeleton of a woman in a flowing ghostly dress extended her claws at Hazel, and she staggered back with a scream.

The ghouls floated around the room, and the hole closed behind them. They bobbed every which way in search of something.

Elle and Hazel stared at them, neither knowing what to do.

The ghouls made several little rushes toward the walls, then circled the room, until they found the window. They rushed towards it all at once, shattered the glass, and flowed out into the black night.

CHAPTER 28

"There must be some way to fight them," Angus began. "They're no' immortal."

"We dinnae ken that," Robbie countered. "They may be, and if they are, we're sunk."

"One thing's for certain," Ewan added. "We cannae stay inside this castle forever. We must get out for food and to tend to our flocks."

"They'll no' leave us to hide in here anyway," Robbie added. "They'll attack the same way they did yesterday. They'll start their bombardment, and once they break down the castle, whatever holds them outside willnae hold them any longer. They'll rush in, and that'll be the end."

"Ye ken them better than we," Angus told him. "What can ye tell us about them?"

"I cannae tell ye naught about them. I never kenned what they were. I thought they were regular people — nice ones." Robbie snorted. "Ye ken as much as I about them. I never wouldae come with them if I'd kenned what they were."

Angus slapped him on the shoulder. "I'd rather face a thousand ghouls with ye here than anything else. Ye're here. That's all I care about."

Robbie looked around the circle of familiar faces. His brother Callum, Fergus and Jamie stared at him in wonder. He never really let himself believe he would see them again, and they clearly never expected to see him alive again.

"One thing I can tell ye." Robbie turned to Ewan. "They're using the name Munro."

"What?" Ewan asked.

"I kenned they were no' Munros. I just never reckoned on them being so far from that. They must have counted on the name of a real clan to convince me. I suppose it worked something."

"Never ye mind that," Angus broke in. "The matter remains — they're out there on our southern boundary, and we've got 'til morning to find a way to defeat them."

"They cannae defeat ye, Angus," Robbie returned. "They cannae take the throne from ye by force. They wouldnae cook up this elaborate plot if they couldae. They needed me to fight ye and defeat ye. They planned this whole invasion to get ye out of yer castle where I would fight ye one on one. That's the only way they could take the throne."

"We dinnae ken it's the throne they're after," Ewan added. "Perhaps they wish to destroy the throne and take the country. They may have any number of motives. They're something beyond human, beyond anything we can understand. We dinnae ken why they're here or why they're attacking us."

Before anyone could reply, a ruckus of screams echoed outside the hall where the men stood in conference.

The door burst open, and Elle ran into the room, her fist clenched around the sleeve of a tall, red-haired woman.

Carmen followed behind, regarding the whole scene with her usual calm demeanor.

Angus whirled around to face them. "What's the meaning of this?"

Elle gestured to Hazel. "I found her casting another spell. Some kind of portal opened up and let in a bunch of those ghouls."

Robbie and Ewan spun around to face Hazel. "You did what?"

"I didn't do anything!" Hazel snapped. "I just wanted to go home! That's all. I didn't know they would—"

"For God's sake! When are you gonna wake up, Hazel?" Carmen said. "You could have made the curse stronger. You could have created a new curse all over again. What the hell is the matter with you?"

"I didn't know!" Hazel shrieked. "I just couldn't stand it anymore. I had to get out of here. I thought I could..."

Angus turned away. "Wheesht! There's no sense in her."

"We ought to kill her," Ewan said with a snarl. "We ought to be rid of her once and for all."

"I'm with ye," Jamie chimed in. "She's been a curse on us from the start. She'll only put us in more danger. We ought to put her down here and now. It's the only way to protect ourselves from her."

"You touch her, and I'll kill you," Elle directed at Ewan and Jamie.

Robbie stared at her; he'd never seen her with such fury in her eyes. But the lass had a point. No one would be harming anyone. The men were undoubtedly out of line.

"What did you think would happen though?" Elle then said, this time to Hazel. "The enemy is camped up on the ridge waiting to slaughter us all, and you had to play around and give them an opening."

Hazel dipped her head. "I'm sorry, okay?" However, when she peered back Elle and Carmen, her voice didn't waver. "*You* both might've accepted this place as home now, but not me. I don't belong here, and in all honesty, neither of you do either."

Angus spoke up. "Take it easy, all of ye. If the things went out through the window, then there's no harm done as yet. So far, the castle still protects us, even if the things do come through. Now, afore we go any further, we all need to settle down some and think of a way to defeat these things. If we attack each other, we dinnae stand a chance." Angus turned to his brother and Ewan, his voice firm and threatening as he told them, "And as far as killing Hazel, I forbid it under any circumstances. And if I hear ye talk about such a thing again, I'll throw you to the ghouls myself."

Hazel's head snapped around to stare at him, and to Robbie's surprise, his brother smiled at her.

Ewan smacked his lips in annoyance but said nothing.

No one said anything.

Carmen broke the silence. "If those things came through the same portal of the spell, maybe they're part of the curse."

Everybody turned around to look at her.

"The curse?" Angus asked, furrowing his brow.

"It was something you said, Elle, that made me think of it," Carmen went on. "If the three of us are still here, it must mean the curse is still in place. If they came through the portal when Hazel cast the spell, there must be a way to send them back through it using the same spell. If we break the curse, we'll send them back where they came from."

"If we did that," Elle pointed out, "then we would get sent back where we came too."

Everyone in the room looked at each other.

Robbie's eyes met Elle's.

Sent back?

He couldn't do that. Then again, if he didn't send her back, they would all die.

He glanced at Angus and found his brother looking at Carmen. They all thought the same thing. None of them wanted to break the curse.

They wanted to stay together.

"There's another potential and significant drawback though," Elle added. "If Hazel tried to open a portal again, those ghouls might all come through and overrun us."

Angus nodded in agreement. "Aye, but there must be a way," he murmured.

When no one spoke again, no solution coming to any of their minds, he went on.

"We're no' getting anywhere with this tonight. All of ye get to your rooms for a few hours' sleep. We'll meet back here at sunrise, and hopefully, one of us will have come up with a brilliant idea, eh? Go on. Get ye out of here."

One by one, the women wandered away — Hazel being the first to make an escape.

Soon, it was just the men left in the room.

Ewan let out a shaky breath. "I best get down to the armory and check on the Guard. Ye're with me, Jamie and Callum."

"Aye," the younger men replied.

Callum then came up to Robbie. He opened his mouth, but then shut it without saying anything.

Robbie saw the emotion on his face. He clapped his brother on the shoulder and pulled him into an embrace.

"It's all right, lad. Everything's all right now."

Callum's shoulders shook, then finally he tore himself out of his brother's arms and exited the room after Ewan and Jamie.

Robbie turned around to find Angus and Fergus standing together.

Angus smiled at Robbie. "Ye being back is still the highpoint of this day. No number of ghouls can or will change that."

"It's no' the best of circumstances," Robbie returned. "I'm sorry to be the one to deliver misfortune on ye. It wasn't my idea of a cheerful homecoming."

Angus chuckled. "It's the best homecoming we couldae hoped for. Now get upstairs to yer woman and dinnae let me see ye down here again afore morning. I'm still the King around here."

Angus left the room laughing to himself over his own wittiness.

Robbie watched him. He was still the same old Angus, but being King had changed him too. He no longer carried the burden of leadership. Being responsible for all these lives no longer oppressed him. He came into his power. He could give orders to his own brothers and laugh at himself in the same breath.

Robbie started to leave the room, too, when he again became aware of Fergus standing there. The young man regarded him with his huge dark eyes. For the thousandth time in his life, Robbie wondered what those eyes saw that the rest of them could not?

Robbie studied his younger brother. "Lad?"

"Rob?"

"Aye?"

"That woman... Hazel..." He stopped.

"What about her?" Robbie asked curiously.

"She... uh..."

Robbie took a closer look at the young man. He knew something. He just couldn't get it out.

"If ye ken anything that'll defeat these things, lad," Robbie told him, "ye must tell me and Angus. It's the only way we can survive this. Ye ken that. Tell me what ye're thinking."

"She can cast the spell," Fergus blurted out. "She must be able to. She sent herself and the others here, so the spell worked. She just opened the door to let those things through. She can do it. She just has to do it in the right way."

Robbie cocked his head. "I'm still not following ye?"

"She *can* do it, or she, Carmen, and yer lass wouldnae be here. Do ye see?"

Robbie blinked at him. He never thought about it before, but now that Fergus pointed it out, he was right. Hazel cast the spell that brought her here. She cast another one upstairs to let those ghouls through. She must be able to do it again. Surely it would only take a small adjustment to make it happen correctly.

The only problem was that no one, not even Hazel, knew what the adjustment needed to be. All the same,

227

Fergus' words had inspired Robbie not to forsake their cause and despair over what they currently could not control.

Fergus had some power. The whole clan had already sensed that. The lad had never cast a magic spell before, but he knew something about Hazel. Robbie felt it.

He nodded toward the door. "Ye try talking to her, lad. I don't know why, but I think ye might be able to appease Hazel enough for her to figure out what's missing in the spell."

Fergus nodded as if he agreed.

Good luck, brother, Robbie thought as the day's events started to sink in. *Ye might very well be our last hope.*

CHAPTER 29

Carmen came out of Hazel's room to find Elle standing in the hall.

Elle leaned against the wall with one foot propped up. "Is she okay?"

"She's okay," Carmen replied. "She's just sitting in a chair in front of the fire right now. She's not ready to go to sleep."

Elle hung her head. "She'll be more reclusive than ever, now that Ewan and Jamie said they want to kill her."

"No one will kill her," Carmen stated, her tone firm. "Angus will protect her. I can't be certain she won't try to cast the spell again, though, and that could be disastrous."

"I should go in there and talk to her," Elle remarked. "I should apologize for just blurting things out like that."

"You didn't overreact if that's what you're worried about. I wouldn't talk to her right now if I were you. You both need rest. You should just get some rest and talk to her later – after you've both had time to let all this craziness sink in. Ha, I'll include myself in that too."

Elle cast a sidelong glance at the door. "I don't like leaving it. She always counted on me to support her before. I feel responsible for anything that happens to her."

Just then, Robbie came down the passage with one of the younger Cameron brothers – Fergus, Elle thought his name was. They stopped outside Hazel's door.

"How's the witch?" Robbie asked Carmen.

Carmen bit back a smile. "That's not funny. She's fine, but she's a little fragile. I was just telling Elle to leave her alone for now."

"She'll be better when she kens she can cast the spell that'll save us all," Robbie replied. "She's got the power."

Carmen gaped at him. "What?"

Robbie pointed to Fergus at his side. "My brother is going to talk to her about it."

"Is that really a good idea?" Carmen asked.

"Do ye have a better one?" Robbie waved Fergus toward the door. "Go on, lad, and good luck to ye."

Fergus walked through the door and shut it behind him.

Elle, Robbie, and Carmen stared at the plain wooden door until Carmen sighed.

"I sure hope you know what you're doing," she told Robbie.

"I dinnae ken what I'm doing," Robbie replied, "but he does. That's all I care about."

"What's he going to say to her in there?"

"Heaven only kens." Robbie turned to Elle. "Come on. Let's get out of here."

Elle gave Carmen a sheepish smile, then fell in at his side on their way back to the room Angus and Carmen had allocated to them.

Robbie stopped outside it and studied Elle for a moment. "Did ye hear what Angus said?"

"About what?"

"Ye didn't hear? He said it after ye left. He called ye my woman."

Elle chuckled. "Well, is he wrong?"

Robbie put his arm around her shoulders. "Aye, if ye want to be, that is."

She buried her face against his chest. "I really do. I just hate to think about everything that could happen to stop us being together. I hope you understand that."

He hugged her tighter. "Let's trust Fergus to come up with a way."

"About that... I'm with Carmen – what is he going to say to Hazel?"

"There's something about him." Robbie shook his head. "I cannae explain it to ye. I dinnae think he can explain it himself. He's got something. He's like Hazel that way. He says she's got the power, and he should ken if anybody does." He jerked his head toward the room. "Come on inside, lass."

At that moment, footsteps came hurrying down the passage behind them.

They turned around to see Fergus and Hazel coming toward them.

A bright smile lit up Fergus' face. "She's going to do it! She agrees."

Elle glanced at Hazel.

Hazel didn't look all that happy about it. She hung back and kept her eyes fixed on the floor. She wouldn't look Elle in the face.

Robbie patted Fergus on the back. "That's fine, lad. Get ye downstairs and roust Ewan and Jamie to the conference hall. I'll get Angus and meet ye there to discuss how we're going to do it."

Fergus hurried off one way, and Robbie went the other.

They left Elle standing there, staring at Hazel. She took a deep breath.

"What on earth is going on?"

"This is all my fault," Hazel murmured. "None of this would have happened if I hadn't messed around with the spell in the first place."

Elle reached out and touched her arm. "It's all right. Maybe Carmen's got a point, and this is all a good thing."

"How could it be a good thing? Do you know how many people have died because of this curse?"

"Just look at Carmen and me," Elle replied. "Carmen wouldn't have Angus, and I wouldn't have Rob if you hadn't sent us here. That's a silver lining, right?"

Hazel lifted her eyes to Elle's face. "Do you think so?"

Elle gave a weak smile. "Listen, Hazel. Carmen told me you have a problem with the Urlus. You should give them a chance. They're good people."

Hazel blinked at her. "You love him, don't you?"

Elle blushed. "Yeah. I guess I do."

"I know they're good people. I've seen it myself, and Angus has been a lot kinder to me than I probably deserve. I just don't seem to be able to make the first move."

"It looks like Fergus made the first move," Elle remarked. "What did he say to you in there?"

"He didn't really say anything. He just said I could do it. He... he has a way of working on your mind. His eyes did something to me. I can't explain it."

"I think I understand. If this works, we'll all be saved. I'm sure the Urlus would be very grateful to you for that."

"It's the least I can do to make up for this curse I suppose. You were right about that."

"Never mind. Let's get back downstairs."

Hazel accompanied her down the passage. "I still don't think I can do it."

"You don't? Why did you agree to it, then?"

"I didn't, really. Fergus... well, he didn't really ask. He just sort of stood there and looked at me with those eyes of his. It just sort of happened that I knew I really could do it. It just sort of became obvious that I *would* do it. I don't know how, but as long as he's standing there, I guess I'll do it. I'll have to."

Elle regarded Hazel with her head on the side. She didn't understand half of what Hazel said, but something in Fergus' manner apparently made people trust him. Robbie trusted him so Elle could go along with it. For now. The situation couldn't possibly get any worse... could it?

They came to the great staircase leading down to the castle's main entrance.

Ewan and Jamie crossed the foyer below.

Elle and Hazel started to descend when a mighty blow struck the castle walls. The floor vibrated under Elle's feet.

Hazel stumbled and fell down a few stairs.

Ewan and Jamie stopped in their tracks and looked around.

Elle hurried to Hazel's side and tried to raise her to her feet. "Are you okay?"

Another concussion hit the castle. The edifice rattled, and a chip of plaster dislodged from the ceiling.

Ewan shouted, and he and Jamie raced away somewhere.

Elle groped for Hazel's arm. "Come on."

Hazel got to her feet when another shivering blow struck.

Elle hustled her down the stairs. "Come on. We have to get out of here."

"What's happening?" Hazel cried.

"They're attacking again," Elle shouted over the noise. "They've started another bombardment."

Elle shoved Hazel down the stairs and across the foyer. Her mind turned in a thousand directions at once. They had to rendezvous with the men in the conference hall. She had to get to Ewan. He would give her some weapon to fight those things out there.

People rushed in every direction at once. Women screamed, and men shouted orders, but no one could hear them over the din of one concussion after another.

Elle tightened her grip on Hazel's arm and propelled her forward. They only made it a few paces when an enormous boulder crashed through the roof. Beams, stone, and plaster rained down on Elle's head. The boulder plunged into the floor and shattered the stones underfoot.

The shockwave knocked Elle and Hazel off their feet. Dust and smoke filled the foyer.

Elle coughed plaster dust out of her throat. She couldn't see a thing through the debris.

Screams tore the air. The low pounding of more strikes echoed in the distance, and the floor vibrated with continual tremors.

Beams, rock, and destroyed chandeliers piled all over the floor around the two women. The rubble blocked their passage to the conference hall. A few servants and yeomen struggled through the disaster, but Elle couldn't see Rob or any of his brothers anywhere.

She took hold of Hazel. "Come on."

She couldn't see any avenue of escape except the huge front entrance. Black night crowded close beyond the open door. Elle headed that way, Hazel limping after her.

They only took a few steps when another massive projectile collided with the door, smashing the wall in. Brick fragments and mortar pocked Elle's face and stung her eyes. She threw her hands in front of her face to protect herself.

A block struck Hazel in the forehead, and she crumpled at Elle's feet.

Elle blinked the dust out of her eyes and fell on her knees at Hazel's side. "Hazel! Hazel!"

Hazel didn't answer. She lay still and pale on the carpet, white with plaster dust. Blood streamed from a gash in her forehead and ran into her red hair.

Elle cast her eye around the foyer. She couldn't stay here, and she couldn't leave Hazel behind either.

Think, Elle, think!

Deep groans and rumbles of more falling missiles sounded all over the castle. Elle couldn't think of anywhere in the castle where she would be safe. She only knew she had to flee. She had to get out of here before the whole castle caved in on her head.

If only Hazel would wake up – she could tell Elle how to navigate through the strange castle. Elle prayed for

Carmen or just about anybody to tell her where to go, but she was alone.

Not able to hesitate for a second longer, she seized Hazel around the waist and heaved her off the floor, having no choice but to drag her.

Only one thin passage of open space led to a dark hallway behind the sweeping staircase. Elle followed it.

It curved behind the conference hall into a kitchen where no light burned. Only the fire flickering on the hearth illuminated a path to a double door leading out to the castle gardens.

Elle pushed the door open and stopped. A solid wall of ghouls flew in a steady circle past the door. They flowed over the garden wall and around the other side of the castle. Elle caught sight of individual ghouls. Their hideous faces showed through the eerie glow. They rode ghost horses and waved their hellish weapons in her face.

Elle faltered.

Dammit!

She couldn't go out there, and she dared not go back.

She was trapped.

CHAPTER 30

Robbie knocked on Angus' door.

"Angus, mon, ye must come right away!"

Angus appeared in the door bare-chested. Robbie caught sight of Carmen stretched out on the bed behind him. She wore her old pants and down vest the way she did when the brothers found her on the road. She rested her head on her arm and kept her eyes closed.

Angus glared at his brother, clearly having been interrupted from some... "private time".

"This better be pretty bloody good, Rob."

"He's done it, mon. Fergus has come up with a way to cast the spell to send the ghouls back."

"What?" Angus snapped. "How could he?"

"He isnae to do it. It's Hazel. Fergus convinced her to try. Come on – he's collecting Ewan and Jamie. Ye must come back to the conference room. There's no' a moment to lose."

Angus didn't budge until Carmen stood up and came to the door.

"What's this about Hazel casting another spell?" she asked.

"I wouldnae believe it myself," Robbie stammered. "It's Fergus I believe in. Ye ken what he looks like when the power comes over him. He says she'll do it, and I believe him. I'm going downstairs. Come as soon as ye can."

He turned his back on them. He didn't want to think about what they were doing in there before he disturbed them. He'd delivered the message. Now he had to go.

He headed down the passage when the first concussion hit.

The castle shook, and the doors rattled in their sockets.

Robbie pulled up short and listened.

Angus' door was yanked open one more time behind him, and Angus rushed out, in his shirt this time.

Carmen followed on his heels. "What's going on?"

Another blow boomed somewhere far away.

The three of them listened for a moment before racing for the stairs.

Robbie put his foot on the first stair when a projectile catapulted through the wall next to them. It smashed into the steps, and the supports beneath it gave way. The whole staircase collapsed under his feet. He wheeled to retreat to the landing, but he couldn't catch his balance.

Angus rushed forward and snatched at his arms. "Rob!"

Robbie floundered in mid-air. He grabbed at his brother. Angus tried to pull him back, but the stair under Robbie's feet crumbled to powder. He plummeted into space and pulled Angus with him.

Carmen screamed. Her hand shot out, but both men fell away into nothing. The stairs sank into a pile of rubble on the floor far below.

Angus and Robbie fell on top of it still clasped in each other's arms.

Robbie hit the stone hard. It bruised his ribs, and he groaned in pain.

Carmen's voice echoed down the empty space from above. "Angus! Robbie! Are you all right?"

"We're all right," Angus said with a growl.

He didn't have time to say any more before another missile struck the roof over their heads. The ceiling trembled, and plaster broke loose.

Angus' hands took hold of Robbie and hauled him to his feet. "Get up, mon. We must get out of here afore they destroy the whole castle."

Robbie struggled to his feet and shook the dust out of his face.

Carmen hopped down from the crumbling floor above them and landed next to Angus.

Angus started climbing over the debris.

"Where'll we go?" she asked.

"This way," he murmured.

He steered them to a door to one side. They ducked through into the servants' quarters. Not a living soul remained in any of the rooms.

Angus led them down a dim hall to a back entrance into the guardroom. He eased the door back and stole a peek into the courtyard.

"They're out there," he said.

"The ghouls?"

He nodded. "Aye, they've got the castle surrounded. We'll never get out alive."

"We have to," Robbie insisted. "We cannae stay in here, or they'll knock the place down around our ears."

He started forward, but Angus yanked him back.

"Ye're no' going out there, Rob. I cannae allow it. I lost ye once, and I cannae lose ye again — no' like this."

Robbie grabbed him by the head. "Listen to me, mon. You're the King here, no' me. They cannae beat ye without me fighting ye. As long as we're together, they cannae touch us. We must get away from the throne. They may smash the castle to powder, but they cannae destroy the throne. We'll get away and hide ye somewhere. It's our best shot to defeat them."

Angus frowned. "Are ye sure?"

Robbie burst out laughing. "Of course not. I'm no' sure of naught but ye, mon. I cannae let them take ye. Now come on, the both of ye. We must get away from the castle afore one of these stones crushes us all."

He didn't wait a moment longer to argue. He headed through the door into the courtyard. The stable sat across the yard. Robbie went over the whole castle in his mind to recall what he saw the first time he came here. The stable was still inside the walls. The horses stamped and screamed in their stalls, but the ghouls couldn't get inside the walls. As long as Robbie and his companions remained inside, they were safe.

He darted forward. "This way, mon."

Angus followed his lead.

Robbie ducked into the stable and paused to let his eyes adjust to the dark. Carmen breathed next to Angus at his side. He had to find a way out. He had to save Angus. He trusted his brothers and Elle to find their way out.

Elle.

No, he had to force his mind away from Elle. She could take care of herself; he knew it. He didn't know how, but if she were hurt, he'd feel it.

And he would find her again if it was the last thing he did.

He crossed to the nearest stall and lifted the bridle off the wall. "Go and get your horses. Dinnae bother saddling them. Just bridle them and get ready to mount."

"What're ye doing?" Angus asked, catching his breath.

Robbie didn't linger to answer. He rushed to the next stall and opened the door. He flew down the stable from one door to the next.

Angus and Carmen went to work. They bridled three horses and held them until Robbie opened every stall. He herded all the horses into the open stable.

Angus and Carmen watched him, breathless.

Robbie nodded at them. "Ready? Mount ye up."

Angus and Carmen swung onto their mounts. Carmen held Robbie's horse by the bridle while he swung open the wide door at the far end. That door led onto the open field between the castle and the river.

The ghouls cast their weird light over the moon-drenched grass.

Robbie fought for breath. His heart exploded in his chest, but he had to keep going until he accomplished his mission. The horses crowded around him. Their sides shivered in terror and excitement. Their eyes gleamed in the dark, and their warm breath puffed in the quiet.

Robbie hurried to Carmen's side and slung his leg over his mount.

He took his seat. "Now!"

He slapped the nearest horse on the rump.

Angus and Carmen waved their arms and shouted to the horses. The whole herd rocketed forward with a squeal. They plunged into the dark and set off galloping at top speed across the field.

Angus kicked his horse in the flanks. He exploded out of the stable in the midst of the herd.

Carmen barely got a hold of her mount's mane before the animal leaped forward.

All the horses lunged into the open at once.

Robbie bent his head over his horse's neck.

The horses plunged and kicked up their heels in their desperate flight out of the stable. They streaked under the mass of ghouls circling the castle. They ran for the river, jumped across, and disappeared into the forest.

Robbie glanced around and spotted Angus and Carmen cantering with the herd to safety. His spirits soared.

This is really going to work!

He tightened his legs around his horse to urge it forward when an otherworldly shriek echoed above his head. He glanced up, and his heart skipped a beat.

The ghouls had stopped their circling to turn their dark eye sockets on the fleeing party. Angus and Carmen had already gained the river and disappeared into the forest. Only Robbie remained behind. He kicked his mount, but at that moment, a bolt of lightning slammed into the ground in front of the animal's head. The horse veered so fast Robbie almost hit the dirt. He struggled to correct while the animal rushed off at an angle to the rest of the herd.

Robbie didn't try to turn the horse. He gave the creature his head and a good thing he did. Lightning crashed into the ground all around him. The animal swerved one way and then another to miss it. The bolts crackled through the air. The horse screamed and plunged. It dodged and danced every which way at once. Robbie focused all his power on staying on the damn beast.

The horse cantered all over the plane. It ran away from the river and even headed back to the stable where it belonged, but a wicked slash of lightning sizzled down ahead of it. Turf and grass spattered in Robbie's face.

The horse reared and pawed the air. Robbie dared not look up at the ghouls moving in on him. The horse came down running. It streaked over the grass toward the ridge where the ghoul army was camped. Robbie considered jumping clear when another wave of ghouls came flowing over the ridge. They swept down the mountain heading straight for him.

Robbie held his breath. He couldn't stop the horse or turn the creature in its headlong flight. He could only hold on and hope for the best.

The ghouls unleashed their fire on the desperate animal. More lightning whizzed around Robbie's head. The horse screeched in terror and broke sideways. It plunged down the hill back toward the castle where the ghouls still circled to cut off anyone from going in or out.

Robbie let his eyes sink closed.

A mass of ghouls separated from the circle to trap him between the castle and the rank coming up behind him. Lightning flew thick and fast. It raced horizontally past the horse and vertically all around. Robbie couldn't ride through that thick hail of fire without getting hit.

A few more vicious strikes crashed on either side before a hellish bolt struck the ground right in front of the horse. The impact blew a crater in the sod and flung the animal backward. The horse landed on its back with Robbie pinned beneath it. Only a miracle saved Robbie from getting every bone in his body pulverized to a bloody pulp.

The horse shrieked and rolled off him, lunging to its feet. In the blink of an eye, it rocketed away and disappeared into the night.

Robbie struggled to get his legs under him, but when he looked around, he saw the horse gone and the ghouls moving in for the kill.

He let out a shuddering sigh. Was this it? Would he die out there? Would he never see Elle or his brothers again?

He kept his head held high though, not letting the fear pervade him any deeper. He prepared to meet the inevitable.

The ghouls gathered above his head. Their lightning winked against the black sky, and electricity weighed heavy in the air.

The light got stronger. They gathered their lightning to blow him to kingdom come... when another wild shriek echoed across the field.

Pounding beats shook the air.

Robbie barely had time to turn around before a massive black dragon soared by him.

Aye! Why hadn't Robbie thought of that before? He should've changed into Ushne, and they could have escaped the castle a lot bloody faster.

The Dragon King slowed its flight enough for Robbie to leap onto his back, then he raced across the grass and banked over the castle.

"Thank ye, brother," Robbie said with mirth, slapping Angus' scaly skin.

The Dragon King grunted steam as if to say, "Yer welcome, ye loun."

Robbie laughed.

It was a small win, but a very much needed one.

CHAPTER 31

Elle set Hazel down on the floor by the kitchen fire while she thought her problem over. How could she get Hazel out of the castle without facing the ghouls? Her courage flagged every time she looked outside.

A groan behind her caught her attention. She turned to see Hazel rubbing her head.

"Oohh! What happened?"

Elle fell on her knees next to her friend. "Oh, thank goodness you're awake. You scared me there for a second."

Hazel looked around. "What are we doing in here?"

"It was our only option, but we can't stay here. Those things are out there, and they're bombarding the castle with their siege machines. Is there any way to get out of here without confronting them in the open?"

Hazel blinked. "Yes, actually. Carmen showed me. Here, help me up."

Elle propped her shoulder under Hazel's arm. "Lean on me. I'll help you, but we can't go the usual way."

"Over here." Hazel steered her back down the hall to a side door into the butler's pantry. "Now into the grand dining room."

Elle opened the door into the dining room, but they found their way blocked by piles of broken sticks and rubble. "Now what?"

"Around here." Hazel started to balance better, and could now walk by herself.

She guided Elle back down the hall to another entrance to the dining room.

Hazel crossed the floor to the big stone fireplace. "Here."

"Where?" Elle asked. "I don't see anything."

Hazel ducked into the fireplace. She pressed a brick, and the back wall swiveled back to reveal a black hole.

Elle stared down into it. "What is it?"

"It's a passage under the castle. Carmen showed it to me. It leads out to the forest without ever coming above ground."

"Wow. It's like something out of a storybook."

"I guess these Urlus thought of everything." Hazel ducked into the tunnel. "Come on."

Elle followed her, and Hazel closed the door behind her. They found themselves in a pitch-dark cavern under the castle.

Elle dared not speak above a whisper. "How will we know when we get there?"

Hazel groped for her hand. "Come on. I've never been down here before, but we can't go back to the castle. We'll just have to find out what's at the end."

Hazel set off. Her hand gave Elle courage. Why did she ever entertain thoughts of Hazel being incompetent and silly? Hazel dragged her free hand against the wall to guide their way. Elle trailed her into the dark.

One concussion after another rocked the surface far above, but the sound diminished the farther they went. Elle started to take heart. This might just work.

Hazel didn't hesitate. She hurried down the tunnel into nothing.

All at once, a draft of chilly air hit Elle in the face. The dark took on a different cast, and the two women broke into the open forest.

Stars twinkled between the branches overhead, and Hazel let go of Elle's hand. "We're here."

Elle sank down at the base of a tree and sighed. "Thank you, Hazel. You did it."

Hazel gazed into the distance toward the castle. "I hope the others are all right."

"Where should we go now?"

"There's a cottage over there. An old lady lives there – I've seen her pottering about from my bedroom window. I hope she's all right too. If the others got out, they'll probably head there."

"We can check." Elle got to her feet, and Hazel led the way into the greater forest.

How Hazel found her way in the dark, Elle couldn't understand.

In a few minutes, they caught sight of a light shining in the darkness.

Elle slowly pressed forward, urging Hazel to be on guard.

"Hazel, there's some sort of light up ahead. We need to be careful in case it's one of those damn ghouls," Elle whispered.

"Okay," Hazel whispered back.

As Elle was creeping closer and closer to the light, something hard hit her.

She fell to the ground with an *oof.*

"Elle? What happened? I can't see you anymore," Hazel asked as loudly as she could without accidentally alerting a potential ghoul.

"Who goes there?" came an all-too-familiar voice.

Elle quickly got back up onto her feet. "Rob! Is that you?" she asked, hope lacing her voice.

"Elle?" he answered, and then the light that she had previously spotted lit up the space around them.

There stood Rob, looking as dashing and handsome as ever.

She threw her arms around him.

He laughed out loud. "Aye, it's good to see you too, lass! I've been worried sick about ye."

"Ditto. How did you make it out?"

"Never ye mind." He took her hand. "Come along. The others are waiting in the cottage."

"I've got Hazel here with me," Elle told him.

Robbie spun around. "Hazel! Oh, that's a lucky stroke! We'll be needing her."

Elle felt Hazel tense at her side, but Hazel said nothing on their way to the cottage.

A short while later, they were at the little house. Robbie opened the door, and Elle stepped into the light and warmth. Bodies packed the room.

Angus and Carmen sat together on the one bed, Ewan and Jamie stood by the blazing fireplace, and Callum sat on a stool at their feet.

"We're all here except Fergus," Robbie announced. "He'll be along any minute now."

Elle sat down at the table, and her shoulders sagged. "Thank the heavens we all made it out. We can stay here until we figure out what to do."

"We'll no' stay here," Robbie replied. "We were just trying to figure out how to find Hazel. Now that she's here, we're going back out there. We've no time to lose."

"Me!" Hazel cried. "What were you looking for me for?"

"To cast the spell. You're the only one who can do it. As soon as Fergus arrives, ye must go back out there and make the spell to send those things back where they came from."

Elle's head shot up. "She can't go out there alone. Are you crazy? The ghouls would cut her down long before she got anywhere near completing the spell."

"She'll no' go alone," Robbie replied. "We'll all go out there together. We'll have to, like ye say. We'll have to defend her while she does it. It's the only way."

Elle stared at him. "Are you insane? This will never work. It's suicide."

Robbie didn't answer.

Elle looked around at the rest of them.

None of them would look at her, not even Carmen. They all knew it was hopeless. As soon as the ghouls realized what Hazel was doing, they would attack in all their terrifying fury. They would destroy the whole group and Hazel last of all.

The door burst open, and Fergus strode in. His cheeks were flushed, and he smiled at everybody.

"Did ye get it all?" Robbie asked.

Fergus nodded. "I got it. It wasn't easy, but I done it. Here." He handed a pile of stuff to Hazel.

She backed away with her hands raised. "I'm not doing this. I can't, so don't ask me to. It's impossible."

The smile vanished off Fergus' face. "Ye can do it. We talked about this."

Hazel's tone changed. "How am I supposed to concentrate on the spell with those things all over the place? You guys will be fighting tooth and nail. It'll be noisy. I can't do it."

Fergus lowered his voice to a confidential murmur. "Ye can do it. Ye willnae be alone. I'll be right with ye."

Everyone in the cottage watched on with bated breath.

Hazel searched his face. His deep black eyes sparkled when he looked back at her. They locked together for what seemed like an eternity before she took a breath.

"All right. If you think I can, I'll give it a try. I can't promise anything."

"You'll do it. I ken ye will."

Hazel shook herself. "When do you want to do it?"

Angus jumped to his feet. "Right now. We must strike immediately."

"The five of us will take our dragon forms," Robbie added. "Ewan, ye and Carmen and Elle will take the ground position and defend Hazel. The five of us will do our best to draw the ghouls away from ye, but I'll make no promises how successful we'll be. Ye must all do the best ye can with it, and we'll hope for the best."

Hazel rounded on Fergus. "Don't fly off. Stay close in case I need you. I might not have the power to cast the spell on my own."

He stood closer to her than anybody expected. He never left her side. "I'll be there. I'll no' be far away. Ye focus on the spell and dinnae think about me. I'll be with ye. If ye cannae do it or ye need my help, I'll come to ye."

A brief smile flashed over Hazel's face and immediately vanished. "Okay. I'll do it."

Robbie threw the door open.

The night had faded to a dim gray.

He headed outside when Elle laid her hand on his arm to stop him. "Give me your saber, Rob."

"What?" he asked.

"I don't have a weapon, and you won't need it in your dragon form. Give me your saber. Please."

Angus unbuckled his scabbard. "She's right. We'll no' be needing these. Disarm, lads, and give your weapons to the others. They need them more than we do."

The five brothers took off their weapons and loaded them into Ewan's, Carmen's, and Elle's arms.

Elle buckled Robbie's saber around her waist. It didn't give her any more courage to face what was out there. A saber wouldn't do much against those things, but it was better than facing them empty-handed.

"You should take a weapon, too, Hazel," Carmen remarked. "You might need it out there."

Hazel stared down at the stuff in her hands and shook her head. "I won't need it. If I can't defeat them with this, we're all finished. I only wish I could cast the spell here, in peace and quiet. I don't want to go out there with them screaming in my ears the whole time."

"You have to do it out in the open," Carmen told her. "You have to open the portal where the most ghouls are likely to get sucked into it."

"There's only one thing," Hazel replied. "If I succeed, the curse will be lifted. You and I and Elle will probably get sucked into the portal too. We'll be sent back."

The company that prepared a moment before to rush out to battle paused on the threshold.

Elle looked up at Robbie, and he gazed down at her. She couldn't hold back. She threw her arms around him all over again. She had to hold him at all costs. She couldn't get sent back. She couldn't stand the thought of losing him.

Angus and Carmen regarded each other from a few inches apart. Angus raised his arm to lay his hand against Carmen's cheek. "Lass."

They fell into each other's arms kissing. No one turned away. The King and Queen of the Urlus kissed right there in the sight of everyone.

Elle rubbed her face against Robbie's chest. She tasted one last time the sweetness of his sheltering presence.

Ushne. My Ushne.

She didn't say it out loud. That was their own private secret. She carried that name in her heart. She would never forget, even if she did get sent back to a world bereft of dragons and magic and ghouls.

He kissed her head and held her as long as she stayed in his arms. He never let her go until she separated from him of her own free will. She couldn't kiss him – not then with all the others standing around. She would save that for another time when they could be alone.

She touched his cheek once and walked out the door.

CHAPTER 32

Robbie and the others lined up beside the trees and looked out over the plane. Dawn now lit the sky, but that day held no warmth or comfort for anyone hiding in the forest. No ghouls fluttered around the castle anymore. They were all up on the ridge.

None of the castle towers remained standing. Most of the wall surrounding the castle sagged into piles of loose rock. Would anything be left by the time they got back — *if* they got back? Maybe that's why the ghouls didn't fly around anymore. They didn't have to. They probably already destroyed the throne and left. Now Robbie and Angus and all the rest of them might as well go home, too, because they sure weren't going back to that castle.

Robbie glanced down the line of people standing at his side. His brothers, Ewan, Carmen, Elle, and Hazel. Nine people against an army of ghouls from Hell didn't sound like wonderful odds, and everybody knew it. No one wanted to make the first move to step out on that plane. The castle didn't inspire much confidence either.

Robbie fixed his eye on the ridge overhead. They were up there, and he had a score to settle with Alan. If

Hazel succeeded in making the spell, so much the better. In the meantime, Robbie had a job to do.

Tension crackled down the line. The brothers itched to spread their wings and get out there and fight. The women didn't show the same anticipation to face the deadly ghouls, but they would rise to the occasion. Robbie knew he could count on Elle and Carmen.

Hazel was a different matter. She kept looking at Fergus, who stood at her side. He alone gave her the courage to face what she had to do.

"Get ye out there. Get your spell started now while they're quiet. Get as much of it done as ye can afore they twig to what's afoot. Do ye understand?" Fergus told her.

She nodded but didn't move.

He waved to the plane, but she still didn't go out there.

Robbie didn't blame her. No one in their right mind would want to go out there alone, much less cast a magic spell that would bring the demons down on her head.

In the end, Fergus took her by the hand and led her into the open now that the sky had lightened a little more. He guided her out into the field and stopped. The group under the trees watched in breathless anxiety while Hazel went down on her knees on the grass. Fergus stayed on his feet and surveyed the hills all around.

What Hazel was doing out there, Robbie couldn't guess. Anticipation burned in his chest. He couldn't stand the wait much longer. Part of him hoped Hazel would hurry and get the spell done soon to cut the ensuing fight short. On the other hand, she was better off working slowly and making sure she got it right.

How could anyone be sure she would do it? What if she failed and they all wound up dead or dispersed? He couldn't think that way. Fergus believed. Nothing else mattered. Fergus made the decision to trust Hazel.

The rest of them would follow his lead in this for a change.

Something rumbled out of the distance.

Robbie took a step forward to fly out into the field, but Angus held him back.

"Not yet. Stop a moment."

Robbie's brain roiled in the tension. He couldn't stop another second under the trees. He had to get out there and face this, whatever happened.

Then he saw them. A smoky white haze poured over the ridge on a direct line for Hazel.

Fergus turned around to face it.

Hazel stopped what she was doing to look up. Fergus bent down to say something in her ear, and she lowered her head to concentrate on her work.

At that moment, Angus exploded out of the trees, roaring to the heavens. In an instant, his huge black body broke the branches, and he rose to the sky. His brothers responded in a flash, transforming into their dragon forms.

Robbie as Ushne jumped, and the air hit his scales whooshing past him. At the same instant, Callum and Jamie launched into the air, too.

The four brothers zoomed low over the grass to intercept the enemy.

Ewan raised his sword on high and shouted, "Come on!"

He charged onto the field with Elle and Carmen right behind him.

At the same instant, Fergus changed into a glowing blue dragon, but he didn't take off. He planted his crooked legs in front of Hazel and screeched his challenge to the onrushing ghouls.

Hazel screamed at the noise. She jumped back, and the Tarot cards fluttered over the grass. Elle and Carmen rushed over to her.

Elle exchanged a few words of conversation with Hazel, and Hazel fell on her knees one more time. She fumbled to gather up the cards and get back to her spell.

Ewan took his place next to Fergus, and that was the last thing Ushne saw of his brothers and his friends. He whizzed up the mountain toward the ridge.

The rest of the battle would take care of itself.

He streaked inches over the grass and rocketed into the sky over the ridge. He stalled there in mid-air and stooped to plummet down the other side when he saw something that made him hesitate. There was Alan – not the devilish, wavy ghoul from their first battle. It was really Alan, Prince Alan the man, his former friend.

Ushne hovered in the air. He flapped his wings a few times, but he couldn't attack him. As long as Alan kept his human form, he diffused all Robbie's human murderous venom. He wanted to kill Alan in the bloodiest, most excruciating way, but he couldn't.

He drifted to the ground, landed, and straightened up. Still as Ushne, Robbie stared at the man who used to be his companion.

"Alan?"

Alan smiled. "You've done well, lad, but ye cannae keep the castle."

"What in the name of Heaven are ye doing this for, Alan?"

"The Phoenix Throne is evil, mon. We and our kind were sent to eliminate it from the world entirely."

"Evil! How can ye say that? It's our rightful inheritance. My brother is King. He came through the fire to claim it and break the curse."

"He never broke the curse, and well ye ken it," Alan replied. "We are the ones who'll break the curse of the Phoenix Throne, no' ye and yours. The wraiths that attacked ye in yer castle back home were sent to destroy ye and the evil of yer kind. We'll no' rest until we destroy the throne and all that belongs to it. Ye must accept that, for ye'll no' drive us away with tricks and baubles."

Ushne shook his head. This couldn't be right. He couldn't believe it.

"Ye're lying. Ye cannae destroy the throne by any means. That's why ye needed me to defeat Angus, 'cuz ye cannae defeat him yerself. Ye cannae destroy the throne without us destroying it ourselves. Ye'll never defeat us. As long as even one of us remains alive, we'll fight ye to the death. Ye cannae win."

Alan chuckled and shook his head. "Take a look down the hill at yer beloved castle. It stands in ruins. It'll only take one more bombardment like that to pound yer castle to the ground. Once the castle ceases to be, the throne will fall to us, and ye'll die. Once the throne is destroyed, ye and yer brothers will lose yer dragon forms. Ye'll die from our lightning, and ye'll cease to trouble the world any longer. Give it up, mon. Save yer lives and fall back. Leave the Phoenix Throne the way ye found it and live."

Inside Ushne, Robbie's head spun. This couldn't be happening. Alan was right about one thing. The castle couldn't survive another bombardment. What if he was right about the rest of it? What if the Phoenix Throne was part of the curse? What if the wraiths and the ghouls *had* all come through the portal to correct Hazel's terrible mistake – the same mistake she was getting ready to make down on the field right now?

Ushne cast a glance over his shoulder. What if he and his brothers could take Elle and Carmen and disappear into the forest? Wouldn't he rather travel this country with Elle than confront the ghouls? He would give anything to become nothing more than an ordinary man with his woman by his side. He would pay any price to forget the Phoenix Throne ever existed.

At that moment, a bright red dragon burst into the sky ahead of him. It rocketed into the heavens with a thousand ghouls on its tail. It was Jamie.

The battle down on the plane called Ushne back. Whatever else he could be or wanted to be, his destiny remained caught up with his brothers. They extended themselves to their limit to save the Phoenix Throne, and he would too.

Elle was down there somewhere, battling with the others. He couldn't believe she or his brothers or Carmen or Ewan or Hazel or any of them were evil. This whole tragic situation was a terrible mistake, but he couldn't change sides, not now.

He turned around to walk away.

"Come back, Rob," Alan demanded.

Ushne spun around to face him. "No, Alan. Ye lied to me, to trick me and turn me against my own brother. Ye used me to try to kill Angus. Ye made me believe he was dead. I never would have joined ye if I'd kenned the truth, and ye kenned it when ye lied to me about it. I'll no' believe a word ye say for the rest of my life, and if ye touch me again, I'll roast ye where ye stand."

"It isnae like that, Rob, and well ye ken it. I never lied to ye. I told ye the Urlus took the country and Angus burned up in the fire. All of that was true. I told ye the Urlu King took the Phoenix Throne. I told ye the truth."

Ushne glared at him. "Are ye finished yet? Ye're naught but full of lies, and you're trying to trick me again. Now leave me be. I've a wee piece of business to attend to, and ye're slowing me down."

Alan stepped back, and the benign smile faded from his face. "Ye'll live to regret this. Mark my words."

Ushne grunted out steam. "I'll be long dead afore I come anywhere close to regretting it. Now stand back if ye dinnae wish to get hurt."

Ushne didn't wait for him to answer. He turned his back on Alan and spread his arms to take flight when something hard gripped him from behind. A vise clamped on his shoulder, and icy tendrils crept up his neck to choke the life out of him.

He spun around. Alan stood in front of him, the same Alan Robbie convinced himself he cared about. Alan didn't transform into a ghoul, but he'd done something to Robbie to stop him taking off as Ushne.

Ushne struggled against the unbreakable grip as Alan dragged him across the grass. He couldn't breathe. He clawed at his throat, but there was nothing there.

He staggered forward against his will, the inexorable force hauling him in.

It buckled his knees under him, and he went down on the grass at Alan's feet.

CHAPTER 33

Elle threw herself on her knees next to Hazel and started talking fast.

"Get the spell cast, Hazel. Do it now. Don't look around. We'll defend you. Just get it done. Do you hear me?"

Hazel nodded, but she couldn't speak. Her hands shook sorting the Tarot cards. She fumbled righting the bowl of lavender water. She touched the sage smudge stick to a live coal in another bowl. Smoke blew across the field, and she set the smudge stick aside.

Elle rested her hand on Hazel's shoulder to steady her.

Fergus' constant screeching only flustered Hazel more. She kept glancing up at him, but he didn't see her. The blue dragon stood with his back to her and faced the onrushing ghouls.

The first watery wave of the things rushed down the mountain. They aimed their lightning at Fergus. He bent his head low and let rip a steady stream of fire on them. It blasted straight through their ghostly bodies. It didn't affect them at all. They flowed around Fergus in two streams that missed Hazel crouched behind him.

Hazel bent her head over her cards.

She mumbled the magic words *"Mnistoh, mnylnin, ini dheflo llyatta lladdepas sefrimi viaphreen urlu..."*

"Not Urlu," Elle interrupted. "Don't say Urlu. That's what got us here in the first place. You have to open the portal to somewhere else."

"Where?" Hazel asked. "What place should I ask for?"

"I... I don't know," Elle replied. "Anywhere, I guess. How about Antarctica? Or the bottom of the ocean? How should I know? Just send them somewhere."

Hazel's eyes darted around the field. Then she gasped.

"I know!"

She started over with the incantation.

"Mnistoh, mnylnin, ini dheflo llyatta lladdepas sefrimi viaphreen Atlantis..."

Elle nodded. That should do the job.

Hazel nodded back and went to work setting out the Tarot cards. The wind caught them. She had to hold them down to keep them in position.

Elle saw the problem and held down two. She couldn't stop looking around at the battle heating up all around her.

Ewan swung two swords, one in each hand.

The ghouls split around Fergus and doubled back. They shot their lightning at him and peppered his sides.

Ewan deflected the attacks with his swords, but he couldn't hold back the whole mass of ghouls rushing in to attack.

The ghouls split a second time and a third until several streams of the white ghosts raced all over the field. No one could keep up with them, and their lightning crackled in all directions.

Carmen backed into position. She took her place next to Ewan and turned to defend his side.

"Come on, Elle!" she cried. "We need you."

At that moment, another bolt cut the air above Hazel's head. It singed her hair, and Hazel screamed.

Elle leaped to her feet and scrambled into position behind Hazel to protect her rear.

Once she got upright, Elle's heart quailed at what she saw. Ghouls raced all over the field, blasting dragons out of the sky.

Fergus reared on his hind legs and beat the air with his wings under constant fire. Lightning flashed all over him. It hit his chest and sides and wings and neck and head, causing him to flail in agony.

Ewan jumped in front of him to refract the blows away, but a vicious blast struck him in the leg, knocking him to the ground. He struggled up, only to be cut down by another blow to the head.

He slumped at Fergus' feet and lay still.

Elle didn't have time to help them. Ghouls crowded all around her. They came from both her sides and in front. She drew her sword, but she already knew it was hopeless. She couldn't defend herself from all these things at once.

Carmen cried out, and Elle glanced over her shoulder in time to see Carmen go down on one knee. Carmen still slashed right and left. She cut the ghouls in half, but they only reformed to throw their lightning bolts at her faster than ever.

Down on the ground, Hazel's voice rose to a shriek:

"*Mnistoh, mnylnin, ini dheflo llyatta lladdepas sefrimi viaphreen Atlantis...*"

Dear God, Hazel, hurry up, Elle thought.

She didn't say it out loud though. She didn't dare distract Hazel. How on earth could Hazel get the spell right in all this chaos? What had Fergus been thinking?

At that moment, two of the whizzing streams of ghouls joined into one catastrophic river of whiteness. They barreled into Fergus, and a massive explosion of lightning and force lifted him off the ground. He levitated over the grass for one terrible moment. Electricity fizzled all over his skin and around his head. It shook him in the air before slamming him into the ground right in front of Hazel.

He shrank back into a man, and lay spread-eagled on the ground. His head lolled to one side, and his black hair fell across his face. His eyes rolled half-shut, and his gaze rested on Hazel.

For a fraction of an instant, their eyes met. Then Hazel started the words again in a different tone. Her voice echoed across the field, all the way up to the ridge where the ghoul army was camped. She boomed out the spell for all the world to hear.

Ghouls gathered all around for the final assault.

Jamie, Callum, and Angus fought the ghouls in the air.

Elle didn't want to check how they were doing. Where was Robbie?

A hideous ghoul in the shape of an old hag drifted over her face. The ghoul extended disembodied claws to catch Elle. Her skin crawled. She had to defend Hazel, even if she only did it for a few more seconds.

The ghoul inched closer. A blue-white zigzag of light appeared in the old hag's hand. The demon pulled back its arm to take aim.

At the last second, Elle raised her sword and struck the bolt in the ghoul's hand, causing it to bounce back and hit the ghoul instead.

The ghoul flew away shrieking.

Elle got to her feet. She could do this. Those things weren't as invincible as they seemed. She brandished her sword.

Carmen fought on the other side of Hazel. She and Elle were the only ones left to protect her. How much more work did Hazel need to do before the portal opened?

Elle danced one way and then the other. She snatched up one of Ewan's swords and faced the ghouls two-handed.

Then, Carmen screamed. Her tone wasn't high or shrill; it was deep like a wailing grunt.

Elle spun around to see two ghouls grab hold of Carmen's arms. They lifted her off the ground and sailed off into the sky with her.

"Elle! Elle!" Carmen shouted. "Help!"

Elle dropped her swords and raced to her friend. She seized Carmen's legs and tried to pull her back down, but the ghouls held on tight.

Carmen's boot came off, and Elle fell to the ground along with it.

She didn't have a chance to save Carmen now.

Ghouls rushed at Hazel going a mile a minute. Elle snatched up her swords and lunged for Hazel just in time. She pranced one way and then another. She whirled in a full circle, but the ghouls still closed in. They would be on top of her any second.

Hazel's voice rose to a bellow. She shouted the magic words at full volume. She no longer cowered on the ground over her Tarot cards and lavender water. She rose to her feet and extended her hands above her head. She called out the magic words to the ghouls in a booming command to do her bidding.

Elle couldn't look at her. Hazel wasn't a bumbling wallflower anymore. She was a witch of enormous power. It took this moment to unleash it. It took Fergus' faith in her and the threat against all their lives.

Her words echoed far and wide to the distant mountains and forests. The sight of her gave Elle a glimmer of hope. She turned her back on Hazel, ready to fight and die to make this spell happen.

The minute she turned around, her jaw dropped, and her eyes bugged out. A ghostly apparition cantered into the air above the ridge, and Elle recognized the ghoul rider.

Alan sat on his ghoul horse, his arms raised above his head. One hand held a sword shooting lightning in all directions. The other hand held the limp, floppy body of a man by the neck.

It was Robbie.

Rage swelled within Elle at the sight, but there was nothing she could do. She slashed her sword at every bolt that came near her, but she changed her strategy. She tried to bat them at Alan, but she couldn't aim them well enough to do any good.

Alan charged on the winds toward her, his sword pointed right at her.

She didn't care. Let him come and face her if he dared. One of them would die on this field, and as long as she remained standing, she would fight him.

His horse picked up speed. He thundered down the mountain and over the plain.

Elle crouched to spring. The field fell silent all around her, or was that just her intense concentration? She swore she'd destroy him for what he did to Robbie.

Halfway across the field, the horse paused to rear. It pawed the air and squealed its otherworldly challenge to anyone in sight.

Elle couldn't wait another moment. She darted forward and grabbed Robbie's dangling leg. She tried to haul him out of the ghoul's grasp, but the horse only cantered into the sky again.

Elle hung on for dear life. She wouldn't let go of Robbie for anything. The horse got fifty feet off the ground, and the ghoul turned around and struck her on the head with its fist.

Elle cringed from the blow, but her grip held.

The ghoul urged its horse toward Hazel.

Elle had to stop this thing getting to Hazel, and she had to get Robbie free from its clutches. Even if he was dead, she had to do something.

She swung her sword at the ghoul, and to her surprise, the metal clanged against the ghoul's sword, knocking it out of its hand.

The ghoul rounded on her in a rage. It beat her again and again around the head. The ghoul might be made of mist and smoke, but those blows were very real.

Tiny pricks of stars flashed in front of her eyes. Her head swam, and her grip loosened.

Hazel's voice touched her ear. She still spoke the magic words, but something in Hazel's tone told Elle this was it.

Elle gave a mighty wriggle and wrenched Robbie out of the monster's grasp.

She and Robbie plummeted toward the ground far below.

The ghoul snarled down at the humans' pathetic efforts to defeat it. It spurred its horse and drove in fast toward Hazel.

At that moment, a blinding flash of light exploded out of the bowl of lavender water. It burst across the plane, all the way to the limit of the sky. At the same instant, the ghoul that used to be Alan fired its lightning at Hazel.

A tremendous blast of flaming white fire hit her full in the chest and flung her backward.

Elle hit the ground hard and bounced. Searing pain shot through every cell of her body.

She floundered up from the black pit of unconsciousness to see the ghouls rushing at Hazel in a huge white cloud. They galloped on their horses and sailed through the air, but instead of colliding with Hazel, they all sucked into the bowl of lavender water.

They vanished, and Elle succumbed to the darkness.

CHAPTER 34

Robbie opened his eyes and stared up at the high lofty ceiling of the grand dining room. Groans, screams, and sobs echoed all around him. He lifted his head, and his eyes went dark. Nausea threatened to overwhelm him. He put his head down and closed his eyes.

"Ye'd do better to lie still, lad," a voice told him. "Ye'll no' be going anywhere for a while, I reckon."

Robbie opened his eyes one more time, but he didn't try to move. He spotted Angus sitting on a chair next to him.

"What... what happened?"

"It's all over," Angus replied. "She did it. Ye and Elle and Carmen and Ewan and Fergus and Hazel – ye all did it. I didnae think ye would, but it's all done. The ghouls are gone. Now it's a simple matter of picking up the pieces." He looked around and chuckled. "And there's a mite lot of pieces to pick up, too."

Robbie dared turn his head one way and then the other. He was lying on a straw pallet. Large holes gaped in the plaster of the ceiling overhead, and the grand chandeliers no longer hung in their places, but the roof and walls and floor remained intact.

Pallets just like his lay in rows all over the floor.

Ewan, Jamie, Callum, and Fergus all lay nearby. Blankets covered them, and they kept their eyes closed.

"Are they... are they going to be all right?"

"Aye, lad," Angus replied. "Everything's going to be all right now."

Robbie swallowed hard. How could he say these next words? How could he say them to Angus, of all people?

"And... and the womenfolk?"

Angus bent over him. He tried to smile, but his mouth twisted.

"They're here. They're in other rooms. Elle has a broken leg and a broken arm from saving ye from that thing. Ye both landed hard from high up. I saw the whole thing. Carmen has a few broken ribs and a nasty tear across her shoulder. Hazel..."

Robbie waited. His heart screamed for Elle. He had to get to her. "And Hazel? Is she all right, too?"

"We dinnae ken if she's all right or no'. She took a heavy blow. She's no' regained consciousness since it happened. Beyond that, she's unharmed. We can only watch and hope for the best."

Robbie sank back on his pallet. "I must get up. I must go to see Elle."

"Ye're no' going nowhere, lad, and that's an order. I suppose I'm still King around here, for now at least, at least until ye get on your feet and start throwing yer weight around."

"I'll no' throw my weight around, mon," Robbie sighed. "Ye're the King, and ye'll stay that way as long as I live."

Angus smiled down at him. "Dinnae make no promises ye'll no' be able to keep. Ye never could keep yer place afore, and I'll no' trust ye to do it now."

Robbie struggled up onto his elbow. His head ached, but he had to move. He couldn't lie here a second longer.

He put out his hand and seized Angus by the wrist. "Ye're the King. Ye're my King. Ye're the only King in this country, and I'm yer most loyal servant. Dinnae ever forget that. Ye hear?"

Angus pressed his hand. "I hear. After the way ye've handled yerself these last few days, I'll never doubt ye again."

Robbie pushed himself up. He had to stop there and wait for his head to cease pounding.

"Ye're a damn fool, is what ye are," Angus told him. "Ye're seeking your death warrant, getting up after the fall ye took."

Robbie heaved himself to his feet and steadied himself against the enormous fireplace on the wall. "Perhaps, but I must see Elle. I must make sure she's okay. I must..."

Angus rose to his feet. "I ken what ye mean. Ye must see that she's still here, that the spell hasnae taken her away."

"Was it so different with ye and Carmen? Dinnae tell me she wasn't the first thing ye checked on when the spell ended."

"I willnae tell ye that because she was. She was the only thing I checked on. I dinnae give a thought to ye or the other lads until I saw she was alive and here with me."

"Then ye'll ken why I have to see Elle." Robbie took a deep breath and pushed himself off the wall.

Once he got moving, his head settled down to a dull roar. He stumbled out of the dining room.

Urlus in various states of injury, some near death, lay all over the floor. Servants moved between them doing what they could.

Angus followed Robbie into the hall.

Robbie looked around. "Where is she?"

"This way." Angus led him down the hall toward the servants' quarters, but they found their path blocked.

Angus turned off into the Throne Room.

Robbie started to cross it when he stopped. He stared up at the huge black dragon perched behind the throne. The castle lay in ruins all around him, but the throne was untouched.

"I guess it's all right," he murmured.

"It's all right. They couldnae touch it. I still dinnae understand what they were trying to do, but I suppose that's a story for another day."

"Alan... I mean..." Robbie stopped. He couldn't explain.

"Go on and tell me," Angus urged. "I want to hear it all."

"He said the throne was evil. I dinnae believe a word he said, but it may do to consider why these forces keep coming over to stop us. He said the throne was evil and we were in the wrong. He said the wraiths came to destroy our family to stop us gaining the throne. He said they would destroy the castle and the throne to correct the mistake of the curse."

Angus frowned. "There's one thing to remark in all of this. The women are still here. They havenae left. The curse must still be in place."

"So... is it good or is it bad? Are we fighting on the wrong side?"

"What're we supposed to do? Lie down and die when those wraiths came to our home? Let the wraiths wipe us out? I think no'. We're here, and I'm on my throne, and I for one will never stop fighting to stop anyone from taking it off me. I dinnae care what anybody else does. This here is mine, and I'll defend it with my life."

Robbie nodded. "That's about like I see it too. Come on – or ye stay here while I visit Elle."

"I'll show ye where she is. Then I'll leave ye alone."

He led Robbie to a bedroom in the servants' quarters.

Angus stopped outside the door. "She's in there."

Robbie put out his hand for the latch, but Angus stopped him.

"Wait a minute, Rob."

"Huh?"

"The Throne is no' evil," Angus told him. "I dinnae care what that ghost thing said. None of us are evil. Ye must understand that."

"Of course we aren't," Robbie replied. "I never believed we were."

Angus nodded in understanding, then turned away and walked off down the hall.

Robbie gazed after him. He knew the Phoenix Throne wasn't evil, so why did he hesitate? The Phoenix Throne might not be evil, but the curse certainly was. The curse allowed all those hellish forces through to attack him and those he loved. How could a force for good do that?

It couldn't, and yet here he was, standing outside Elle's room. She'd beenbadly injured saving him from the ghouls. She defended Hazel until the last possible second. If they all lived in peace in this castle for the rest of their lives, they had Elle to thank for it – and Hazel.

Robbie shook those thoughts out of his mind. The curse – or whatever it was – brought Elle to him. That was enough to make it good.

He pushed the door open and saw Carmen sitting on Elle's bed. Elle lay pale and disheveled on her pillow. Pain contorted her face, and white bandages held her arm against her chest.

She turned her head, and he beheld her stricken countenance. He ached to heal her, to take away the pain he'd caused her. She'd saved him time and again, and he never wanted to stop looking at her. She was the only woman he'd ever wanted. She was a thousand times more precious because he never knew when fate would yank her out of his hands.

Carmen patted her leg. "I'll leave you alone now. I'll tell the servants to send you over some more of that tea for the pain. You need to sleep. I'll come back and see you later."

Elle grasped her hand. "Thank you."

Carmen smiled at her. She brushed past Robbie on her way out of the room and closed the door behind her.

Robbie gazed down at Elle.

She gasped for breath, and she couldn't rest against the pillow. She writhed in pain.

Robbie came to her side and sat down. "Ye're no well, lass. Ye're in pain."

Elle smacked her lips. "I'm burning up. I need to move. I can't stand being stuck in this bed."

He got to his feet. "I'll go find that tea for ye. Ye cannae stay like this."

"No!" Her hand shot out. "Don't leave. Please."

"I cannae see ye like this," he told her. "I must do something to help ye the way ye've always helped me."

She kept her hand extended toward him. "Please don't leave. I want you here. If you want to help me, sit down here next to me. I... I need you here."

He sat down, but he didn't like it. He couldn't bear to see her suffering.

She took his hand and closed her eyes. Her breathing evened out, and she started to settle down.

"Tell me what's going on out there. Tell me what's going on in the rest of the castle."

"Castle!" He chuckled wryly. "It's a pile of loose stone. It'll take a project to put it back to the way it was afore. I can tell ye that."

"Where are your brothers?"

"They're all flat on their backs in the dining room, which is where I was afore I came to see ye. They're all in a bad way – all except Angus. At least our King has his health. We need that right now."

She opened her eyes and fixed her ferocious gaze on him. "Are they all right? Are your brothers all right?"

"Angus says they're fine. Everyone's fine, all but..."

Elle sighed. "I know... Hazel..."

He hung his head. "Aye. No one kens if she'll wake up."

Elle sank back on her pillow. "I knew it."

He leaned down and kissed her hand. "Ye did it, lass. Ye defended her until she cast the spell, and ye got me back from Alan. Ye're the best of them all, lass."

Elle sighed, a lone tear streaking down one cheek. "I hear what you're saying, Rob. But for me, being painted as some kind of 'hero' means nothing. Not if I've potentially lost one of my dearest friends."

She turned away from him then, and Robbie didn't dare say another word about it. He understood. He would've felt the same way if it were one of his brothers or closest companions.

However, despite all the destruction, failure and grievances, they all had to be grateful for one thing. The dawn would once again rise, and they would stand tall, ready to face the next menace that dared to try and expel them.

CHAPTER 35

Elle eased the coverlet back in her own grand bedroom.

Robbie slumbered in the bed next to her. He sighed in his sleep, but he didn't wake up. He'd carried her up here by a back staircase that wasn't destroyed in the bombardment. He insisted she would be more comfortable here than in the servants' quarters, and he was right.

She used her one good arm to slide her heavy part-cloth part-wooden cast across the sheets. She propped her broken leg against the floor and stopped to rest. Moving the cast around with one arm while her other arm hung in a sling wasn't as easy as it sounded. Every movement cost her a huge effort, but she had to do this.

She took hold of her walking stick and hauled herself off the bed. She hobbled to the door before she caught her breath.

She glanced back at Robbie. He lay oblivious.

She quietly swung the door back, let herself out into the passage, and shut the door with a soft click. She limped down the passage to the far end, but she didn't bother to knock at the last door.

She opened it and went inside.

Moonlight streamed through the window to brighten the room. It threw an eerie square of blue light on the carpet, but Elle no longer feared to look out into the night. No ghouls or demons hunted her out there anymore.

She stumbled forward a few steps to the bed. To her surprise, the thin figure laid out under the coverlet turned to stare at her. The moon glittered on two bright eyes in the darkness.

"Elle?"

"Hazel!" Elle exclaimed. "You're awake! Oh, thank goodness! We've all been so worried about you. We thought you might never wake up."

"What happened? Where am I?"

"You're back in the castle. You did it. You cast the spell and sent all those ghouls to Atlantis, or wherever." Elle couldn't hold back her laughter. Sheer relief burst out of her. "Oh, I'm so glad you're all right."

"Where are the others? Is..."

"They're all okay. Everybody's okay. You're the last one to come out of the woods. You're a hero, Hazel. You saved us all."

"I couldn't have done it without you, Elle," Hazel replied. "You kept me going, and you and Carmen and Ewan and—"

"Hey, it was the least we could do to help you. I just can't believe you actually did it."

"Neither can I," Hazel replied with a small chuckle. "To think I could have cast that spell all along and sent myself back home, and I never did it. I tried, but it didn't work until now."

Elle froze. "You what?"

"I wanted to go home. That's why I cast the spell that let those ghouls through in the first place. I never really knew I had that kind of power."

"You can't think about casting the spell again," Elle told her. "Don't try again to send yourself back."

"Why shouldn't I? I don't belong here. I thought I could, but I just don't fit in. Carmen keeps trying to get me 'out and about', but not even she can understand what it's like here for me. I don't want to be around the Urlus. It's not that I hate them, I just... They're just not my people. I miss home."

"Do you still feel that way even after everything Fergus helped you?"

"Fergus!" Hazel shook her head. "I don't get your meaning?"

"He defended you, just the way Carmen and Ewan and I did. He believed in you when no one else did. You should be thanking him."

"Look, he encouraged me to cast that spell for his own purpose. He didn't do it because he likes me or cares about me."

Elle gave a teasing smirk. "Are you absolutely sure about that?"

Hazel's head shot up. "Of course. Besides, he's a dragon. I could never... have *feelings* for a dragon."

Elle laughed at that. "I see where you're coming from. I felt that way too, at first, but they're not monsters. Rob certainly isn't a monster. He's beautiful, and I love him."

Hazel stared at her with wide eyes. "You really do, huh?"

Elle let out a shaky breath. "Yes, and it wasn't by choice. It just naturally happened. And I think, deep down, you might have some feelings for Fergus too."

When Hazel didn't answer, Elle continued on.

"What's more, Hazel – if you succeed in sending yourself back as a result of this, you'll again have Fergus to thank. Doesn't that mean anything to you?"

Hazel sighed and turned back to the window. "Of course it does. It means the world to me. I don't know how to show him how grateful I am, but that doesn't mean I *like* him. Plus, finding a guy is definitely not a priority for me here. In fact, it's just not something I've considered before this point. It's not the context for it, no offense."

Elle regarded the frail form of her friend before sitting down on the edge of the bed. She had no idea how to get through to Hazel. Maybe it wasn't possible. Hazel would never know the bliss of giving herself to one of them. She would never enjoy the exhilaration of riding on a dragon's back when he zoomed over the landscape. She would never know the intoxicating bliss of pleasure rushing through her when he loomed over her.

However, all her frustration soon melted away, and heartbreaking pity took its place.

Poor Hazel! She really can't let her guard down and accept this new world. And to be honest, perhaps you shouldn't push her to. After all, she's her own person. She can make her own decisions.

Elle got to her feet. "Okay. If that's how you feel, I won't try to argue with you anymore. If you want to leave, I'll support you. One hundred percent."

"Really?" Hazel looked at her in disbelief.

Elle smiled. "Yes, really. I promise."

The two girls embraced, but when they parted, Hazel was biting her lip.

Slowly, she met Elle's gaze again.

"Elle, will you tell everyone how grateful I am for everything they've done for me? I'm not sure if I can face them."

"Oh, Hazel. I won't tell them for you. You're braver than that," Elle replied, her tone firmer.

Hazel sighed in defeat.

"I'll tell you something else," Elle went on. "If you keep going the way you are, you're going to make enemies of the few people that still want to help you. If you don't thank everybody for defending you and helping you out, if you don't make some effort to reach out to these people, they'll think you're nothing but a rude foreigner. And I know there's much more to you than that."

"I know," Hazel said. "I'll try, okay?"

Elle smiled. It was a start.

"Well, I should get some rest, as should you, so I'll talk to you later," she said.

Hazel nodded, and Elle left her to it.

Once out in the passage, she leaned against the wall to close her eyes. This simple trip down the hall had taken much of her strength. She almost wanted to cry from the exhaustion.

After a few moments of respite, Elle made her way back to her room and snuck into bed next to Robbie.

He roused in his slumber and put his arms around her. She settled into his embrace, but she didn't fall asleep for a long time. She lay awake and thought about Hazel.

What could snap Hazel out of her stupor? What could break down the barrier separating her from the Urlus? If Hazel really did harbor a secret desire for Fergus, why didn't she let it out?

Then again, maybe Hazel was being wiser than them all. If the curse ever lifts, all three of them would most likely disappear – get zapped back to the States. They would lose the men they loved so much.

Elle couldn't stand that, and she wouldn't wish that on her worst enemy.

Yes, perhaps Hazel does have the right idea.

CHAPTER 36

Robbie led a horse through the fields beyond the castle walls.

Elle sat astride the animal, and they wandered at a leisurely pace to the river beyond.

Robbie paused to let the horse drink before he guided it across the gravel bed.

They ambled here and there. Wherever the horse decided to stop and nibble the grass, Robbie stopped, too, until the animal decided to move on.

They worked their way through the woods to another open plane beyond. The hills rose to flat land far away, but Robbie had no intention of going there.

When the country opened out again, he stopped the horse and lifted Elle to the ground. He sat her down and helped her arrange her wooden cast in front of her. Her dress covered it, and she folded her good leg under her skirts. A solid strip of material still supported her arm.

Robbie tethered the horse to a tree and let it graze. He sat down next to Elle.

"Well, lass, here ye are."

Elle gazed up at the sun-drenched sky and sighed. "I love it out here," she exclaimed. "Who knows how many more days we'll have like this before autumn sets in."

"Aye. Ye can feel the slight frost in the air these mornings."

"At least you'll have the castle fixed up before it gets too cold," she remarked.

"Aye. All the country's rallying to Angus' banner. He's a great King."

Elle cocked her head. "You don't regret coming here, do you?"

"Why should I regret it? I'm happy to be with my brothers again, and I'm glad we're living in peace instead of fighting all the time. That was sheer hell."

"I mean the part about Angus being King. You don't wish you were King in his place?"

"Not at all. I'm glad I'll never be King, and I can serve him the way a king ought to be served. I'm right glad of that."

Elle looked away.

"What're ye thinking, lass?"

"You asked me…" She stopped.

Robbie waited. She always came out with it eventually. "I asked ye what?"

"You asked me if I wanted to be your Queen. So, where does that leave us now?"

He laughed out loud. "Is that what ye've been stewing on all this time? Ye're disheartened that ye won't be my Queen?"

"I never said that," she replied curtly. "I asked if you didn't regret not being King. Do you regret not being King and having me as your Queen?"

He leaned in to kiss her. "You're still my Queen, now as much as ever. Dinnae ye ken that, lassie?"

She blushed and rested her head on his shoulder. "I'm not a queen. Carmen, technically, is Queen."

"Well, ye're as much a queen to me as if ye were and I was on the throne. That's all I care about."

"I just don't want you to be unhappy here. I don't want you to secretly resent serving Angus if you really want to be King yourself."

"Well, I dinnae want to be King. I couldnae be happier. He carries all this responsibility, and I'm free as a bird to take ye out riding whenever I wish."

She laughed. "That's true."

Robbie took a deep breath. He'd delayed saying it for long enough. He wouldn't get any happier sitting on it when he wanted it out in the open.

"The real question is ye."

"Me!" she exclaimed. "Why is the real question me?"

"The real question is: are *ye* happy here?"

"Of course. I love it here, and I love being with you."

"Ye're no' worrying about the curse being lifted and being sent back?"

Elle visibly thought for a moment. "Well, it seems like the curse won't be lifted for a while. It looks like you're stuck with me... for now."

"That's no' what I asked ye."

"What did you ask me then?"

"If ye can live with the possibility that we'll be parted?"

"It looks like I'll have to."

He shook his head. He couldn't get a straight answer out of her.

"What's the matter?" she asked. "I don't understand what you're asking me."

He turned toward her and picked up her hand. He pressed it to his lips.

"I'm asking ye to marry me. That's what I'm asking."

"What?" She gasped. "Marry you?"

"Aye. Ye're no' going anywhere, and neither am I. We're together and..."

She watched him with her hawk eyes.

He had to say it.

"And we sleep together in the same bed. We share each other's bodies. We're bound to have a few bairns one of these days."

Her cheeks colored and she turned away. "Whoa. Bairns? I take it you mean kids?"

"Kids?"

"Babies?"

"Oh, aye." He frowned but repeated himself. "Please, marry me, Elle. Give yer all to me."

She gazed up into his eyes. "I have given my all to you. Have I ever held back from you?"

"Then give your all to me in this too. Marry me and let go of yer old life."

"But what if I do get sent back? What if we have children and then we get separated? What will happen then?"

He bent low to murmur into her face, "Ye said ye wanted to be there when it happened. Ye said ye wanted to see my face and touch me and hold me right up until the last moment. Ye said ye wanted to spend every moment with me that ye could. Ye said if we're to be torn apart, no' to let it happen afore it was time. Ye said all that. Do ye still feel that way?"

She buried her face in his neck. "You know I do."

"Then marry me. Let us be together until the very last moment."

She whispered the answer into his ear: "All right."

He cupped her chin and raised her mouth to his lips. They swam in a blissful kiss under the shimmering sun. She reclined back against his arm, and he supported her in gentle swaying rhythm.

Robbie stretched out on the ground and scooted closer to Elle. In the weeks since the battle, he'd learned to take everything at a snail's pace to accommodate her broken arm and leg. Her injuries made love-making a special challenge, but he managed it without hurting her. He took his cues from her, and he never did anything she wasn't ready for.

He lifted her into the crook of his shoulder, and they relaxed. He hungered for her right now, but he didn't want to take her right there on the fresh grass — no, he *did* want to take her. He wanted to see her naked body gleaming in the sun. He wanted to see her shining all over with vibrant pleasure and flushed excitement. He wanted to lie back on the ground and let her ride him into explosive pleasure.

However, that would never happen with her leg in a wooden cast. He knew better than to ask. He loved her too much, and now that she'd said yes to his proposal, he cherished her even more.

He held her close. She was all his. How long before they had bairns together? Carmen was already pregnant. For all he knew, Elle could be pregnant right now too.

He leaned forward to kiss her, and she collapsed back into the bend of his elbow. He pressed his body against her and felt the supple softness of her desire under her dress. He could just touch her there.

He ran his hand up her sides and caressed her cheeks down to her neck. Her tongue danced around his mouth and stirred his member under his kilt. He hardened against her, and she whined into the pressure.

She stroked his chest through his shirt, her delicate fingers grazing his skin. She traced the outline of muscle over his heart and down to the cleft where his ribs joined his stomach.

Robbie gazed at her face. Her cheeks seemed to shine with an inner light. Her hair waved over his arm. He dragged his fingertips down her collarbone to the frilled outline of her bodice over her shapely chest.

She moved toward his mouth, and her breast heaved into his hand. He massaged her breasts until she moaned out loud. She arched her back to thrust herself against his hardness.

He never intended to take her like this, but he needed her beyond words.

He squeezed her good leg through her dress and pulled it over his hip. She panted through their kisses as he grabbed a handful of her buttock in one hand and crushed her against him. He raked his bulging manhood across her tender thighs.

His madness threatened to overflow its banks.

He dove his hand under her dress and touched bare skin. Oh, she felt more heavenly than ever now that he knew she was all his. His fingers sank into her wet opening, but before he could do anything, she ran her own fingers down his midsection. Before he could stop her, she tossed his kilt aside. Her small, soft fingers closed around his member, and he thought he would burst right then and there.

He stared straight ahead, but he didn't see her right in front of him. He knew only the heavenly closeness of her hand around his shaft, rolling the skin back and caressing him down to the root.

Dear God, she knows what she's doing.

She stroked him to throbbing hardness. He didn't know what to do. He blinked, and there she was in front of him. He stared into her beguiling eyes as their hands, their bodies, connected them somewhere beyond this world.

Robbie quivered all over.

He yanked his hand away and sat up. His member fell out of her hand, and his kilt draped over it. He jumped up on his knees.

Elle gave a cry. "What is it?"

"We're no' doing this here." He scooped her up in his arms. "We're going back to the castle."

"What?"

He didn't respond. He set her on her feet, where she balanced on her cast and waited while he caught his horse. He stopped the animal in front of her and gently lifted her onto its back.

Robbie set off for the castle without a word. He didn't say anything, not even when he set her down by the stairs that led up to their shared chamber.

Elle waited there like she usually did until he put the horse in the stables.

When he finally came back, he picked her up, carried her to their room, and laid her down on the bed.

CHAPTER 37

Robbie stretched out on the bed next to Elle the same way he had on the grass beyond the river. They'd done it out there in that field a dozen times before like they'd done it in this bed. This time was different though.

Elle knew it, and she read the same thing in his eyes.

She had agreed to marry him, so why was she now considering holding back? Yes, of course, there was the uncertainty of not knowing if they could stay together.

He was right. She wanted to be there at their final moment. She never wanted to miss a minute together if that was how things turned out.

One of these days, it would happen. Even if they spent their whole lives together and watched their children and grandchildren grow up in this castle, one of them would die first. She wanted to be there for that too. She didn't care how they got separated in the end, as long as she was there.

Spurred on by such thoughts, Elle let the threads of hesitancy fall away.

Robbie began to kiss her in long, delicious swoops, and this time, nothing would stand in the way of him taking her. They were alone, and technically, engaged to be married.

What could be better than that?

Elle needed him. She wanted to devour him. She wanted to tackle him and have her way with him, but she couldn't. Her leg and arm wouldn't let her. She could only respond to what he did. She could only show him how much she craved him.

He pushed her dress up to expose her un-casted thigh and ran his rough fingertips over the skin, causing tingles to shoot through her body. Although he clearly wanted to take his time, indulge in the sensual foreplay they often enjoyed together, Elle didn't have the patience tonight.

She reached up and kissed him again, urging him with her mouth to go faster, not to waver.

To her delight, he responded, undoing the laces of her bodice to shift up her dress so that she was free of it completely.

In the subdued light of the chamber, he raked his eyes over her... the curves and hollows... the contours of her breasts... the column of her throat.

"Christ, Elle," Robbie said, his words coming out almost as a whisper. "What did I do to deserve such a beauty?"

She smiled and tugged at his shirt, hoisting it up so she could revel in the sight of his rock-hard abs. She would never tire of gazing upon his body. His broad shoulders... firm muscled skin... bulging arms...

He was what women back home would call the definition of an Adonis.

Peering down, she frowned at the kilt he still wore, and so made swift work of removing it.

She wasn't at all surprised to see what was then revealed – his proud manhood rising up to greet her.

"Aye," Elle finally replied, putting on a Scottish accent, "what did ye do?"

Robbie bit his bottom lip and grunted. "Ye're such a tease, ye ken that?"

"Aye," she taunted again.

"Right. That's it, lass..."

He kissed her again, first on the lips, then on her chin and then down her throat before pausing at her breasts.

He gave each mound equal attention, gently sucking on the erect nibs like they were filled with sweet nectar.

Elle writhed at his touch, feeling herself getting wetter and wetter by the second. She ached for him to be inside of her, mounting her, claiming her again and again and again.

Luckily, Robbie didn't hold off on taking her for long. He climbed on top of her, and she helped guide his manhood to her throbbing entrance.

With one simple push, he slipped inside her moist cavern, sliding slowly in and out, in and out.

She opened for him like a parched flower in desperate need of water.

Although they'd had sex numerous times before now, this time felt new.

Different.

Their bodies were connecting deeper, stronger, as if they were two jigsaw pieces that had finally found their missing half.

They moved together in a primitive-like rhythm, like animals lost to nature's call.

Elle felt her climax building, coming then receding, coming then receding.

She started to shake, the blood rushing to her cheeks as she held her breath in anticipation.

Above her, Robbie grinned, knowing she was about to come for him.

"That's it, my lass. Ye're mine, and only mine," he said, panting out the words.

She moaned as her nerves almost breached their breaking point.

"Tell me ye're mine, Elle," he commanded.

"I'm..." Words were lost on her tongue as a blissful sensation took over.

"Say it," Robbie demanded.

"I..."

"Say it!"

"I'm... I'm yours!"

"Again!"

"I'm yours, Robbie Cameron!" Elle wailed as her orgasm crested to its highest peak, pushing herself upward to meet his lunges, giving herself over to him, mind, body, and soul.

Robbie followed her into the wave, giving a few last thrusts before he groaned and eased his pulsing. He stared into her eyes as he emptied his seed inside her, all the while telling her that she was his and his alone.

Somewhere in all that pleasure, Elle had felt like she'd lost all sense of where she ended and he began. And now, in the aftermath, she still quivered from how intense their lovemaking had been. More intense than any other time.

After a minute, Robbie broke the intimate contact and flopped down next to her on the bed.

They both gave long, deep sighs, trying to catch their breaths.

"Just when I think having ye cannae get any better, ye go and prove me wrong," he finally said, turning on his side to look at her.

She beamed and reached out to cup his face with one hand. "I've never had sex like that with any other man," she told him, still flushed from all the exertion. "You're all I want, now and forever. I mean that with all my heart."

Her words seemed to light up something within him, as a broad smile carved itself across his ruggedly handsome face.

"Ye have no idea what it means to me to hear ye say that," he said, taking one of her palms and kissing it tenderly.

But Elle knew exactly what it meant to him. Because his words of love had a profound effect on her too.

Out of the men she had known, he was the only who'd actually done it.

Robbie Cameron had shown her what could be possible once she allowed herself to open up her heart.

CHAPTER 38

Robbie paced back and forth in the guardroom. He stopped in the door and gazed across the courtyard to the stables. Then he turned around and walked back to the window looking out over the fields.

Ewan and Robbie's three younger brothers sat on a nearby bench. They all wore their dress kilts with silver and gold decorations pinned to their plaids. They carried silver-hilted daggers in their socks and wore seal-skin sporrans instead of their usual leather ones.

Callum rubbed his hands together and kept turning his head right and left.

Fergus stared straight in front of him, the way he did when he had something on his mind.

Jamie leaned back against the racks of armor and weapons behind the bench. He kept his eyes closed and feigned sleep, a sure sign he was as nervous as everybody else.

Ewan smacked his lips. "Do ye have to pace about like that, mon? Ye're driving all of us to distraction. Sit ye down and wait like the rest of us."

Robbie paid him no attention. He adjusted his plaid for the hundredth time and picked invisible specks of stray wool off his kilt. He straightened his shirt and shrugged his shoulders one more time, but it didn't help him much. His heart crashed back and forth between exploding out of his chest and stopping altogether.

He couldn't stand the strain much longer.

Ewan started to stand up and collided with Robbie coming back the other way. The impact knocked Ewan off balance, so he sat down heavily on the bench again.

Robbie stepped back and waved his hand. "Wheesht, mon! On ye go."

Ewan bowed his head and gestured toward the door. "No, mon. After ye."

Robbie hung back. "No. Ye go ahead."

"It's yer bloody wedding day, mon. Ye'll go ahead, and I'll sit right here until ye go."

Ewan crossed his arms over his chest and crunched his face into the closest thing to a scowl he could muster. He pretended not to see Robbie standing there.

Robbie sighed and walked on to the door. He stopped at the threshold – not because he wanted to, of course. He wanted to keep walking. He wanted to get out there in the clear, fragrant air. He wanted to keep walking to the woods and fields beyond the river and even into the mountains. He would go anywhere to get away from what he had to do, but he didn't dare. He got himself into this. He just had to get through the next hour, and he would be free.

He walked back to the window, but the view outside didn't give him any encouragement. Where was Elle right now? Was she as nervous and excited as he was? What would she look like right now? Was she entertaining second thoughts? What if she didn't come?

The guardroom door opened, and all four men leaped off the bench at once.

Robbie whipped around.

A servant boy stood in the doorway and stared wide-eyed at the five big men menacing him.

Robbie's shoulders slumped. "All right, lad?"

"Aye," the boy replied.

The brothers filed out first, followed by Ewan, and Robbie brought up the rear.

Thank the stars they didn't get tangled up with each other. They proceeded with calm, quiet dignity to the grand entrance foyer outside the Throne Room.

Robbie felt anything but calm and dignified, but at least he managed to keep his feelings hidden.

In the foyer, they found about a hundred nobles from all over Urlu assembled in their finery with their ladies on their arms.

Ewan's lieutenant of the Guard organized the procession, and a good thing he did, too, as Ewan himself couldn't be more useless in his state of heightened nerves.

The lieutenant instructed everyone where to stand. He positioned all the nobles in pairs at the front. He waved Ewan into place at the very end of the line.

"Now then, Captain, if ye'll take yer place here…"

Ewan obeyed the young man like a meek little lamb.

Next came the brothers in ascending order of age: Jamie, Fergus, Callum, and last of all, Robbie. He did his best not to fidget and shift his feet while he waited. The closer he came to the moment of truth, the more his chest hurt.

He couldn't go through with this. It was asking too much of any man to wait like this.

Why in Heaven's name didn't he just take Elle to Angus and marry her in private? Why did everything that happened in this castle have to turn into an affair of state? He might be the King's brother, but he was still just an ordinary man.

The lieutenant said something Robbie didn't hear. All of a sudden, the great doors swung open, and a blast of music gusted into the foyer.

Robbie's heart felt like it was lodged in his throat. He wanted to run. He could duck out the castle's front door and no one would see him until it was too late. He was at the back of the line.

Yes, that's a good plan.

But then he caught sight of the black wooden dragon stooped over the throne at the far end of the hall. It narrowed its eyes at him. He couldn't disobey that silent command. He served the Phoenix Throne, just like everybody else here.

He had to go through with this.

Before he could do anything, the procession started moving.

The nobles and ladies filed forward into the Throne Room. They marched down the long red carpet between crowds of other admirers in rich clothes and gem-encrusted crowns. They turned either way and lined up in front of the throne.

At last, the lieutenant himself moved forward and left Ewan and the brothers alone in the foyer.

For one terrible moment, Robbie doubted Ewan and his brothers could go through with this either. Would Ewan have the fortitude to walk into that room?

Ewan, though, started forward.

After he started walking, Jamie fell in line behind his Captain.

The three brothers entered the Throne Room, filed down the carpet, and turned off into their places in front of the nobles.

Robbie came to the doorway. The whole assembly turned around to look at him.

Angus and Carmen stood on the platform in front of the throne. Angus wore his family tartan with a diamond-studded belt around his waist. Silver tassels sparkling with gems hung from his sporran, and his crown glittered in the sunshine streaming through the stained-glass windows overhead.

Carmen wore a sweeping gown of snow-white organza. Gold thread trimmed the seams, and pearls and diamonds shaped her scooped neckline. Her dainty crown showed off her glistening black hair, and she smiled down the long hall to Robbie waiting in the doorway.

He took a deep breath and squared his shoulders. He didn't have to see anything else in this room. He only had to concentrate on Angus. As long as he did that, he couldn't go wrong.

He rested his hand on his sword hilt and started walking.

The assembly turned to watch him pass. He faced this moment like the last battle of his life.

He would conquer this.

He marched to the throne and planted his legs wide in front of Angus.

His brother gazed down at him in calm assurance. He waited until the chorus of trumpet blasts died away to nothing.

Robbie had never heard the Throne Room so quiet. Tension hung thick and dangerous in the air.

Angus took a step forward, and his voice echoed off the walls. "Kneel."

Robbie went down on one knee and bowed his head. He couldn't see the dragon perched there above the throne anymore, but he sensed its piercing eyes watching his every move. Robbie bowed to the dragon too. He never thought he was bowing to his brother. That dragon was Angus' power. Robbie would always serve that power.

Angus strode down the steps to stand in front of Robbie. He draped something over Robbie's head, and a heavy medallion swung into Robbie's view. A huge sapphire sat in the middle of a ring of diamonds set in gold.

Angus drew his sword and laid the blade across Robbie's shoulder. He moved the blade from Robbie's right shoulder, to the left, and back to the right.

"I knight you Sir Robert Cameron. Rise."

Robbie got to his feet, and he no longer saw a king in front of him. It was only Angus; the same old Angus Robbie had known all his life.

Angus' face cracked into a huge grin. He shook Robbie's hand, but they ended up hugging each other anyway. Angus slapped him on the back and squeezed his shoulder.

Robbie's heart ached, and a lump was still stuck in his throat, but he wasn't free just yet. The most agonizing part was yet to come, and his eyes already stung with the tears he longed to shed. His emotions raged inside him, but he had to quash them down just a little longer... just a little longer.

Angus took a step back, but he didn't return to the throne. Upon the platform, Carmen touched a white silk handkerchief to her eyes.

Robbie didn't dare look at his brothers, or he would lose his wits completely.

At that moment, a side door opened and the whole company craned their necks to stare.

Robbie turned and lost his breath at the sight he beheld. There stood Elle in the most beautiful gown he'd ever seen. A white veil hung over her hair, and a string of gold-set diamonds surrounded her ivory throat. She no longer needed her arm in a sling, but she still walked with a slight limp due to her leg not being fully healed yet.

He couldn't stop staring at her radiant face.

All his doubts vaporized to nothing.

She came to his side, and he offered her his arm. Her eyes spoke volumes. He never should have doubted her. She would never change her mind about this.

They couldn't stop staring at each other, not even when Angus' voice boomed over the crowd.

"We are gathered here today for the union of this man and this woman. Ye, Sir Robert, and ye, Elle, have rendered this land invaluable service the likes of which it can never repay. It is with great joy and gratitude, then, that I have the honor to bring ye both together at last and make ye both valued members of this court. Do ye, Sir Robert, take this woman in marriage?"

Robbie swallowed hard. "I do."

"And do ye, Elle, take this man in marriage?"

Her eyes sparkled when she looked up at him. "I do."

"Have ye the rings?"

Jamie stepped forward. For one eternal moment, he and Robbie couldn't get their shaking hands to function. It took every ounce of Robbie's resolve not to bellow at his brother to hand him the bloody rings already.

At last, they got the two rings safely into Robbie's hands.

He faced Elle, but he could scarcely breathe.

"Repeat after me, Rob," Angus instructed him. "With this ring, I thee wed, to love, honor, and cherish thee until death parts us forever."

Robbie took a breath and quickly found his nerve. He said the words without wavering and slipped the tiny circle of gold onto Elle's finger.

Then, he passed his own thicker band to her.

"With this ring, I thee wed, to love, honor, and cherish thee until death parts us forever," she vowed, her eyes catching his in their powerful sway.

Angus' voice finally startled Robbie out of his reverie.

"I now pronounce ye man and wife. Ye may kiss yer bride, brother."

The whole Throne Room erupted into deafening cheers.

Streamers and confetti rained down on the couple.

Callum, Jamie, and Fergus all clapped and laughed with mirth.

Tears streamed down Carmen's cheeks, and Angus put his arms around her.

However, Robbie didn't see any of that. He saw only Elle, his love, his bride, his prize.

He took her in his arms and kissed her for all to see, but that kiss didn't symbolize the beginning of their union.

For they had already said it all and done it all long before this day.

CHAPTER 39

Elle leaned on Robbie's arm while one dignitary after another came up to shake Robbie's hand.

The ladies hugged Elle and kissed her on the cheeks, most of them crying and saying how happy they were for her.

Robbie held himself together during the hours of feasting, congratulations, and festivities following the ceremony. He still wore the jeweled medallion Angus gave him, and almost everyone called him Sir Robert.

The name sounded strange to Elle. He was just her Rob, even if he did look magnificent in his fancy kilt and medals. He accepted all the accolades and well-wishes. He kept hugging his brothers and Ewan and Carmen again and again.

Elle never let go of his arm. Her leg still ached a little despite being almost healed, but she didn't have to move around. She just had to stand there and get through it. That was the price of marrying a knight.

She finally sat down at the long feast table with a sigh of relief, but by the end of the meal, her leg hurt just as much as if she'd been standing.

She had to get out of there and rest.

After a few more hours in partial agony, she patted Robbie's arm. "I think it's time we head upstairs."

He nodded in agreement. "Aye, let's go then."

Robbie pushed back his chair and helped Elle up from hers. People called out to them as they passed, but they only waved them their goodbye and kept going.

Elle paused in the foyer. She still couldn't get up the stairs by herself.

Robbie didn't hesitate. He picked her up in his arms and carried her.

Once in their chamber, he laid her down on the bed.

She propped herself against her pillows and took off her veil. "If you want to have another ale or two with your brothers, that's all right with me, you know? I don't mind just resting up here by myself for a little while," she said.

He shook his head and grinned. "No, I'd rather spend most of my wedding night with my bonnie bride."

"Are you sure?" she asked, with a teasing tone. "Everyone might miss seeing the 'great Sir Robert Cameron' knighted and married." She changed her voice to the closest thing to a throaty rumble as she could manage. "Oh, yes, Sir Robert. Oh, thank you, Sir Robert. If you please, Sir Robert."

He narrowed his eyes at her. "Ye better no' start calling me that."

She laughed out loud, then a firm knock resounded on the door.

"Now who the devil could that be?" Robbie scowled.

With visible reluctance, he went and opened it to find Angus standing in the passage outside.

Robbie stood back. "Angus, mon. To what do we owe the honor?"

Angus gave a sweeping bow and brushed the floor with his hand. "The honor is all mine, Sir Robert."

"Quiet now," Robbie snapped, still scowling. "What can I do for ye?"

"Can I come in for a moment?"

Robbie looked annoyed, but his brother was the King, which meant refusing him would be frowned upon – even if it was Robbie's and Elle's wedding night.

"Aye, make it quick though," Robbie replied, stepping back to allow his brother to enter the chamber.

Angus strode inside and nodded to Elle. "I've got something to say to ye."

Elle sat up on the bed, curious as to why he was there.

"Ye ken Carmen is pregnant. I'll have an heir, but that willnae be for a fair few years yet. I need a regent to be my second in case anything happens to me."

"That's no bother," Robbie said. "Ye ken ye can always count on me, mon."

"That's no' all I have to say to ye, Rob. Ye and me, we always shared the leadership. Ye were always as much a leader as I, if no more. The lads listen to ye."

"Aye. Isnae that why ye asked me to be yer regent?"

Angus shook his head. "It's more than that. I want to share the Kingship with ye. We can do it together – half and half, ye and me, the way it should be. What do ye say?"

"I cannae be 'half King', mon. Urlu can have only one King, and that's ye. Ye've united yer power while I've been wandering the back blocks. Ye cannae share that out with anyone – especially no' me. I serve the Phoenix Throne, the same as Ewan and the other lads."

Dragon Quest

"Ye dinnae have to serve it, mon. Ye deserve to sit on it as much as I. Take yer place, mon. Dinnae think to hold ye back."

Robbie crossed the room and gazed out the window. Dusk had descended over the fields, and a cool wind ruffled the grass on the plain.

Elle watched him from the bed. What would he choose? Would he take Angus up on his offer? Robbie once thought he would be King. Did he still harbor any ambitions of ascending the throne himself?

"Ye think on it," Angus told him. "I want ye to. I dinnae want to lord it over ye, Rob. But ye're as fit to be King as I."

Robbie turned around to face him again. "But I'm no' the King. Ye are, and that's as it should be. Ye were made for this, mon, and right glad I am of it. All's right with the world, and I'd no' change a thing."

Angus walked to the door. "Ye think on it. Ye may change your mind by and by. If that happens, ye let me ken, and we'll see what we can do about it."

"I have a better idea."

Angus raised his eyebrows. "Oh? What is that?"

Robbie didn't answer. Instead, he crossed to the bed, picked up Elle, and left the room, leaving a wide-eyed king behind them.

"Robbie Cameron, what on earth are you doing?" Elle protested, half in shock and half in utter amusement.

"Ye'll see, lass," he replied with a wicked smile.

Robbie climbed a hidden flight of stairs to the roof and set Elle on her feet in the bracing breeze.

"Okay, so out with it. What's this all about?" she asked.

"Just a wee wedding present I prepared for ye."

"A wedding present!" She frowned. "I don't need a wedding present."

"Ye need this. Trust me. Now, stand back a little way."

Elle immediately knew what he was about to do and stepped back a few paces.

Robbie bent forward, and his sides exploded into the huge haunches and scaly coils of Ushne. He slithered over the roof, his scales scraping the stones under his belly.

He returned to Elle, but he didn't bend down to let her climb on. He looped his tail around her and lifted her off the turret to set her down astride his neck.

She held on tight as he flexed his wings then launched into the open air.

He circled the castle in the gathering twilight. A hint of deep green and fading gold touched the western horizon. Stars pricked the dark blue firmament in the east, and a pale crescent moon shone over the landscape.

The wind whipped Elle's hair back and tore at her dress. She narrowed her eyes as he picked up speed. He raced over the ground and zoomed up into the mountains. His body rippled between her legs. His muscles contracted to pump his powerful wings.

She didn't think to check where they were going until he'd already flown far away. He whizzed out to sea and around the coasts.

The darker night fell, and still, he flew on.

She laid her cheek against his neck, and his heat warmed her. She no longer cared where they were going as long as they went there together.

She opened her eyes to see a familiar landscape below. She spotted Obus' cottage. She raised her head to see the mountains standing tall and proud in front of her.

Ushne flew up and hovered over the caldera. She stared down into the glowing inferno.

Why does he want to come back here?

He landed on the bare rock and lifted her down. A pallet of wool with a spare change of his clothes sat next to the caldera in the place where she used to sleep with him as Ushne. He must have prepared this especially for her.

The rock radiated its heat through the pallet into her legs, and she sat down to soak up every drop of it. Ushne walked around the caldera, but he didn't change back into a man. He dragged his long body across the hot stones.

She lay back on the bed and let out a deep, contented sigh. The events of the past few months came full circle. He couldn't have chosen a more fitting present to give her. She gazed up at the stars, and her happiness became complete.

Ushne slithered over next to her and stretched out on the rock at her side. His head bobbed above her head, and his gleaming eyes slit the night. She loved him like this, so powerful, so alluring, so attentive. Her heart dissolved in a puddle of desire. Anything he could do or give her now would only top an already perfect day.

His head drifted lower until he hovered right above her face. She raised her hand and touched his cheek. She ran her fingers over the spikes on his head and down his neck. His breath smelled smoky in her nostrils. Her own aching need for him no longer bothered her. She welcomed the electric energy rushing through her skin to infect her all over.

He hummed under his breath as he closed his eyes and ran his head against her. He twisted his head to rub over her chest and neck. His long neck slipped between her arms and coiled all around her.

She gave herself over to the blissful rapture of this moment. She was all his, and he was all hers. The whole world belonged to them alone. They could go back to the castle and serve Angus, or they could stay here.

Either way, happiness seemed to be welcoming Elle to every minute of her future.

Ushne settled down next to her. Elle never feared to touch him or let that overwhelming desire wash over her. She wanted him in all his dragon glory. She wanted to touch him both as a dragon and a man.

Even when she closed her eyes, he loomed over her. He commanded her to serve him and love him with the same intense power as the dragon behind the Phoenix Throne. All the Urlus carried that power within them, and he was no different.

Angus ruled, but any trick of fate could put Robbie or any other Urlu, any other brother of the Camerons, on the throne in his place.

They all carried the fire within them.

Even before sleep took her, her dreams of Ushne washed all the other reality away. Nothing existed but him. He filled her nights and days, her waking and her sleeping. He filled her body and her soul. Another generation of Urlus would spring from her.

They would rise to the Phoenix Throne.

The Phoenix Throne could never be evil. Elle didn't care what anybody said. The Phoenix Throne was shedding its light to the corners of this land, perhaps this world. It called everyone to peace and prosperity.

She'd never known that she'd dwelt in darkness before she came to this magical place. She never knew how much she craved that peace and light, and now she'd found it.

In the depths of the night, she put out her hand to touch Ushne's sides. He breathed and rumbled in sleep. He was still there. He protected her like no one had ever done before.

They never had to go back. That was the wedding present he'd given her.

He wanted to stay out here.

Both Robbie and Ushne were at their happiest with just Elle on the road, with no one else but each other to depend on.

Nothing but the open sky, the elements, and whatever destination they chose.

Heather Walker

Dragon Quest

Heather Walker

Made in United States
North Haven, CT
02 December 2021

11859145R00173